Other titles by Quentin Carter:

Hoodwinked

In Cahootz

Contagious

AMONGST
THIEVES

by

Quentin Carter

This is a work of fiction. The authors have invented the characters. Any resemblance to actual persons, living or dead, is purely coincidental.

If you have purchased this book with a 'dull' or missing cover—You have possibly purchased an unauthorized or stolen book. Please immediately contact the publisher advising where, when and how you purchased this book.

Compilation and Introduction copyright © 2007 by Triple Crown Publications
PO Box 6888
Columbus, Ohio 43205
www.TripleCrownPublications.com

Library of Congress Control Number: 2007943158
ISBN 13: 978-0-9799517-2-5
Author: Quentin Carter
Cover Design/Graphics: www.MarionDesigns.com
Typesetting: Holscher Type and Design
Associate Editor: Dani Rickard
Editor-in-Chief: Mia McPherson
Consulting: Vickie M. Stringer

First Trade Paperback Edition Printing December 2007

10 9 8 7 6 5 4 3 2

Printed in Canada

acknowledgements

As usual I would like to thank the man upstairs for answering my prayers by not sending me back into the world having to start form the ground up.

My family who has held me down from the moment that I was found guilty at my trial, until my release date. Charles & Lois Williams, Christopher Carter, Brad, Black, and my sister, Denisha, Cheron & Joey. My cousins, Barbara Jones, Lillina White, Vickie, TT, Ashley, Tashay, Willie, Mary Ann, June & Ruby, Macoshia Williams and Tay Nunn, & Leggs Diamond.

Those precious children of mine, Quentez, Mikelle, Brianna & Brianna, who just insist on believing that I'm rich.

And my lil partnas Jamauny and his 7-year-old lil brother, who wrote, made and sent me a copy of his book "Invincible."

Thanks to these beautiful women my bid was a little easier to cope. My home girl Kiria Cummings, my long time friend Lakisha Adams, proper talking ass Kelli Woods, my very sweet California gal Shanell C. My gangster girl from the dirty Tamara

Duppins, and the seldom seen Mauri Foster.

I don't know about any other author but I have some great fans that support me. They are just as much appreciated as anyone else that I've mentioned in this. My history teacher and pen pal from Saginaw, MI Latera Washington.

Crazy Crazy ass Katrina McClain, From the DC area, Unique C. My first fan from Richmond, VA Tiara Carmon, form NY to KC Nikie Green, My Puerto Rican fan Lisa Aguilar, from the Chicago Tribune Pamela T. Suprlock, Prison Ministers Gayle Johnson, and Sarah Morning (NY).

To those who wake up in the same hell as I do just in different places. Antwon Thompson (NY) Mike (KAT) Pernel (NJ) Devin Young (Ohio).

My Jamaican queen Patricia Bruce (Miami) and my friend by way of a friend Lomika Hardy.

My home boys who I wake up with, argue with and kick it with on a day to day basis, Freddie Hammons, Gary Jones, Honeyman, Deko, Edward, Gill, my cousin Leggs Diamond, J-bird.

The entire T.C.P. staff that go to work every day and do what they have to, to keep Triple Crown Publications the #1 leader in Urban Fiction. Vickie Stringer, Mia McPherson, Benzo Stringer, and those who are unknown to me.

And last but not least my editor, typist and friend Cynthia Parker who keeps me updated on everything that I need to know. And oh yea, to Lady Scorpio (Kim) of Coast to Coast Readers. You know

I wasn't gonna forget about you.

This will be my final novel written from the cell of a prison. I can only hope that I will not get out there in the world and fall victim to that ugly element that we call temptation.

King Author

dedication

This book is dedicated to my cousin Sheldon A.C. Haynes, who lost his life in the driveway of his suburban home on the night of January 29, 2007, all because he had a chain on his neck that was worth $5,000. And some idiots thought that it would be best to take his life just to get it.

R.I.P. Family

chapter

1

A black mini-van cruised down the block at a slow pace. It slowed even more as it neared the middle of the block.

"Circle the block one more time. Make sure ain't no police coming," said Bryan.

"Man, you sure this dude keeps his money up in that raggedy-ass house?" Eric inquired. "I ain't doing this shit for nothing." He kept driving down the street.

Bryan was sitting on the passenger side, nervously pulling on a joint. "The dude got at least thirty or forty grand up in there."

Eric shook his head doubtedly. "Why I never heard of him then?"

Bryan was becoming frustrated with all of Eric's questions. For a second, he wished that he had come alone. But he was afraid of doing it by himself.

"Because he's not a drug dealer," explained Bryan. "He's a goddamn jacker. He runs with Snug."

"Snug?" Eric asked with surprise. "Aw, he good to go."

Eric parked at the end of the block. They both casually strolled up to the house.

"What now?"

Bryan fished a key out of one of the many flowerpots that cluttered the screened-in porch. He flashed it at Eric.

"I know somebody who knows somebody," Bryan bragged.

Seconds later, they entered the dark living room of the house. The place reeked of cat shit and was decorated with old, worn down furniture. Photographs of country-looking older white people filled the walls and mantle.

Eric couldn't believe what his eyes revealed to him. "What the fuck is this?"

Bryan smiled as he dug a flashlight out of his jacket pocket. "A cover-up. That's all. Follow me."

Eric followed Bryan into the master bedroom. Up against the far wall, next to the bed, was a large fish tank that housed a million rocks and a huge snake.

"Just like she said," Bryan stated with a smile. He rushed over to the tank and removed the top.

A black and red Diamondback was slithering over a small tree buried between the rocks. The sight of the snake sent a chill down Eric's spine.

"What the fuck're you doing?" Eric whispered loudly.

"Chill." Bryan pulled a small white mouse out of

his pocket, and tossed him inside. While he peered over at Eric, the snake struck the mouse.

While the snake was busy feasting, Bryan reached in and took him out. He placed the snake on the bed.

"Help me." Bryan started scooping the rocks out of the tank and onto the floor. Eric joined him.

After the last rock was removed they came upon a piece of cardboard. Bryan reached in and removed it. There, staring them in the face, were two layers of bundled money.

"Ooh, Bryan!" Eric shouted. "There it is, man."

"We're only taking half," Bryan explained.

"Why half?"

"Because I know the dude. Besides, he might not trip so hard if we don't take it all."

After they finished bagging the money, they replaced the rocks and snakes inside the tank. Then they left.

# # # #

While Bryan and Eric were breaking and entering, Ramon and Hershey were walking out of the movie theater.

"That was a good movie," Hershey commented. She wrapped her arm around him. "Thank you, baby." She kissed his cheek.

"Thank me when we get home."

"I can do that." She touched her lip. "Even though my lip is still a little swollen from you slapping me the other night."

Ramon sighed. "Don't start. We've been having a good time."

"I know," Hershey admitted. "I'm sorry. I'll ..."

"Just don't say nothing." Ramon thought about the bag of money under his seat. "I got to stop and put some money up first."

"Aw, man," Hershey pouted. "I'm ready to go home so we can do our thing."

"It's not gonna take no time for me to ..."

"Um hm," she murmured with her lips turned up.

Ramon came to a halt next to his Chevy Blazer and kissed her.

"Let's do it out here," Hershey suggested.

Ramon saw her nipples protruding through her blouse. He stopped and climbed into the truck.

Hershey continued to beg as she climbed in. She clutched his zipper, tugging at his pants.

"Damn, bitch, calm down," Ramon said angrily. "You act like you going dick crazy."

Glaring at him, Hershey said, "That was uncalled for, Ramon." She lifted her head. "You sure know how to ruin a good time." She sat with her arms folded across her chest.

"I'm sorry. C'mere."

The smile that she fought so hard to contain came busting out. "I'm not fooling with you, Ramon."

"Aw'ight."

# # # #

Ramon pulled into the driveway of his safe house before Hershey finally came up for air. She had been giving him head the whole way there. She wiped the slobber from her mouth with her hand.

"Hurry up, baby," Hershey said eagerly.

"Be right back."

When Ramon opened the front door, he did not hear his alarm beep. He placed his hand on his gun and listened for sounds of movement. He didn't hear anything, so he figured he must have forgotten to activate the alarm.

He checked the house for signs of forced entry. When he didn't see anything, he went into the bedroom and cut on the light. After he removed the covering off of the tank, he peered down and saw the mouse's tail hanging out of the snake's mouth.

Ramon reached in and removed the snake, then the rocks, and eventually the cardboard. Someone had discovered his stash spot. But only half of the money was missing.

Backing up against the wall, he glanced around the room while clutching the butt of his gun tucked away in his jeans. After a minute or so of stillness, he didn't hear a sound.

A large birdcage hung from the ceiling over by the closet. It was covered with a sheet. Ramon removed the cover, unveiling Willie, his big green and yellow parrot. Sitting on the floor beneath it was a jar of birdseeds. He shook a few into the palm of his hand, and then fed them to Willie.

"You hear anything good, ole buddy?" Ramon asked.

Willie flapped his wings, and then opened his mouth. "Occccccck! Ooh, Bryan," Willie mimicked.

Ramon smiled. "I knew you'd come through."

# # # #

Once they reached home, Ramon paid the babysitter and sent her home. While Hershey was getting ready to get in the shower, he got on the phone with the people at the alarm company and learned that his alarm had been deactivated earlier that evening. He had not been there in days. There was only one other person who had the code.

Hershey.

Hershey threw on her robe, picked up her towel and walked toward the bedroom door. Soon as she crossed the threshold, her throat was seized by Ramon's strong hand. She gasped as he brought the butt of his gun down on her forehead.

"Ouch!" Hershey hollered as she fell back and onto the bed. Her towel fell from her hand. "Owww!" She held her head in a daze, wondering what happened.

As soon as her head settled, she peered up and saw Ramon standing over her. His arm was wrapped around their daughter, Trishay's, shoulder with the gun in his hand.

"Call your fuckin' brother, now," Ramon demanded in a calm but deadly tone.

Hershey trembled under his cold stare.

"Okay. I ... I ... I ..." she stopped attempting to speak and picked up the phone. Bryan answered. "Bryan, what did you do? Why is —"

Ramon snatched the phone from her hand. The hand that held his gun remained on Trishay's shoulder. When Hershey reached out for her, Ramon took a step back.

"Bryan," Ramon spoke. "You got twenty minutes to bring me my fuckin' money, or I'ma kill your sister ... and if that don't do it, I'ma kill your niece, too. You hear me?"

Trishay peered at her mother with terror-filled eyes. She was only six, but could sense that she was in trouble.

"Man, I didn't ..."

"Twenty minutes." Ramon hung up.

Tears streamed down Hershey's face. "You would kill me and your own daughter over some shit that Bryan done? Huh?"

"Shut up, bitch. You could be in this just as deep as he is for all I know. Tell me, how did he find out where I kept my money? Or better yet, how did he deactivate the goddamn alarm?"

"I — ouch!" Ramon slapped her. She rolled off the bed onto the floor.

Ramon kneeled down and punched her in the face. "Answer me, bitch!"

"I told him where the key was," Hershey admitted. "I turned off the alarm earlier today." She paused to sniffle. "He was just supposed to be taking some girl over there for a while. That's all." She wiped the blood from her nose. "I didn't know he ..."

"You's a dumb-ass bitch. You know that?" Ramon kicked her in the leg.

Trishay grabbed him. "Daddy," she called out.

"Please don't hurt my baby," Hershey murmured.

Ramon raised the gun toward Hershey.

Trishay gasped. "Daddy!"

# # # #

Bryan had to break the news to Eric that they had to return the money.

Eric refused to hand over his half of the $50,000 split. He had risked his life to obtain it, and it was his to keep.

"That's my big sister and my little niece," Bryan pleaded. "Please, man. We have to give it back."

"Unt unh. That's your problem, dawg." Eric grabbed his bag of money and backed toward the exit.

"Eric, don't leave my family hanging like that."

"Trust me, dawg. He's not gonna kill his own family. He's not that crazy." Eric opened the door. "I promise to get at him if he does you, man. I'm out."

"Please Eric!" Bryan begged. "I can't —"

Eric closed the door and left.

Seconds later, Bryan heard the squeal of Eric's tires as he pulled off. "Fuck!"

# # # #

"I should kill your ass," Ramon stated in a cold voice as he lowered the gun. "You'd better pray that sucka of yours brings me my money." He took Trishay and left the room.

Ramon was sitting on the sofa next to Trishay when the doorbell rang. Hershey, who was sitting directly across from them, jumped up when she heard the bell.

"You want me to answer it?" Hershey asked nervously.

Ramon held his daughter close, then nodded.

Bryan saw the distressed look on his sister's battered face when the door swung open.

"Bryan, why?" she cried. "Why you do that?"

He tried to respond but nothing came out. Bryan stepped inside the house, and faced Ramon, who shot daggers at him.

Ramon cocked his gun. "Gimme my fuckin' money," he growled. Bryan tossed him the bag. "Empty it."

Bryan dumped its contents out on the floor, $25,000 short. Ramon could easily tell just by glancing at it that it wasn't all there.

He raised his gun.

Fear covered Bryan's face as he cringed, preparing to take the slugs. Ramon fired.

Boc!

Bryan fell back against the door clutching his stomach.

"Fuck is the rest of my money?" Ramon shouted.

Hershey scooped Trishay up and hurried across the room.

Bryan spit out a clot of blood. "E ... Eric, man. He wouldn't give ... give his half back." Tears formed in his eyes.

Slowly, Ramon rose from the sofa. "You know damn well that I wasn't gonna let you live. Didn't you?"

Bryan's eyes closed shut. His pain was becoming unbearable. "W ... we only took half."

"Well, you should've took all of it and ran with Eric. Now you's a dead thief."

Boc! Boc!

Bryan's body jerked with each blast.

"Nooo!" Hershey screamed out as she shielded Trishay's eyes from the horrific sight. "That's my baby brother!"

"Now he's your dead brother." Ramon spat on Bryan's lifeless face then left the house for the last time.

Fifteen minutes after Hershey called the police, they pulled Ramon's truck over. He was arrested and charged with second-degree murder.

chapter

2

15 Years Later

Snug Brim jumped on the freeway headed south in his blue BMW. The warm night breeze swooshed in through the sunroof as he accelerated. He could see emergency lights flashing about a half mile ahead. Just to be cautious, he clutched his Ruger in case he had to toss it.

His increasing heart rate began to settle after he rounded the bend and saw the cause of the flashing lights. Thankfully, they were coming from a tow truck and not the cops.

The last thing Snug wanted to do was part with his gun. His head was wanted by at least ten people. In fact, the only reason why he was still breathing was because his enemies fired on him from long distances. They lacked the courage to come within ten feet of him. His yen for robberies and homicides was the reason for his popularity around town.

His crew of thieves consisted of five people including himself. There was Bobby, who scouted the hits. AJ supplied the artillery. Chico drove the getaway car. Then there was the beautiful Yawni, who was used like a piece of exotic meat to encourage victims to bite. Together, they were responsible for ten percent of the city's current murder rate.

When the 55th exit came up, Snug got off the freeway. He drove all the way to Brooklyn Avenue, then made a left. As he neared the middle of the block, he slowed to a coast and picked up his cell phone.

"Hello."

"Ramon, bring yo' ass outside," Snug barked into the phone.

Minutes later, Ramon stepped out on the porch. Snug could see from the distance that instead of dreads, he was now wearing a baldhead. And he had dropped at least fifty pounds of fat.

Ramon took his time finishing his cigarette before thumping it onto the grass. "See you in the morning, mama," he hollered over his shoulder as he started toward the BMW.

Ramon had just been released from prison hours earlier. He was the sixth member of Snug's crew before he got locked up. Before he was indicted back in '89, he led the crew. Back then, they were more organized. Now, under Snug's command, they were a bunch of bloodthirsty, money-hungry cowboys.

"Ramon!" his mother shouted. "Try not to kill nobody. You just got out."

Ramon ignored his mother and got inside the

comfortable interior of the BMW.

"A 40-year-old mama's boy," Snug joked.

Ramon peered at Snug, who was now 38, and still the size of a 13-year-old, standing 5'7". He was handsome and an immaculate dresser.

"You got that right," Ramon retorted. "She's the only one who drove three hours to see me every month, too."

"Yeah, well. At least I kept your books straight," Snug said in defense as he drove away.

"That, you did."

"What happened to the dreadlocks?"

Ramon ran his palm over his baldhead. "Stress. It's a muthafucka being locked away, man."

Snug lit a cigarette. "I hope I never find out."

Ramon observed the lavish leather and wood grain interior of the new car. The navigation system lit up the whole front seat.

"Money must be good," Ramon commented.

Snug smirked. "We done came a long way from robbing drug dealers. Now we hittin' big businesses and shit, like on TV." He chuckled.

While they strolled up the avenue, Ramon observed the scenery like a child looking in a candy store window. Streets had changed. The small family-owned businesses that were once around either had moved, shut down or been replaced. Wire wheels were no longer in style. Fifteen inches wasn't even considered a big rim anymore. Now, rims were 28 inches tall. Some of them even cost five figures. Now that Ramon had turned 40, flashy wheels and drugs wasn't where his head was.

Ramon picked up Snug's cell phone. "How do you use this thing?"

"Dial the number, then press send," he instructed. "Who you calling?"

"Sheena. She's at the hotel waiting on me."

"Sheena?" Snug repeated in a surprised tone. "Aw, shit, man. That skeezer was everybody's bitch while you was gone. Now she's got five kids and broken down." He laughed. "Man, you kill me."

Ramon shrugged. "She kept writing letters and sending me change while I was down. Even visited once or twice. The least I could do to show gratitude is fuck her."

"I guess."

"Besides, I'm horny as a muthafucka. Do you realize I'm forty, and haven't sucked a pussy?"

"Really? What about Hershey?"

Ramon went silent.

Snug said, "Aw, man, let that shit go. Her brother stole your money. You had to kill him. The muthafucka shouldn't have done it. I would've killed both of 'em."

"Whatever happened to Hershey?"

Snug sucked his teeth. "I don't know. Last I heard the bitch moved to Columbia."

"I missed my family."

Snug was unsympathetic. "Well, obviously they don't miss you, or the bitch wouldn't have put you away. Point blank."

Snug drove Ramon out to the hotel on 87th Street next to the Amoco gas station. The parking lot was full. A light blue '96 Chevy Impala was parked at the entrance. Snug parked behind it.

"A'ight, you old muthafucka," Snug teased.

Ramon gazed at the entrance doors. "I'ma shack up here for a few days. So you know where to find me if you need me."

Snug turned off the ignition. "I'm coming in to use the bathroom." He pulled a condom out of his pocket on their way inside. "Use this. Right now you're disease free. Keep it that way."

"Good lookin' out," Ramon said as he accepted it.

The two occupants of the Impala both heard the voices and turned around. The driver winced when he saw Ramon's familiar face. The man had aged a little, and had grown a goatee, but it was him.

Eric reached inside his glove box and removed his gun.

"Wha'sup?" his friend asked with concern.

"That's that nigga who shot Bryan."

The dude glanced out the back window at the two figures entering the building.

"What you wanna do?"

"I promised Bryan that I would kill that nigga if something happened to him."

"Let's do it."

# # # #

After Ramon obtained the room key from the front desk, he and Snug found Room 205. Ramon's manhood was throbbing from the excitement. He could already feel the insides of Sheena's warm pussy.

"Here we go," Ramon said out loud. "Room 205." He placed the key in the slot. When the light flashed green he turned the handle. "Hell-ooo!"

Sheena hurried and pushed "play" on her portable radio, then took her position on the bed. Earth, Wind & Fire started playing through the speakers.

She lay naked on the bed with her legs open. As Ramon stood in front of the TV, Snug ducked into the bathroom. Ramon's eyes scanned her chocolate body. Her titties were starting to sag, her belly had a small pudge and stretch marks surrounded her waist like a belt. But she was still fine in the face. There were no laugh lines or dark circles around her eyes.

Sheena cupped her sagging titties and massaged them gently. Ramon forced himself not to laugh. He had gotten used to looking at the flawless young models inside the magazines while in prison. However, since Sheena looked out for him, he planned on making her his main broad. But he was gonna have to find a young, tender mistress to fuck on.

Snug snuck out of the bathroom, out of Sheena's sight, hit Ramon with a smile, then crept out the door. Ramon approached the bed. Sheena got up on her knees and started tracing his muscular arms with her hands.

"I see you made good use of all that time," she complimented, referring to his muscles.

He kissed her. Sheena immediately began undressing him.

# # # #

When Snug walked out of the hotel room, Eric and his partner were strolling up the hallway. Eric's buddy nodded at Snug. Snug, being that hard gangsta, ignored him and kept on walking.

Eric and his friend lingered in the hallway until Snug disappeared around the corner.

"Which room did he come out of?"

"This one here," Eric replied. He took out his gun and knocked on the door.

# # # #

Ramon was lying in bed with Sheena on top of him. He gently caressed her back while she nibbled on his neck and face. He slid his hands down to her butt cheeks, guiding her up and down on his dick.

"Yessss," Sheena murmured. "Give it to me, old man."

Knock. Knock.

Sheena frowned as she turned her head toward the door. "Who in the hell —" the sudden jerking feeling inside her womb alerted her that Ramon was cumming.

"I know you didn't cum."

Ramon grinned bashfully. "I did just get out after doing fifteen years without no pussy. You should be proud that your pussy is so good."

Sheena scowled. "Proud? Nigga, I'm mad that I didn't get mine."

"I'm not through. Just give me a second to rest up. Now go get the door."

She stared at him for a moment. "It better get back up." She kissed his lips, then got up.

He watched her put on her blouse and head for the door. Her unbelievably still-firm ass jiggled as she walked.

"You still got a trunk on that old Buick," he joked.

She smacked one of her cheeks and kept on walking.

Ramon rose from the bed and walked into the bathroom. When Sheena opened the door, Eric had the gun pointed at her face. A horrified look came over her.

Standing before the mirror, Ramon gazed down at his limp organ. He noticed that when hard, it didn't stand as straight as it used to, back when he was 25. Now it was tilted a little to the right.

"Ba-by," Sheena called in a weak voice.

Ramon could tell by her voice that there was trouble. He stepped to the side of the closed bathroom door.

"Yes?" he answered.

"Wasn't nobody at the door," she lied. "Come out so we can finish." Her voice was shaky.

"I'm 'bout to take a shower."

"I'm coming in."

The door slowly eased open. Ramon stood behind it. Through the crack, he saw Sheena walk in. Eric was behind her holding his gun in her back. Ramon waited until he thought she was safely through, then with all the force he could muster, he kicked the door closed on Eric's hand. But not before Eric fired a single round into Sheena's back.

Sheena fell forward onto the sink. Ramon didn't have time to check on her. His own life was on the line. The door slammed on Eric's arm. He fired another shot into the wall. Ramon kicked the door repeatedly until the gun fell to the floor. When he reached down to get it, the door flung open, knocking him on his side. Eric rushed in holding his right arm, kicking at him.

Snug barged in just as Eric's friend entered the bathroom.

Boc! Boc!

Snug fired two shots into his back. His body flew into Eric, knocking him over on Ramon. Ramon grabbed Eric's sore arm and twisted it.

"Ahh!" Eric yelled.

Snug casually walked over and fired a single round into Eric's head. Ramon closed his eyes until it was over. When he felt Eric's body jerk, then go limp, he kicked him off, then hurried to his feet.

Sheena was lying on her back, gasping for air. Blood was all over the floor. Ramon almost slipped and fell trying to get to her.

"Call an ambulance!" Ramon shouted.

Snug didn't move. He had shot enough people to know that Sheena wouldn't make it.

"Ramon," Snug said, "let's go, man."

"No!" Ramon held Sheena's head in his arms. She gazed up at him briefly, then slipped into the world of the unknown. "Snug, call the —"

"She's gone, Ramon." Snug looked up when he heard the police sirens. "Let's beat it, man."

"I'm not running. I'll be here with a story to tell 'em."

"Suit yourself. Just keep my name out of it." Snug left back out the way he came.

Ramon gazed into Sheena's dead orbs wondering, *why did this have to happen?* She looked after him while he was down and out. Now he would never get the chance to repay her.

When the Kansas City newspaper came out the following day, the front-page article read:

Three killed in hotel room
Two gunmen barged inside a couple's hotel room allegedly in an attempt to flee from another gunman. An altercation broke out between one of the gunmen and the male hotel room occupant. The third gunman barged in and shot the first two gunmen. But not before the female

occupant took a bullet to the back, after the first gunman's gun went off. The third gunman fled, while the male victim watched his girlfriend die in his arms.

The survivor is listed as 40-year-old Ramon Delay.

chapter

3

2 Months Later

Ever since the triple homicide at the hotel, business had declined. Guests complained that the place lacked security guards and that the rooms were not secure enough for the cost. Lowering the price of the rooms was not an option, considering the large monthly overhead.

The end result was the hotel was forced to sell, or they would be closed down in the near future. All because a group of black men decided to use the place as a shooting gallery.

Mr. Montel Murphy, the hotel's owner, owned many businesses in the state of Missouri. He used his street smarts and connects to help muscle small businesses into selling out to his company and all kinds of other mischief. His only weakness was that he loved black pussy.

Murphy figured that most black women came from poor backgrounds or were down on their luck; so he showered them with expensive gifts and trips, and often bragged about his business ventures while lying in bed.

But after it was all said and done, Murphy was a lonely old man. He had spent the better part of his life chasing young girls and forgot to settle with someone near his age who he could grow old with. Someone who would love him and not his huge bankroll.

He knew that the young broads only went for him because he was rich. That's why he had developed a soft spot for Yawni.

Yawni pretended to love him with the skill of an old prostitute. She would look him in the eye while he talked, tend to his needs when he was sick, and never asked for anything that wasn't forced upon her. She tried to get pregnant by him, but old Murphy never laid her without protection. Yawni even offered to be his wife, which he regretfully declined. No one would inherit a dime of his fortune when he passed. He planned on spending what he could while he was alive. The rest would be donated to various charities and foundations across the world.

Murphy finished cleaning his dentures inside the bathroom of his downtown loft. Yawni was sprawled over the bed watching TV. She wore nothing but a pair of pink lace panties and a pair of stilettos. They had just finished role-playing a little while before.

She ran her long fingers through her bushy, brownish-golden hair. Yawni was mixed but had more white features than black, with a pointed nose and thin lips. She looked like a rich kitten lying there. She was long in the legs and round in the chest.

"Ready for bed, big daddy?" Yawni purred.

"Yeah. First, fix me a drink, would ya?"

"Sure."

While she prepared his nightcap, he removed his silk robe, unveiling his pudgy, hairy stomach, then sat on the bed. Yawni returned a minute later with his drink.

"Here you go, sweetie." She climbed in bed behind him and massaged his shoulders. "You're tense. What's eating you?"

Murphy took a sip. "Ah! Business ain't so good."

"Which one? You own twenty of them."

"My hotel here in the city." He sipped on his drink. "It's been going down hill fast since those murders happened." He rubbed his sagging chin as if in thought. "I need to sell it fast, before I'm forced to close it."

"Don't worry. You'll think of something." She tapped his shoulder. "C'mon and lay down. Rest your bones."

Murphy finished his drink before getting under the covers with her.

"Yeah," Murphy said. "I'll think of something. Listen, you keep your ear to the street for any potential buyers, okay? Things might get a little grimey, you know what I mean?"

Yawni didn't answer. She was in deep thought. Murphy had just given her an idea. She would run it by Snug in the morning and see what he thought.

chapter
4

Snug and Yawni arrived at Laura's Soul Food diner on 75th. Ramon was inside sitting at a table, enjoying a fried catfish dinner and watching the basketball game. The place was empty with the exception of him and the two owners.

"Duncan can't play for shit," Ramon blurted out. "All that fuckin' money he makes and he can't even make a fuckin' free throw."

The cook, Tank - who was also one of the owners - sat next to him shaking his head in agreement.

Snug and Yawni walked through the door.

"Hey, Tank. What's up?" Snug said. Anybody who was looking could have seen the pistol bulging out of Snug's waist.

Ramon shot Tank a look that said *get somewhere*.

"Good seein' you, Snug," Tank said on his way to the back.

Yawni gave Ramon a hug and a peck on the lips.

"Mm, I've been waiting years to kiss those big,

juicy lips," Yawni joked. She could see fuzz growing on his head around a bald spot. "What's up with the head?"

"Losing my damn hair."

"It's sexy."

"Quit playing."

Snug and Yawni sat at the table with him.

"So?" Ramon inquired. "What's this all about?"

Yawni decided to do the talking. "Well, a friend of mine owns the hotel that Sheena got killed at. Problem is, since them murders happened, business hasn't been good. In fact, it's looking to shut down within the next year."

Ramon shrugged while he continued to devour his meal.

"... me and Snug think that it will be a good idea if me, him, AJ, Bobby and Chico bought it. And we figured since you're the one with the degree and all the brains, you'd be in charge of it. You could act as manager. Only the six of us will split the proceeds."

Ramon spit out a chicken bone. "Doesn't sound very profitable. Not with six people going in on a hotel that's foreclosing."

Snug joined the conversation. "Exactly, Ramon. But we'll be able to clean up the dirty money that we be stealing."

"That doesn't do me any good."

"Sure it does. You get to keep fifty percent while the rest of us get ten apiece."

Ramon rubbed his chin as if in thought. "And I'd

have total control?"

Yawni thumped cigarette ashes in the tray. "Consider it yours."

"How much does the hotel cost?"

"Three million," Snug said as if it were a small amount.

"Y'all already got the cash?"

Snug looked to Yawni, who said, "Not yet, but we're working on it."

"Working on it, meaning you're planning a big score?" Ramon asked.

Yawni nodded.

"I want in."

"Why?" Snug was curious.

"Because. Not only do I want to run the business, but I also want part ownership of it. We do it my way, or I won't get involved. Point blank."

Yawni shifted her gaze over to Snug, and smiled. "You got it," she answered. She stood. "I'll be in touch." She motioned for Snug to follow.

Outside the restaurant, Yawni waited at the passenger door for Snug to unlock the car.

"You owe me a hundred bucks," she said across the hood of the car. "I told you he would come along."

"Yeah, yeah. Get in the fuckin' car."

# # # #

Two Days Later
Ramon was sitting at the same table inside Laura's

Soul Food joint playing dominoes with Tank.

He slammed a bone down on the table. *Blam!* "Fideen!" he shouted. "And domino. Shake that shit up," Ramon heckled.

"You ain't gon' win, if that's what you're thinking," Tank bellowed. "I betcha that."

"If you trick 'em, you can beat 'em, Tank," Ramon joked as he selected seven new bones. "Let's see here."

Yawni walked through the door. She had on high heels, capri jeans and a sleeveless blouse that fastened around her thin neck. Her bare chest hid behind the thin material.

"Goddamn baby," Tank exclaimed. "You know your meal is on the house."

Yawni smiled. "Thanks, baby, but I don't do meat."

"None?"

"I take that back," Yawni peered over at Ramon. "There is one rare T-bone cooked well done that I would love to feast on."

"Ooh wee! What we gonna do with her, Ramon?"

"Put her on tape and sell it in the back of a magazine."

They all laughed.

Yawni said, "Seriously, Ramon. I need you to take a ride with me."

Ramon sucked his teeth. "Is it business or pleasure?"

"Umm, maybe a little of both." She flashed her wide grin.

Ramon stood up. "Tank, hold it down until I return."

# # # #

Yawni ordered Ramon to drive her Lexus truck while she rode shotgun. She instructed him to take Highway 71 all the way downtown. He was relaxing to the Isley Brothers CD when she leaned over and began unzipping his pants.

"Yawni, what ..."

"Relax, nigga. I'm trying to see something." Yawni opened his pants and took out his dick. She put it up under her nose, and then sniffed. "Just like I thought. You ain't had no pussy. Have you?" She shook his dick while talking to him. "Have you?"

"I haven't had time," he replied sheepishly. "I've been so stressed about money that it probably won't ... mmm."

Ramon felt her warm jaws and smooth lips as she took him in and out of her mouth. Yawni positioned herself so she could go all the way down on him, feeling his head bumping her throat.

Slurrrp ... Slurrrp.

Yawni took one of his hands and placed it on her ass.

"Doo wroom mm uck," she mumbled with a mouth full of his swipe.

"I'm not gon' wreck your truck ... sst. Mm goddamn, this shit feels good." He swerved a little bit, but immediately regained control.

There was a slippery sucking noise when Yawni quickly pulled him out of her mouth. "Man —"

"Girl, just keep on going." He pushed her head back down.

"Stick your finger in my butt while I'm doing it."

# # # #

By the time they arrived at Murphy's downtown office, Ramon felt like he had been actually fucking Yawni. Truthfully, he was in shock. Never before had she so boldly thrown herself on him like that.

Ramon pulled into the parking lot.

"What now?"

Yawni fixed her hair and lipstick inside the mirror. "Now we go in." She faced Ramon. "How do I look?"

"Like a white girl."

"Good. Let's go."

A sexy young black secretary of about 22 escorted them back to Murphy's office. He was standing by the window peering through a huge telescope at the downtown area. Ramon could see gray, wavy hair that only grew on the back of his head.

Ramon leaned toward Yawni and whispered, "I see we got something in common."

"Shhh!" She murmured. "Ba-by."

Murphy stopped peeping and turned around. Yawni walked up to him and gave him a short but passionate kiss on the lips.

"That's enough," Murphy joked. "There's no telling where those lips have been. Huh? Huh?" He laughed. Ramon laughed with him.

"Ha, ha," Yawni retorted. "Fuck the both of y'all."

"So." Murphy patted his stomach. "Who do we have here?"

"Montel, this is my longtime friend, Ramon." She led Ramon over to Murphy. "Ramon, this is Montel."

They both shook hands and nodded at one another.

"Have a seat," Murphy offered as he walked behind his desk. "Can Yawni get you anything? A cigar perhaps?"

"I'm fine."

"I'll have a cigarette," Yawni said. She fired one up, then took a seat next to Ramon with her legs crossed.

Murphy sat back in his chair. "Ramon, let me be frank and tell you that I have a problem." Ramon nodded. "I need you to help me solve it. I own three banks. One in Springfield, Missouri. One in Jefferson City, Missouri and one right here in Kansas City."

Ramon sat back in his chair and braced himself for what was next to come.

Murphy sighed before he continued. "I want you to rob all three of them." Ramon attempted to speak, but Murphy raised his hand. "Hear me out, first. I'll supply you with all the inside information that you'll need to carry this thing out. In the end, if it all goes well, you should make out with two million in cash, and two million worth of bonds. Those, I'll be happy to buy back at half price. Plus, I get a fourth of the two million. The money that you'll get will be used to buy my hotel. Since I hear you took part in helping it go under, anyway."

"Let me get this straight." Ramon sat up. "I ... we steal your money, give you a cut, then buy your unprofitable hotel? And then you'll file a claim to get your money back from your insurance company?"

"Yes," Murphy replied frankly. "That's my plan."

Ramon shifted his gaze over to Yawni, who winked at him.

"If you say so," Ramon finally agreed.

Murphy smiled. "Good. My people will be in touch with you soon." He extended his hand.

Ramon shook it.

# # # #

Inside the dining room of Snug's home, Bobby, Yawni, AJ and Chico gathered around a round table. Snug was busy setting up the slide projector.

They were all dressed in black suits and mock neck shirts. Yawni had on a black suit with a white blouse—their typical meeting gear.

Eight minutes later, Ramon entered the room wearing the exact same suit as the men, except he wore a turtleneck underneath. In his hand he carried a black briefcase that he placed on the table. He opened it, took out some slides, and tossed them to Yawni.

"Handle those for me, please," Ramon commanded.

While Yawni pulled down the projection screen and loaded the projector, Ramon addressed the group. "How is everybody?"

They all nodded. Each of them were either sipping coffee or puffing on a Newport.

"First off, people, we got three banks on our list. The first is located in Springfield. The second in Jefferson City and the last, which will be our biggest challenge, is right here in the city. The only good thing about it is that Bobby has put together a good escape plan, so it shouldn't be a problem."

Yawni started up the projector. While Ramon did the explaining, she worked the controls. There wasn't a weak link in the room, and Ramon was aware of that. Trust was not an issue with them. The issue was getting the jobs done and returning safely with the money.

Though Ramon had not pulled a robbery in 15 years and had turned 40, Snug still felt at ease about letting him come along. He remembered how well Ramon handled himself at the hotel that night Eric tried to kill him.

After all of the slides were shown, and Ramon had run out of things to say, Snug added his own afterthought.

"The most important thing," Snug said, "is that each of you know your role. Three minutes is all we have to get in and out of a bank. Y'all know that." He peered at Chico. "Chico, what do you do if you spot the heat?"

"Get on my radio and yell abort."

"If you hear abort, drop whatever you're doing and get the hell out of there," Snug stated. "No ifs ands or buts."

Ramon scanned the well-groomed group with his hawk eyes and was impressed by what he saw.

"Get out of here," he commanded. "This meeting is adjourned."

"And no fucking," Yawni added in a motherly tone. "Y'all know how pussy slows you down."

AJ turned around, pouting. "Aw, come on, ma."

"Especially not you, AJ," Yawni said. "You act like you can't function after you get a shot of young pussy. And we don't need anybody arriving late. A late nigga ..."

"Is a dead nigga," AJ finished her statement. "I know."

Everybody in the room understood that the queen meant business and meant every word she spoke. Their bills getting paid depended on each of them carrying out their jobs correctly.

# # # #

"Ah! Ahhh! Ahhh!" Yawni screamed out in passion. She was in the doggy style position while

Ramon stood behind her, pounding his hammer into her backside. He grabbed her hair. She tried to scoot up toward the headboard, away from him. He put his knees up on the bed, chasing the cat, still continuously stabbing her guts.

"Ooh! Ooh! Ooh! Ramon, p ... please. Un huh. I promise I won't ... urrrgh!"

"Unt unh, bitch. Don't run. Don't run. Take it. Take it." Ramon pulled at her hair.

Yawni held onto the headboard, screaming, "I'm about to ... to ... cum!" Pussy juice came squirting out of her onto his dick and pelvis. "Shiiit!"

Ramon lay down on the bed panting. Yawni crawled on top of him. He could feel her heart thumping against his chest.

"Say you give, bitch. Callin' me no fuckin' old man."

"I give. I give, baby," Yawni surrendered. She placed her hand on her stomach. "Man, I can still feel you inside of there. I probably got bruises on my uterus."

"I was trying to kill you."

"Okay, killer." She kissed his chest and reached for her cigarettes on the nightstand. She fired up two and placed one between Ramon's lips. "It's been a while. You're sure you're up for a gun fight?"

"Yeah. I had one the first day I got out, remember? A killer never loses his touch."

Yawni held her cigarette away from her face while she admired him. "I love you, Ramon."

He ran his hand up her thigh. "I love you, too. But we can never be together. Friends are friends, so let's keep it that way."

Yawni's face reddened. "If you say so." She glanced at her watch. "I've gotta take a shower so I can leave. You're welcome to stay."

"Where you headed? To the old man's?"

"Yes." She puffed on her cigarette. "I like to be at his house when he returns. Makes him feel wanted. Is there anything I can have him get you?"

Ramon placed his hands behind his head, and locked his fingers. "Nah. I'll have everything I need in less than a year."

Yawni stood and put on a sheer robe. Her nipples stabbed at the fabric. Ramon regarded her hairy pubic mound with a lustful gaze.

"Your hair is tangled," he informed her.

Yawni scratched her pelvis. "Better?" She struck a pose.

He nodded in approval.

"Okay." She headed for the bathroom. "I don't know why you're commenting on a pussy you don't want."

Ramon smiled as he shook his head.

chapter

5

The bank in Springfield wasn't crowded. That's why Ramon chose to do it on a Wednesday, because it was unlikely to be busy.

Yawni was inside the bank discussing a loan with the bank's manager. She was dressed in a beige business suit, low-heeled pumps and glasses. Her hair was in a ponytail and she clutched a crocodile briefcase.

Very discreetly, she took in the scenery around her while in conversation with the manager. There were four bank tellers behind the counters. Two of them in their mid 40s. The other two looked to be in their early 20s.

An old guard with a gray handlebar mustache stood by the restroom door, sipping on a cup of hot java while chatting with one of the loan officers. Four customers were standing in line. Three women and a man.

Yawni excused herself so she could use the restroom. She waited around in front of the restroom mirror and pretended to check her make-up until the bathroom cleared. Her super dark foundation, false eyelashes and green contact lenses made her unrecognizable to even her own mother.

Once the bathroom cleared, she shut and secured the door. Then she took her radio out of her bag.

"C2 to C1, over," she whispered.

Chico, Snug and Bobby had just pulled up in front of the building in an old-school Impala.

Bobby raised his radio to his lips. "C1 to C2. Go 'head, over."

Yawni quickly gave them a description of what was gong on inside the bank. The entire crew listened intently until she finished talking.

Bobby said, "Okay C2, we're comin' in. C1 to the road runner, get ready to move in."

Ramon flushed the toilet inside the bank's restroom. He checked the chamber of the P89 that Murphy had stashed behind the toilet. Dressed in black slacks and a turtleneck, he exited the stall, then pulled the ski mask down over his face. Before he walked out the door, he took a deep breath.

The old guard was standing right outside the door, still chatting with the female loan officer. Her blue eyes expanded when she saw Ramon come up behind him. Ramon brought the butt of the gun down on the guard's head.

Thump.

He snatched up the loan officer at the same time AJ, Bobby and Snug came storming in. They all gripped AK-47s. Snug held two of them. He handed one to Ramon who tucked the P89 inside his waist.

"Come with me," Ramon ordered the loan officer.

"Ow!" she yelped as he yanked her.

Snug shouted, "Everybody down, now! This is a muthafuckin' robbery. Do as the fuck I say and you won't be fuckin' hurt."

Bobby and AJ rushed the four tellers with their guns drawn. AJ tossed the bags to Bobby, who threw them at the first teller.

"Take one and pass the rest," he commanded.

The bank manager froze as he watched Ramon, gun in hand, dragging the loan officer his way. The guard attempted to rise, but Snug kicked him in the face, then relieved him of his revolver.

Ramon shoved the loan officer into the manager. "What's your name?" he yelled.

"Huh?" the loan officer replied nervously.

"Your fuckin' name. Tell me your name."

"Sheila. Sheila Crawford."

"Okay, Sheila. Tell your boss to give you the key, now."

The manager's hand shook violently while he went into his desk drawer and produced a gold key. Ramon snatched it from him, then backhanded him with his gloved fist. Light cries and sniffles could be heard while Ramon hauled Sheila across the floor and inside the vault. He took a laundry bag out of his pocket and threw it at her.

"Fill it," Ramon ordered. "You got 45 seconds. Keep a stack for yourself."

One of the older tellers was preparing to hit the silent alarm. Just to be safe, she peeped above the counter to see if anyone was watching her. Over by the women's restroom, she saw Yawni peeking out the door. Yawni signaled her by holding up her cell phone, indicating that she had called 911. The teller nodded, then continued filling the bag.

Two minutes and forty-two seconds after they first entered the bank, the four men walked out the front door, each carrying a duffle bag full of money. Ten seconds earlier, Yawni phoned the police claiming to be a hiding hostage in a bank robbery.

Chico pulled up out front in the Impala. They all hurried into the car.

Early the next morning, they drove to Jefferson City and robbed the second bank that afternoon. The bank in Kansas City would be more difficult. They needed a week to recuperate before they took on that challenge.

During that time, Ramon made plans for his new hotel. Since the place was already down hill, he had to think of something that would bring clientele back. Something that would generate

more income than any other hotel in the city —
enough to make him a known name across
America. He wanted tickets to golf tournaments,
box seats at the stadium. To be a friend of famous
entertainers. To sum it all up, he wanted to conquer the American dream—to be rich.

chapter

6

The alarm clock beeped.

AJ jumped out of bed. "What time is it?" The clock read 3:30 pm. "Oh, shit!" He jumped up and hurried into his clothes.

The girl sleeping next to him raised her head from under the covers. She ran her fingers through her wild hair, and let out a long sigh.

"Baby, where're you goin' now?" she inquired.

"Shut up!" AJ hollered. "You're the fuckin' reason I'ma be late."

She shot him an angry look, then shook her head as she watched him run around. AJ couldn't find his shirt. She could tell what he was looking for by the way he was patting his chest. To assist him, she raised her naked body up and walked to the bathroom. Seconds later, she returned carrying his shirt.

"Lookin' for this?" She held it up with a smile on her face, thinking that she had just pleased him.

AJ scowled. "Bitch, you find something funny?" He crept over to her, clutching her arms. "Huh?"

Quickly he released her right arm to slap her face, then shook her violently.

"Baby, please," she cried.

AJ shoved her down on the bed. Only halfway dressed, he picked up his gun and made for the door.

"And don't call me, either. You funky-ass whore." AJ slammed the door behind him.

The woman put up her middle finger. "Fuck you," she said to the closed door.

# # # #

Chico, Snug and Bobby were waiting outside AJ's house in the Impala. They had been waiting for AJ to show up for over 30 minutes. Snug's temperature continuously elevated as the minutes passed. He had become tired of glancing at his watch ten minutes before.

Bobby looked at his. "Where's this nigga—"

Before he finished his sentence, he saw AJ's Suburban flying up the block. He whipped into the driveway and was out of the truck in a hurry.

Snug said, "Nobody say a word when he gets in here."

AJ climbed into the backseat. "Man, I had to ..."

Chico bolted away from the curb.

Eerrrrrk.

# # # #

The bank was unbelievably crowded. The fact

that it was near closing time didn't make a difference, like Ramon had planned. But the robbery still had to be carried out.

Yawni walked in, dressed in her usual garb. Through her dark glasses she scanned the room. Cameras were on every wall and above every counter. Those wouldn't be a problem, since the bank's owner was in on the job.

There was a line of people at the ATM machine and at each of the five teller windows. There were even a few people standing in the commercial account line. This time the security guard was in his 20s and looked to be in good shape. He casually walked around tapping a flashlight against his thigh. He seemed anxious, like he was waiting on something to kick off.

Yawni discreetly walked to the restroom and ducked into a stall. She texted Snug and Ramon all the information they needed. Since the place was so crowded, Yawni herself would have to get involved.

She left the restroom and stood in line for teller #3.

"Hi," she heard a child's voice say.

Yawni peered down and saw a little white girl staring up at her. She put on a false smile.

"Hello."

"My stepdaddy is a cop," the girl stated.

"Is that so?"

"Um hm." She pointed to a black man with a clean cut and a goatee. He was standing at the counter filling out a deposit slip. "There he is right there. He's the best ..."

The little girl's voice faded out as Yawni lowered her glasses and watched the man closely. His back-up revolver was bulging out of his tight-fitting rugby shirt. How could she have missed something as crucial as that? The man's face had cop written all over it. That wasn't the kind of thing that she would have missed five years ago. Age did have its downfalls.

She looked at her watch and saw that it was almost showtime. *Damn!* Too late to call it off. Yawni would just have to play it by ear.

"... him and my mommy are getting married soon," the little girl's voice registered again. "Did you hear me?"

"Huh? Yes, yes, I heard you." Yawni walked away. She didn't see the little girl stick her tongue out at her.

The cop was having a difficult time filling out the deposit slip. He was already on his third one. Yawni snuck up behind him. He glanced back at her, smiled, then continued with what he was doing.

Yawni watched him mess up another slip before offering her assistance.

"Excuse me," she said, tapping his shoulder lightly.

He turned around.

"Do you need some assistance?"

The cop smiled.

# # # #

Ramon hung up the pay phone outside the bank after he saw the Impala drop off its occupants. The people outside the bank and around the area were too busy doing their own things to notice three armed men walking toward the bank. If they had, they probably wouldn't have believed what they were seeing.

They were ten feet away from the entrance when Ramon slipped in ahead of them.

The security guard was at the entrance. He was just about to start locking out customers. "Excuse me, sir. We're closing." The security guard held up his hand.

"Ah, can't you just," Ramon hit him with his taser, "make an exception?"

The guard collapsed onto the floor.

Snug passed Ramon an AK-47 on his way over to the tellers. One of the tellers tensed up when she saw Snug storming toward her, rifle in hand. She went for the emergency button.

He pointed the rifle at her. "Remove your finger from that button," he commanded.

The crowd turned around at the sound of Snug's voice. Seeing the powerful rifle in his hands sent them into panic.

"Ahhh!" Screams came from all directions.

Bobby took one side, AJ took the other and Snug jumped up on the counter.

"Everybody on the floor. Now!" Ramon shouted as he walked through, brandishing his weapon. The people did as they were told, but they weren't moving fast enough. Ramon snatched up the policeman's little girl. "Do it now, or she gets it."

Snug handed the bags to the tellers. "Fill 'em. And no funny money."

The cop hesitated as he slowly got down on the floor. Yawni waited for him to comply before she dropped. She kept one hand above her head, and one on the .38 inside her blazer pocket.

The manager stood silent, hoping that the robber would go on without bothering him. He almost shitted on himself when he saw Ramon storming toward him.

"You," Ramon yelled, pointing a stiff finger at the manager. "Come with me." He snatched the man by the collar, and dragged him to the vault.

"W...what are you looking for?"

"Bonds," Ramon replied. "All of 'em."

The manager's hands shook while he opened the safe. Then he took a step back.

"On your knees and lock your hands behind your head." After the manager obeyed his command, Ramon put the AK around his neck and started filling the bags.

The police officer felt helpless lying there, watching his scared stepdaughter. She was facing the wall with her hands up, having a hard time counting backward from 100. Ramon told her that if she reached one before they had left, then she cheated, and would be punished.

After the tellers filled the bags, they handed them to Snug. He threw two of the bags at Bobby, who in turn slung one to AJ.

The cop on the floor thought that it was the perfect time to make his move. He gazed at his partner, Officer Bierman, who was on the floor near the teller counter, staring back at him. He gave Bierman the signal to make his move.

Bierman jumped and drew his .38 revolver. "Police! Nobody move!" he ordered. He aimed it at Snug.

The officer next to Yawni got on his feet as well, drawing his gun. "Drop 'em, now!"

AJ moved. Officer Bierman removed his aim from Snug, and shot at AJ.

Pop! Pop!

AJ dove behind the counter.

By the time Bierman swung his gun back to Snug, Snug had the rifle pointed at him. Just as he was about to shoot, the other officer fired, hitting Snug in the arm. The cop got to take one step before he felt the barrel of Yawni's Glock buried in the small of his back.

Boc! Boc!

The crowd started screaming as they jumped up and ran around. The little girl closed her eyes tight and kept on counting. No one attempted to rescue her.

Bobby ran to check on AJ. Bierman ducked behind the manager's desk. Yawni crouched low and fired two shots in his direction.

Boc! Boc!

Inside the safe, Ramon immediately stopped bagging after hearing the gunfire. Then he heard Yawni scream, "Abort!" over the radio. He zipped the bags and peeped out the safe's door.

He saw Bierman crouched behind a desk with a gun in his hand, speaking into a radio. Across the room, he saw Yawni kneeling down with her gun aimed at the desk. Snug was getting up off the floor. Blood soaked his sleeve. Bobby and AJ were hiding behind two pillars. Sirens could be heard nearby. Ramon leveled his AK at Bierman's head.

Du-Du-Du-Du!

The bullets ripped through Bierman's chin, neck and upper chest. The radio fell from his hand. Ramon walked up on him and pointed the rifle.

Du-Du-Du!

Ramon tossed Yawni one of the bags. "Let's go."

A blue unmarked Crown Victoria pulled up in front just as they were coming out. Before the detectives got a chance to do anything, Ramon and Snug fired on the car.

Du-Du-Du-Du! Du-Du-Du-Du!

The hail of bullets ripped through the metal like it was cotton. The detectives inside fell to the floor for cover.

"C'mon," Yawni yelled. She took off toward the back of the building. Her adrenaline was pumping. She had never come this close to being caught before.

Another car pulled up trying to cut them off. The driver jumped out, using his door as a shield, then pointed his weapon.

"Freeze!" he commanded.

Yawni pointed her pistol, firing at the door's window. The officer fell backward.

Ramon brought up the rear. "Go! Go! Go!"

Shots started coming from behind them. They ducked behind Popeye's Chicken and ran until they came upon a manhole. Ramon stood guard until everybody was down the hole. Then he climbed down and covered the hole with the lid.

"Run!" Yawni urged.

Funky sewage water splashed up on the legs of their pants as they ran through the dark tunnel. No one could see ahead, but they knew the direction in which they were headed.

"I can't see," AJ whined.

"Shut up and c'mon!" Yawni yelled back at him. "Damnit!" The heel had broken off of her shoe, causing her to fall.

Ramon ran into her. He felt around until he found her foot, then took off her other shoe.

"I got too much baggage to carry you," he said. "Get up and run barefoot. C'mon, it's just water." He helped her up, and they were on the move again.

They ran for several long blocks until they came upon the opening that they were looking for. The Impala's powerful engine could be heard roaring.

That eased their nerves a little.

Chico saw all the police riding and a helicopter patrolling the area. He was too far from the bank to see what was going on, but he had heard the gunshots. His first mind told him to get ghost, but somehow, he knew that they would make it out. As long as they made it to the sewer.

Seconds later, he heard the doors opening, then bodies getting in. AJ and Bobby hid inside the trunk. Ramon and Snug hid on the floor of the backseat. Yawni sat in the front seat with her head between her legs.

Chico was driving up Paseo Boulevard when a policeman pulled up beside him, with his wide nose all up in his car. Chico shot him an angry stare. The policeman looked away as he sped off with his lights flashing.

AJ and Bobby felt the car finally come to a stop 30 minutes later. The car rocked slightly as the occupants exited. Light shone inside the trunk after the door was raised. Yawni reached in and helped Bobby out. AJ lifted his head waiting to follow Bobby. Snug placed both hands on the trunk, then brought it down hard on AJ's head.

Thunk!

AJ screamed out.

Snug lifted the trunk, then brought it down again.

Thunk!

Then again, and again.

When Snug lifted the trunk again, he peered down at AJ holding his bleeding head. Yawni glared down at him with her gun held tight in her hand.

Pussy had always been his downfall, she thought to herself, just before she fired three slugs into his body.

Yawni tossed the car keys to Bobby. "Get rid of it."

chapter

7

Ramon and Yawni sat on her living room floor for hours counting up the score with two money counters and two note pads. They took several breaks before finally finishing early the next morning.

Yawni returned from the kitchen carrying a plate of eggs and bacon. Ramon sat on the floor in front of the sofa wearing a white wife-beater and pajama bottoms.

"Breakfast," Yawni announced in a cheerful tone. She stuck the plate under his nose.

Ramon stared at the plate like it had a dead rat on it.

"That's not turkey bacon," he commented.

Yawni looked at the bacon. "I know. It's pig bacon."

Ramon sighed briefly. "Baby, c'mon. You know after a black man gets out of the joint, there's one rule that he sticks to."

"And that is?"

"Eating pork is a no-no. Now take that funky-ass

shit on somewhere else."

Yawni sat down Indian style next to him. "I'll eat it if you won't. My mama's 68 and been eating pork all her life."

"It's a filthy animal."

"So are catfish and chicken, but I'll bet you eat that."

Ramon refused to respond because she was correct. In fact, he really couldn't give her a good reason as to why he didn't eat pork. He just knew that most incarcerated black men didn't eat it.

"Shut up," he said.

"That's what I thought. You jailbirds kill me." She chewed on the bacon. "So ... how much did we come up with?"

Ramon fired up a cigarette. "Ah ... $3.8 million in cash and $1.6 million in bonds. Minus that $10,000 that we already gave the boys."

Yawni whistled. "Looks like we'll have a million-one to split after we buy the hotel and pay Murphy."

Ramon shook his head. "I'm keeping the extra."

Yawni stopped chewing and swallowed hard. "What do you mean by keeping the extra?"

Ramon hit his cigarette before stubbing it out in the ashtray. "Just what I said. I got big plans for my hotel. And I need that money to spread around. Rub elbows with some rich people who'll spend big money. I'm thinking much bigger than just a hotel. I'm picturing a room for gambling, an inside swimming pool, an after-hours club, suites and my office overlooking the south end of the building."

Yawni sat down her plate. "What do you mean, *your* hotel?"

"C'mon, baby. You know what I mean. It's all of our hotel, but I'll be running it." He placed his hand on her shoulder and slid it down her slip. "Anything I do on the side will involve you also." He planted a kiss on her naked shoulder. Her body quivered under his touch. "You're my woman."

"Mm," Yawni murmured softly. "I am your woman. And you bet not ever ... ever ... turn your back on me." She rested her head on his chest.

"Let's keep that extra money thing between us, okay?"

"Whatever you say. I'm with you."

# # # #

Murphy sat behind his desk talking on the phone while holding a burning cigar between his chubby little fingers. Paper and books were scattered across his desk. His right hand man, Francisco, sat in a chair reading a business magazine. His two .357 Magnums dangled under his arms.

Francisco dropped the magazine and went for his guns when the door flew open. He relaxed after he saw that it was Yawni. She had Ramon in tow.

"'Ey, Yawni," he said in a thick Italian accent. "Try knocking next time, eh?" He noticed the bag she was clutching.

Yawni cut her eyes at him as she walked past.

"This is not your office, Francisco."

Francisco remained standing, his gaze on Ramon.

Ramon returned his stare without blinking. He gripped the black bags in his hands, ready to swing on them if it came to that. Francisco would be the first person Ramon ever knocked out with 3.5 million dollars.

"Who's this?" Francisco asked without taking his eyes off Ramon.

Murphy removed the phone from this ear and covered it with his shoulder.

"Everything's cool, Francisco. Have a seat." Murphy started talking into the phone again. "Sammy, let me call you back. I got business over here. Un huh. Yeah, okay. Fax it over this evening. Goodbye." He hung up and caught his breath. "Now, Mr. ahh ... Delay. Everything went as planned I hear. The police and insurance company have been eating at my ass all morning. They have a problem believing that all my banks getting robbed is just a coincidence."

Yawni took out the bonds and placed them on Murphy's desk.

Ramon sat the bags of money on the floor.

"That's everything," Yawni explained. "Now. You have something for us?"

Murphy picked up a stack of bonds and regarded it carefully. Then he went into his desk drawer and took out a stack of documents.

"It's all there. The deeds, everything. Take 'em and have your lawyer go over everything before you sign. You guys did a good job. Maybe ah ... you know. Maybe we can do more business in the future, huh?"

Ramon gathered the papers. "Maybe." He started for the door. Yawni trailed him.

"'Ey," Murphy called out.

Yawni turned around.

"Where you going, babe? I need you to stick around for a moment. There's a few things we need to discuss."

Yawni looked at Ramon and nodded her approval. She kissed Ramon's cheek. "Call me later."

Ramon nodded, then shot Francisco one last glare before exiting the office.

After Ramon left, Murphy stood and walked around his desk over to the window. He motioned for Yawni to come to him. She did.

Murphy pointed out the window. "See that?"

Yawni glanced down toward the street. Cars were coming and going, roadside construction was being done, and people walked around like little ants.

"What?" she asked, confused.

"The sidewalk. It's a *long* way down. Isn't it?" He stared at the side of her face.

"Yes."

Murphy clutched her jaw in his hand. She

grabbed his forearm.

"Don't fight me," he warned. She released her grip. "If I find out that you're fucking that black slick bastard sonofabitch." He pointed down at the street below. "You're gonna find out the distance between here and there. And you're gonna know how long it takes to get there. Only you're not gonna live to tell." He squeezed her face. "Understand?"

Yawni turned beet red in the face. Her instincts told her to knee his short ass in the balls. But she knew that she wouldn't make it out of the building alive if she did.

"Good," Murphy replied. As soon as he released his grip, she stormed to the door. "Let me find out the black half of you is starting to override the white. You're fuckin' dead."

She slammed the door closed.

Francisco regarded Murphy with a puzzled look on his face.

"What the fuck're you staring at?" Murphy asked harshly. "Get the hell outta my office."

Francisco started to say something, but instead acted like the flunky he was by doing what he was told.

# # # #

Ramon drove his rented Cadillac out to his new place of business. The first thing he would do was hire an architect to redesign the whole building. He wanted another floor added on top to hold six luxurious suites, complete with Jacuzzis, stocked bars, Internet access, balconies and kitchenettes.

Somehow he had to obtain a permit from the gaming commission so he could open a casino on the bottom floor. There would be a real live gentlemen's room, stocked with leather sofas, card and crap tables, and slot machines. Several flat screen TVs, a lounge area and top-of-the-line stereo equipment. His office would be built at the very top, surrounded by a bulletproof window that overlooked the entire banister area.

Ramon pulled up in front of the hotel, got out and inhaled the fresh air. For the first time in his 40-year-old life, he was gonna really be somebody. It felt damn good.

From that day forward, his life would consist of business meetings, expensive suits, coffee breaks, luncheons, flights and power moves. And if it came down to it, cold-blooded murder. He had to commit robbery, in some form or fashion, to get rich, and robbery sometimes ended with murder.

"You got your chance, Ramon," he said out loud. "Don't fuck it up."

# # # #

The doctor blew his warm breath onto the cold stethoscope before placing it over Detective Molina's heart. He listened carefully while the detective took slow, deep breaths.

"Sounds good, Mr. Molina," the doctor informed

him. "I think you're finally ready to leave this place." He pointed a wrinkled finger at Molina. "Don't forget to pick up the medicine I prescribed. We have to get that blood pressure of yours down."

Molina's wife helped him into his suit jacket.

"He will, doc," she assured him. "Don't you worry."

Molina grunted as he rose from the bed. Luckily, he was wearing his vest when he took the slugs to the chest that the woman shot through his car window during the bank robbery. He growled in agony as he took his first step.

"Careful, honey. You have to take it easy. You've been lying in a hospital bed for two days. You have to take it easy."

"Take it easy my ass," Molina howled. "I can't wait to catch the scumbags who killed Bierman and Brady." He patted his sides searching for his gun holster out of habit. "Where's my gun? Who's got my gun?"

"Baby, calm down," Sarah, his wife said, softly. "It's in the trunk of the car with the rest of your things."

Outside in the car, Molina strapped on his holster then reloaded his gun. Sarah shook her head at him. For the last ten years, her super-cop husband had become obsessed with his job. She cursed the day he became head of the Robbery and Homicide Division.

Molina picked up Sarah's cell phone and started

dialing numbers. He turned her rearview mirror facing him to get a look at his reflection. His eyes were red and baggy - signs of old age. A beard was starting to sprout on his usually clean-shaven face.

"Yes, hello," Molina said into the phone. "Get me Detective Lawton, please." He glanced at Sarah, who was staring out of the window with anger on her face. Lawton came on the line. "Lawton. Look, get me everything you can on every group of bank robbers that has a woman, starting from ... '95. Then pull all their files, and the files of their known accomplices, and have 'em on my desk by eight o'clock tomorrow morning. Thank you." He hung up.

Sarah sighed. "There goes my quality time. It seems like the only time I get to see you is either when you're sleeping or wounded."

Molina shook his head. "You know I got a job to do, Sarah. And part of it is to protect the citizens of this city. Look what happened. Two outstanding young cops lost their lives while trying to cash their checks."

"I'm sorry about that. I feel for their families, but sometimes officers die in the line of duty. That's their job."

Molina slapped the dashboard. "Not under my command, it isn't!" he yelled. His voice lowered. "And the fuckers who did this are gonna pay."

"Our justice system will just let these criminals ..."

"Those bastards will never live to get brought to

justice." He peered out his window. "Not if I can help it."

# # # #

"Francisco, would you hurry the fuck up!" Murphy shouted impatiently. He and Yawni were standing in his office's garage clutching bags of money while they impatiently waited on Francisco to bring the limo around.

"Calm down, baby," Yawni said.

"Wha'da ya mean, calm down? We're standing out here holding over 5 million dollars and he's bullshitting."

The tires squealed as Francisco bolted the stretch limo around the corner. He came to an abrupt halt directly in front of Yawni and Murphy.

Murphy snatched open the back door, let Yawni in, and got in behind her. Francisco bolted away.

About a block away from Murphy's loft, the limo began jerking violently. Francisco pulled over to the side of the street, where the engine died out. Murphy instantly became nervous. He let down the privacy window.

"Francisco, what the fuck is going on?" he asked in a nervous tone.

"I don't know, boss." Francisco turned the key with no luck. He opened his door. "Let me look under the hood."

"Hurry the fuck up, would ya?" Murphy's body moved about in nervous gestures. "Brand new fuckin' car breaks down. What kinda shit is that?"

Yawni put her hand on his shoulder. "Calm down, baby. Everything will be okay."

The back door opened suddenly. Murphy looked up and saw a bleeding Francisco being held by a masked man. A second masked man appeared out of nowhere. He reached in with his pistol drawn, and grabbed one of the bags that Murphy was holding.

"What're you doing?" Murphy held on tight. "These are important business papers."

Without any hesitation, the man hit Murphy upside his head with the gun. Murphy finally released the bag as he fell over on Yawni's lap. The man handed the bags to a third man, who waited outside the limo.

"You're not gonna get away with this, you fuckin' ..."

The man stared at Murphy as if he was contemplating killing him.

"Shhh!" Yawni murmured. "Don't do nothin' to make them kill us." She held his head in her lap.

Finally the masked man began to retreat by backing out of the car. He stood, pointed a gloved finger in the shape of a gun at Murphy, then pretended to shoot him.

Murphy blinked. By the time his eyes opened back up, the man was gone. Seconds later, he heard tires squealing.

Francisco collected himself, then opened wild gunfire at the fleeing Impala.

chapter

8

Snug, Chico and Ramon sat gathered around the table in wife-beaters, smoking cigars and laughing. Snug had remarked about how scared old Murphy looked while he was being robbed for $5 million.

Chico was dismissed after he was handed a small stack of cash, and was told that the rest would be put into the hotel fund.

After Chico's departure, Ramon handed Snug a large stack of cash.

"You know he knows it was us," Ramon said.

Snug shrugged. "Fuck 'em. What do we care? If he makes a fuss about it, we'll bury his fat ass under the Paseo Bridge. Makes me no difference."

Ramon patted him on the shoulder. "Chill out ole buddy. I wanted to keep him alive for my own personal reasons. I heard that he has mob ties. And if I can get in close with him, then he may be able to help me get funded for what I'm trying to do."

Snug studied him carefully. "You mean we."

"Hm? Oh, yea, that's right ... we."

"Good. So what's our next move?"

Ramon cleared his throat. "Next, we find some-one to take the blame for what happened tonight ... then get rid of 'em. That way, we'll earn old Murphy's unconditional trust." Ramon stubbed out his cigar, and stood. "Make sure you pay Francisco. Tell 'em he did a good job."

Ramon slipped on his shirt. "Oh, yeah. Before I forget. We need to find somebody to replace AJ."

"You got somebody in mind?"

Ramon nodded. "Name's Tulu from out of Chi-town. I did four years with him in Leavenworth." He scribbled his name and number on a piece of paper, then handed it to Snug. "Call him tomorrow and tell 'em to get down here. We got work for 'em."

Yawni stormed into the restaurant, headed straight for Ramon. They stared at each other briefly before she drew her arm back and slapped him across his face. With the quick reflexes of a buck, he slapped her back. She swung again, but he caught it, and twisted her arm behind her back.

"Ow. Ouch!" she cried as he bent her over a table.

"Bitch, what the fuck is wrong with you?" he asked in a harsh tone. "'Cause if it's what I think you mad about, you'd better choose sides, fast."

"You fuckin' bastard! You could've warned me, Ramon."

"We had to make it look good."

Ramon released his grip as Yawni snatched

away from him. Breathing rapidly, she pushed her hair out of her face.

"They scared me half to death. What do you need his money for, anyway? Huh?"

"Yawni, we talked about this. You know what I'm trying to do. And to do it, I'll steal from my goddamn grandma. Don't act like you don't know me and my ways."

"You're right, I do know you. That's how I figured out who done it."

Murphy walked into the restaurant followed by Francisco and another lean-faced goon. He regarded Yawni with contempt. He snapped his fingers at her. "Over here, now!"

Yawni did as she was told.

Francisco grabbed her by the arm.

Suddenly, Murphy bolted toward Ramon and swung at him. Ramon side-stepped, then pushed Murphy onto one of the tables. An ashtray and salt and pepper shakers fell to the floor.

Francisco hesitated. The other goon drew down on Ramon. Just as quickly, Snug opened his thumper. No one saw Tank, who was over by the grill, grab his 12 gauge.

Murphy got back on his feet, wiping blood from his lip. Yawni ran to his aid.

"Get away from me," Murphy barked. "I followed your black ass over here."

"They're friends of mine, Montel," Yawni explained.

"Don't give me that friend crap. You're fucking this nigger."

Ramon sneered. "Call me another nigger, you ugly ass cracker, and we gon' tear this place up. Now what's going on?"

Murphy pointed his finger at Ramon. "You fuckin' n ... y'all robbed me."

Ramon looked at Snug, then back at Murphy. "Who robbed you? Point him out."

"Don't get smart with me. You know goddamn well what I'm talking about."

Ramon took a seat. "You're right, I do. Yawni just told us everything. I'm sure that ..." Ramon paused and nodded toward the goon who had the gun pointed at him.

Murphy looked back and slowly gestured for him to put down the gun. He did. Then Snug holstered his.

Ramon continued. "Like I was saying, I'm sure that I can put my ear to the street and find out what happened. Maybe even get some of the money back."

"Why not all of it?"

Ramon threw his hands up. "You're asking the wrong man. If these guys are black, they're sure to be spending your money as we speak." He lit a cigarette. "But if I do ... If I do, you have to invest it into my hotel. Either that or you can find your own goddamn money."

Murphy chewed his bottom lip while glaring

upside Ramon's shiny dome. He wanted the man in front of him dead, but then, he would never see his money again. All that money. He couldn't see himself just shrugging it off and taking that big of a loss. His hands were tied. So for the time being, he had to do things Ramon's way.

His head bobbed up and down in thought. "Alright, Ramon. You've got a deal." Murphy put on a false smile and offered his hand.

Ramon just stared at it. "Smiles and handshakes don't fool me, Mr. Murphy. I know you'd love to shoot me right now."

Murphy snickered. "Many men have also wished death upon me, Ramon. But just like you, I'm still here."

Ramon finally accepted his hand. "Tell me. How can I go about obtaining a gambling license?"

Murphy smirked as if the man standing in front of him was joking. After he saw that he was not, he cleared his throat and began to speak.

"First off, you're a felon. And second, what for?"

"Assume the hotel and license will be under my mother's name. I'll secretly run it under another title. I want to open up a casino inside the basement of the hotel. I plan on hosting fights, entertainers' after parties and things like that. That's the only way I can see the hotel making a comeback. Otherwise, my friends and I are out of $3 million."

Murphy rubbed his sagging chin. "Sounds like a great idea. I want in. I can help get the funds to build this thing. But I'll be expecting a big return."

"No deal," Ramon stated firmly.

"No deal? The only way you'll ever be able to obtain a gambling permit is if I'm in on it. Who in the hell do you think you are? You'll never get it done without me. A lot of palms have to be greased. State politicians and people of that nature. Talk money out of investment bankers, and make deals with Union pension fund officials. People you didn't even know existed. Ones that carry big names and titles that you've never even hard of."

Ramon had never thought of it that way. Yes, he was getting in way over his head, and would definitely need Murphy's pull to get him started. He looked to Yawni, who nodded.

"Okay, Murphy. You do whatever it is you gotta do, and I'll guarantee your money back, plus a large kickback for your trouble."

"I thought you'd see it my way. My people will be in touch."

Murphy walked over to the door and turned around. "Don't forget to find my money." He snapped his finger at his two goons, then disappeared out the door. Yawni joined them.

After they were all gone, Ramon turned to Snug and said, "Sic Tulu on whoever you decide to take the rap for the robbery. Then leak to Murphy that Francisco was in on it. That way, we'll tie up any loose ends."

"Sure thing."

# # # #

Molina and Lawton sat inside an enclosed room watching the film of the bank robbery. They were near tears after they saw two of their fellow officers get shot. The tape showed unclear images of the gunmen's faces. Courtesy of Murphy.

When Molina saw the outfit of the woman who shot him, he ordered the tape stopped.

"Zoom in on her shoes," said Molina. "You see that? We found the heel of that shoe inside the sewer."

Lawton said, "Now we know exactly how they escaped."

Molina stared at the screen with determination in his eyes. "Does anyone besides me wonder how they discovered that escape route?"

Lawton knew his boss well. "What're you thinking?"

"I think it was an inside job. Either that or these assholes had blueprints of the city. Did we find anything on crews that have female accomplices?"

"Yes sir," Lawton said. "Two of them. One is a group of street punks, but they're small time, and way too unorganized to pull off something like this. And the other is run by this man." He opened up a file and placed a picture in front of Molina.

"His real name is Jesse Jones. Goes by the street moniker 'Snug Brim'. Our snitches say it's because he's a sharp dresser who wears brim hats that fit snug on his head."

"Un huh. What else? Give me something that we can use."

"He has a five-man crew that consists of one female. We haven't been able to get name on her yet. They started out robbing and extorting drug dealers. And I heard Snug's name mentioned in that jewelry heist a while back. Never had enough evidence to get an indictment."

Molina smacked his gum. "Tell me more."

Lawton continued reading the file. "The crew members are Alvin Johnson, who coincidently has been reported missing by his family, Bobby Walker, Hector Gomez a.k.a. Chico. Like I said, we haven't got a name for the girl."

"Alvin Johnson," Molina repeated. "Where do I know that name from?"

"His sister, Alvina Johnson, stole that baby from Truman Medical Center nine years ago."

"Oh yeah, the babynapper." Molina finally stopped smacking his gum. "Okay. I want a full surveillance team on these clowns. Around the clock, night and day. I wanna know how busy they have been, and their next move. And I want the name of the mysterious female on my desk some time this week." He peered at the screen one last time.

"We're gonna catch these scumbags."

# # # #

Snug picked up Tulu from the airport. Chico was in the backseat reading a newspaper. To Snug's surprise, Tulu looked like a grimey, cold-blooded killer. It was an unusual look for a guy that Ramon would hang out with. Ramon usually rolled with men who appeared trustworthy on the surface, but were sneaky as foxes.

"So, Tulu," Snug began. "Tell me about yourself."

Tulu was black as shoe rubber, with a long, slender face and a baldhead. His eyeballs were as red as hot coals. Jailhouse tattoos covered his entire upper body.

"I'm a cold blooded mutha fuckin' killa," Tulu boasted in a scratchy voice. "I'll knock a nigga's head off. I just did 20 years in the penitentiary, stabbing and bustin' niggas' asses an' shit. I'm tellin' you man, I just don't give a fuck." He made funny gestures and motions with his hands as he spoke.

"A killa, hunh?" Snug asked.

"Hell yeah. Like I said, I just done 15 years in the muh fuckin' penitentiary."

Chico cut in. "I thought you said 20 years."

Tulu looked at Chico as if seeing him for the first time. "Man, look, I done did so much time, I really don't know how long I've been locked up. I do know this, give me a gun and a target, and I'ma nail his ass." He hit the dashboard with his fist. "Believe that."

# # # #

Murphy sat on his ass behind his desk hollering at Francisco about all the shit that had been going on. First the hotel, then the robbery. Since Yawni wasn't around for him to vent on, he threw the coals at Francisco.

"... And I'm telling you, Frankie," Murphy spat. "If ..."

He was interrupted when the phone rang. "Hello. Un huh. Are you sure? You're positive? I see. Thanks, Bobby. I'll get right on it." He slammed down the phone, and rubbed his eyes.

"Francisco, we have a problem." Murphy pushed a button under his desk.

Francisco sensed something was wrong. He stood with concern on his face. "What's wrong, boss?"

Seconds later, four guys dressed in suits walked into the office.

"It seems," Murphy said, "that Ramon has found the guys who stole my money."

"That's great. Isn't it boss," Francisco said.

"Hunh? Oh, yeah, right, it sure is." Murphy looked away. "Look, uh, Frankie. I want you to make a run with the guys for me. I gotta little problem that I need handled."

Frankie turned and looked at the men standing behind him. They all wore blank expressions.

"Boss, you sure?"

"Yes, I'm sure. It'll just be a short ride. It'll be over in no time."

Francisco stared at Murphy for a long moment. He wasn't a fool. He'd been around long enough to know what Murphy meant by *it'll be over in no time.*

Ramon gave him up. Now he had to pay the ultimate price for dealing with niggers.

Two of the goons placed hands on both of Francisco's shoulders.

"Let's go."

Francisco turned on wobbly legs, and left the room with the goons in tow.

Murphy hated to punish his longtime friend, but what had to be done, had to be done.

"Get off me! Get off meeeee!" Francisco's cries could be heard on the other side of the door.

chapter

9

It took over a year and $88.6 million to reconstruct and rebuild the Resthaven Hotel & Casino. In order to do so, Murphy had to bribe certain state politicians, make donations to churches and surrounding businesses. Plus, he had to obtain special permits and licenses. Things Ramon could not do.

Several investors chipped in to help manifest Ramon's dream into reality. Murphy had convinced them that Ramon, being black, could generate a young crowd by providing the right entertainment and various events, even make Resthaven a popular tourist attraction where millions would come from around the world to sleep and gamble. Murphy believed in Ramon, and the investors believed in Murphy. He had made them so much money in the past that they couldn't refuse him.

If they had, Murphy would have brought in his extortion team to muscle them until they broke. So what other choice did they have?

The Resthaven Hotel & Casino was beautiful. It

was built with 300 rooms, 20 suites, conference rooms, several restaurants, a children's playroom, a small arena, an after-hours club, and the casino was located in the basement, secured by 30 guards, closed doors and cameras everywhere.

The casino area was called the The Den. It had all the comforts of a lounge, equipped with leather sofas, glass tables, laptops, designer lamps - all of which surrounded the gambling area. The walls were red brick and the floors were wooden to add the cozy feeling of home. A 60-inch flat screen accommodated every wall in The Den. Palm trees gave the room an exotic flavor.

They had to purchase and knock down the gas station next door and across the street to build parking garages. Ramon's office was built at the very top, on the edge of the building. But The Den was be his favorite room. Now all he had to do was find a group of fine females who could keep the ballers gambling until they were broke. Some money-hungry groupies without a conscience, or a soft spot for suckers. Straight thoroughbreds.

To find them, he placed ads in the papers, ran a commercial on TV, interviewed strippers, but hadn't found the right group until the day that he was standing in the Resthaven parking lot, watching his "Reserved for Owner" sign being posted up.

Loud rap music came blaring through the air. Ramon faced left and saw an old classic '69 Camaro drop-top whip into the parking lot. It was painted bright red with tan Gucci seating. Twenty-two inch gold Daytons held the monster up.

The beautiful car got his attention. But what had him most was the beautiful young woman who sat in the driver's seat, gripping the wooden steering wheel. She got out wearing black and white pin-striped slacks, high heels and a white blazer. The diamond-studded choker around her neck almost blinded Ramon from a distance.

Her long, jet black, curly locks hung to her shoulders. She had pencil thin eyebrows, with full pink lips and an exquisite nose, like that of a poodle. The young woman gazed in Ramon's direction and squinted her eyes. The sun must have been too bright for her, because she put on a pair of over-sized shades.

Ramon scurried over to her in his tailor-made suit, Gucci glasses and gators. "Hello," he said cheerfully. "I'm Ramon Delay, the owner of the hotel."

She shook his hand. "Jayde." Her tone was firm, yet very seductive. She had a sneaky look about her. He believed that she could slip the diamond ring off his finger without him knowing it.

"How can I help you?"

Jayde removed her shades. "I heard that you were looking for a group of bitches to work your player's den."

Ramon almost smiled at her bluntness. "Yes, I am."

"I command a group of young, fine, scheming hoes. Some of the best around, myself included, who will work any man who enters The Den. No matter the size of their bankroll, if they leave with fat pockets, it's because they've filled them with the complimentary peanuts from the bar."

Ramon smiled. Jayde smirked.

Without further interviewing, he found himself saying, "You're hired."

"I promise we won't let you down, Mr. Delay." Jayde put her shades back on, then got back into her car. The loud pipes came to life when she turned the key.

Ramon put his hand on her door. "How about dinner?" he asked.

Jayde pursed those full pink lips of hers. "How old are you?"

"Forty-one," he replied with a hint of embarrassment, though being locked up for 15 years preserved his youth, and had him looking a crisp 32.

"I'm only 22. You're old enough to be my daddy. Sorry." She giggled as she backed her car up, then sped out of the parking lot.

# # # #

Opening Night

Everything was set to go. The entire staff was in place, from the manager to the housekeepers. Snoop Dogg was in town, in concert, and was having an after party at After 7, the hotel's after-hours club.

Jayde and her crew were lounging in various seductive outfits inside The Den. The girls were as fine as Jayde promised.

There was Roberta, a 5' 7" Dominican chick with smooth slender legs, a round ass and mouth-sized breasts. She had a small round nose and long sandy brown hair.

Then there was Freaky Francine, a little Korean beauty who stood all of 5' 3", Jayde's height, but she was stacked. She came equipped with plump breasts, a sharp nose, and back-length brunette hair. A tattoo of a yellow dragon covered her right foot and ankle.

And last but not least was Lashay. She was a redbone leggy chick who stood 5' 9" with short crinkly hair and innocent schoolgirl looks.

They all wore different eye shadow and bright colored lipstick. Skimpy, exotic clothing covered their well-shaped bodies.

Jayde wore a glittery thong with stilettos, her diamond-studded choker and a fur stole draped around her naked shoulders. The only thing that shielded her huge, round, false boobs were glittery stars that covered her nipples.

Ramon stood on the staircase above The Den observing them. They were all sitting next to different men on the sofas, chatting and sipping champagne. He observed their false smiles and gay laughs while they sipped with one hand and caressed pockets with the other.

"Look at 'em, Snug," Ramon said with a smile. "A den full of thieves. All rested and made up for one purpose ... to help me get rich. Isn't it beautiful?"

Snug smiled. "I have to admit. You done it, baby. That's why we handed it over to you."

"Goddamn right it is," Ramon boasted. He had that hungry gleam in his eye. "Waitress. Get us a couple glasses of champagne. I wanna make a toast." He faced Snug, then gave him that same devilish smile and handshake that even he wouldn't trust.

# # # #

The next day, while sorting through his mail inside his office, Ramon ran across a letter addressed to him with no return address. He regarded it carefully before opening it.

Snug, who was lounging on the sofa adjacent Ramon's desk drinking cognac, saw the suspicious look on his face.

"Everything alright?" Snug asked.

Ramon looked up at him. "Yeah." He opened the letter and read it.

A fool and his money will soon part.

That was all it said. Ramon put the letter inside his desk drawer. *What the hell is that supposed to mean?* he wondered.

He remembered how brutal he used to treat both men and women when he was young. There were so many victims that he could hardly name them all.

Knock! Knock!

His secretary entered the room. "Miss Jayde's fast tail is here to see you."

"Send her in, ma."

Jayde appeared in the doorway looking fine as fur.

"Hey," Snug said with a smile. He was short enough to look her eye to eye.

"Hi, Snug," she replied. "Is the boss ... oh, there he is."

Snug observed her rear through savage orbs as she swayed over to Ramon's desk. He winked at Ramon, then left the two alone.

"One of the rappers from last night is staying in Suite 313. He's planning on staying the whole weekend, so I'll be clinging to him for the next 48 hours. Just so you know."

"How much did he lose last night?" He let his eyes wander down to her crotch, where it looked like the shape of a perfect letter V. A tingling feeling jolted through his loins.

Jayde took a seat across from him with her legs agape.

"I'd say ... close to thirty grand, give or take." She spread her legs, giving him a clear view of her pantiless crotch.

Ramon sat up in his chair. "Boy, you really know how to set it out, don't you?"

"And you're referring to ..."

He nodded toward her opened legs.

She smiled. "That's not for your pleasure, Mr. Delay. It's for mine."

Ramon was confused.

"See how big your eyes became when you saw it? Sweat started rolling down your bald head." She leaned forward. "You call that a kind of power 'pussy control.' It gets me off."

He shifted in his seat as he felt his dick stiffen. "Let me be frank."

"Please do." Jayde kept good eye contact.

"Am I ever gonna ... you know ... be able to hit that? I mean, I am the boss here. Isn't that how it's supposed to happen? The pretty girls set it out for the boss hoping to climb the corporate ladder?"

"In some situations," she admitted.

Jayde removed her blazer, revealing a pink lace bra. She stood and walked around Ramon's desk to where he sat. After she turned his chair facing her, she realized he was in his boxers. His dick was, in fact, hard. He kept a rack of slacks in his office closet, and never lounged in them.

"My pants are in the closet." He answered her question before she could ask it.

Jayde straddled him, pressing her round breasts up against his nose. He took slow, deep breaths as he caught her Burberry perfume.

"You see that, Mr. Delay. Look at how you're sweating. I could do anything to you I wanted right now."

Ramon kissed her chest. She felt his dick jerk, poking her butt cheeks.

"See, you're the boss, but I can take control any," she licked his nose, "time I want."

She rose and walked back over to her chair, leaving him dumbfounded.

While she put her jacket back on, Yawni walked into the office. Her eyes were looking at the real estate brochure in her hand.

"Baby, I saw some bad houses out in —" She froze when she saw Jayde buttoning her blazer. "What's going on?"

Jayde smirked at her. "Nothing." Then, she gazed at Ramon. "Nothing at all." She headed for the exit. As soon as she opened the door, Yawni pushed it closed.

Yawni leaned over, putting her face close to Jayde's. She noticed her poodle-like features.

"If the little pooch wants some more milk, she needs to find another bottle to suck on."

Jayde inhaled Yawni's scent while she peeked down her blouse. "You'd better watch your own back. It could be breast milk that these lips crave. Good day." Jayde opened the door and left.

Even though they hadn't done anything, Ramon still had a guilty look on his face. He came out of the closet with his slacks in hand.

"You were saying, baby?" He was hoping to avoid the inevitable.

"What were you two doing?" Yawni asked hotly.

Ramon sensed her jealously and decided to toy with her.

"Nothing that you and old Murphy haven't done." He put on his diamond *R* cufflinks.

Yawni's mouth fell open. "That's not fair and you know it. Now you wanna lay it all out on the table. I am too old to be competing with some firm-breasted 22-year-old child, Ramon."

He slipped on his suit coat. "Hush up, old girl. I was just teasing you." He walked up on her and kissed her cheek. "I love you."

Yawni pulled away from him. "I love you too, but I am not about to play a game of chess with Jayde."

Ramon admired the beauty that Yawni still possessed to be nearing forty. She was equally as beautiful as Jayde; only Jayde had that wonderful thing called youth on her side. While in the next five years or so, Yawni's breasts would begin to sag and she would experience menopause; Jayde would just be beginning to blossom. And be able to bare the fruit of Ramon's seed.

"Man are you fine." Ramon reached out for her. "C'mere."

Offering little resistance, Yawni allowed herself to be pulled. Ramon nudged her earlobe with his nose.

"That tickles," Yawni murmured. "Stop. Stop,

baby!"

"No matter how old you get, you'll always be new to me."

Those words took her breath away. "Aw boo. Give me a kiss."

They hugged and kissed passionately for about two minutes. Yawni felt moisture in her underwear and pulled away.

"Stop, now. We have to meet the lady about your house."

He desperately started humping her leg. "She'll wait if she wants the money bad enough." He tried to kiss her again.

"Unt unh. I'm starting to leak in these little-ass panties."

"Let me suck 'em dry."

"No silly." Yawni giggled. "I want you to follow me out that door so we can go." She made for the door.

When the elevator opened, they saw the rapper and Jayde on there going at it. She was kissing his neck while he lifted her skirt. He propped her foot up on the rail.

The rapper turned around and saw Ramon. He had on shades, a sweatsuit and a long platinum chain dangling from his neck.

He said, "You better get on dawg, if you comin'. There's plenty of room for you and your lady friend in here, too."

Yawni and Ramon stepped on. They faced the

front. Jayde was behind them purring like a helpless kitten. She knew that she was getting Ramon aroused.

Ramon was aroused and jealous, but he couldn't get mad. She was only doing what she was being paid to do. Take care of the guests and keep them spending.

"Mm," Jayde purred. "Gambling makes me horny."

"Does it?" The rapper said in a rehearsed cool voice. "Well, let's go down to The Den and get about $10,000 worth of chips and try our luck."

Jayde smirked. "Win or lose baby, I'm still gonna ..." she whispered the rest into his ear.

They both giggled when she finished.

"It's all good, baby."

Yawni leaned in close to Ramon and whispered, "Want me to suck your dick on this elevator so you can look cool, too?"

Ramon looked at her and frowned. "C'mon, now. You're a lady. Act like one."

"I was only gonna do it for you."

As Ramon was stepping off the elevator onto the first floor, he wished like hell that he would have at least one shot at getting Jayde. No matter what the cost.

chapter

10

Ramon and Snug trailed behind Murphy while he entertained some big men from the governor's office. They came down personally to get a look at the new hotel and casino.

Just by looking at Ramon, you couldn't see that he was nervous, but he was dropping fingernails everywhere he walked. Snug snuck away for a brief moment, then returned with a drink for him.

They toured the restaurants, then the club, and stopped and chatted by the pool. The two big shots were really checking out the bathing suits.

After about an hour of bullshitting, Murphy led them down to The Den. It was crowded with all kinds of different income: drug dealers, ball players, businessmen and whoever else could afford to gamble big.

When they reached The Den, Ramon took control. He led them over to the lounge where they ordered drinks and enjoyed the scenery.

Roberta sat at the bar as planned, sipping on a

Sex on the Beach, while Lashay stood over her with their legs intertwined, caressing her shoulder.

Every card dealer in the club was female. They were all made to wear boy shorts and stilettos to look appealing to the customers. Halter tops were also standard dress so they couldn't conceal any stolen chips.

The governor's assistant, Carl Peterson, stared at Roberta and Lashay. He saw Roberta's strap slide off her smooth shoulder. Lashay dabbed a pinch of salt on it, took a drink of tequila, then licked it off. Then they tongue-kissed one another.

"Sweet Jesus!" Carl bellowed. "Would you look at that!"

The five gentlemen all shot flirtatious looks across the room toward the bar. Lashay had her hand on Roberta's crotch, rubbing it, while Lashay sucked liquor from her finger. Jake, who was also from the governor's office, cracked a smile.

"Nice place you got here, Mr. Delay," Jake complimented. "Love your choice of female company."

Ramon finished sipping his drink. "Thank you. Say, how would you gentlemen like to get to know those two lovely ladies?"

Carl waved Ramon off. "Stop it. What do we have that they want?"

"I'm 'bout to find out." Ramon sat his drink down on the small square table.

The four guys watched him strut over to the bar. He made conversation with the two women, who found him humorous. After about a minute, the girls climbed off their stools and followed Ramon back over to the lounge.

"Oh my God! Here they come," Carl exclaimed.

He and Jake both straightened their ties and ran their fingers through their hair. Jake's was receding badly, so he didn't have much to do.

Ramon had a girl on each arm. "Gentlemen. These lovely ladies here are Roberta and Lashay. I told them that y'all work for the governor, and they wanted to meet you two personally."

"May we sit with you guys?" Roberta asked.

"Sure, sure." Carl was excited. He scooted over on the sofa so the girls could relax between him and Jake.

Ramon gestured for Snug and Murphy to stand up.

"Ladies," Ramon spoke, "why don't y'all show these two a good time."

Lashay clutched Jake's crotch. "Ooh! Don't worry. We will be good." They giggled.

"Remember gentlemen, you have to pay to play. Nothing in this world is free." The three of them walked away.

The girls were getting acquainted with the two dorks when Freaky Francine appeared out of nowhere. She had on a two-piece swimsuit, fishnet stockings and knee-high boots.

"Somebody order a five-some?" she asked.

Carl loosened his tie. "The more the merrier."

Francine hopped on his lap. "You're gonna have to show some green if you wanna freak Francine."

Both dorks raced for their wallets.

# # # #

"Ooh! We won, baby!" Jayde shouted. She was at the crap table throwing the dice for her rapper friend.

When Ramon stopped to watch her, he saw her cut her eyes at him. She winked, then continued with what she was doing.

Murphy grabbed his balls. "Boy would I like to stick my prick inside that kisser."

"You're not the only one," Snug retorted.

Ramon observed her for a second longer before walking away.

Yawni stood in the security room watching the whole episode on camera. She could tell by the look in Ramon's eyes that he had an ache for Jayde. One that could only be healed by hours of passionate sex. Then hopefully, after his cravings were satisfied, he would come back to her.

If not, Yawni was in a world of trouble. She had killed for cash, but what would she do for love? That was the question that she had to ask herself. Truthfully, she didn't know. Probably because she had never been in love with anything but money.

# # # #

During the next six months, the business prospered enormously. Every week there was some kind of event going on at the Resthaven. Whether a title bout or an after-party, something was going on.

Ramon had rigged the machines so that a certain gambler would win a $250,000 jackpot. It made the news and the gamblers started pouring in from everywhere. He leased four brand new Cadillacs for the company executives, and purchased a $500,000 home on Ward Parkway.

The crew was all becoming salty because Ramon had started spending the majority of his free time with Murphy and a bunch of other powerful white men. He joined clubs they couldn't join. Hung out in places where they were not wanted. Even avoided them whenever they tried to meet with him.

Snug was still his main guy. Only now, he was more like a right-hand man rather than a business partner. Whatever Ramon needed done, Snug did without question. That's how it had been since they were kids.

Yawni was still his girl, and wherever he went, she went. She was a lovely woman who worked the room at all their parties. She even accompanied him to the governor's mansion and to conventions in Vegas. She regretted not being able to move in with him because of her promise to Murphy, but now she was ready to break it and marry the man she loved. Unknown to her, Ramon was content with the way things were. That way, he could spend more time chasing Jayde.

He had tried everything. Gifts, free suites, sweet talk and hadn't struck gold yet. Ramon felt defeated and was beginning to believe what she had told him in the first place. He was too old for her.

Smokey Robinson sang, *"Ba-by let's cruise, a-wayyy from herrrre,"* through the factory speakers. Ramon had the top down on his new Cadillac XLR, bumping, cruising.

The sun beamed down on his slick dome while he rounded Hillcrest Road on his way to work. The world was his, he thought, and the law couldn't touch him. He had gotten too big too fast, and was in cahoots with all the right people. From lower level mafia men to state politicians.

Prosecutors, judges, teachers and athletes were now part of his guest list. They would do anything and spend any amount to keep laying his den of whores. In fact, Jayde and Lashay had been proposed to by several top federal authority figures, but they declined, claiming that they were hoes and not housewife material. Breaking bankrolls was not only their occupation, but their narcotic as well. It was what woke them up in the morning. They loved who they were, and Ramon loved them. Especially Jayde.

Ramon himself had contemplated proposing to Jayde, and he hadn't even had a drink with her, let alone sex. So what was it that made him crave her so? Jayde played hard to get. No matter who it was, or how much cash he had banked, she always remained in control of herself and the situation.

Loud rap music could be heard over the sounds of Smokey. Tailpipes growled behind him. Ramon glanced at his mirror. Jayde's Camaro was rounding the bend at a fast pace. She had on her shades and was singing along with the song. Her three road dawgs were with her.

They looked like they were kicking it. Their long hair blew with the wind. Jayde was a car length behind him when she crossed over the yellow no passing line into the northbound lane. About a block or so up ahead, a small car drove straight toward her.

Jayde pulled alongside Ramon. He peered over at them like they were crazy. The passenger women all sat up in their seats, then flashed their titties at him. He fought for control of the wheel while trying to watch them and the road ahead.

They continue to shake titties and blow kisses at him.

Beep! Beep!

Jayde waited until the car got within 100 feet of her before she stepped on the gas and swerved over in front of Ramon.

"You bitches wanna play?" he said.

After the car passed, Ramon crossed the no passing line and floored it. Jayde saw him passing on the left. She shifted gears and accelerated as well. They both gazed at each other while their cars approached max speed.

Vrooom!

They were running neck and neck when a truck came driving over the hill. The driver saw the Cadillac and immediately began honking his horn.

Ramon hit the gas some, hoping to pass Jayde, but she kept accelerating.

"This bitch is crazy," Ramon said to himself.

As the truck neared, Ramon thought fast. He didn't want to let up and let her win, but he didn't see any other choice. Francine and Roberta started doing the chicken. Ramon thought about running them off the road, but her Dayton helicopter knock-offs might have taken out his tires.

The truck continued to honk.

Ramon released the pedal and swerved back over to the right lane behind Jayde. The girls all clapped in triumph as they pulled into the hotel's parking lot. Jayde smirked as usual.

Ramon parked in his private spot. Jayde parked ten feet away. Loud laughter was heard while the girls exited the car. He regarded the four women with admiration. They were bad, witty and classy all at the same time. And, they were young.

Jayde strutted up to him wearing army capris, stilettos and a tank top. "I told you I was in control ... boss," she said with unhidden sarcasm.

When she tried to walk past, he seized her arm. She peered at his hand.

"When're you gonna learn what a woman's

place is?" he asked.

"When I become one. Right now, I'm just a gangsta-ass bitch who wants to have fun."

Ramon smiled at her. "And what is your idea of fun? A cruise to Jamaica? Thousand-dollar shopping sprees? What? You name it, I can make it happen."

"My idea of fun is having hard, butt-naked sex while thizzin' on Ex, all the while plotting to steal his check." She smirked while looking him up and down. "You ... all you wanna do is spend big bread with hopes of taking me to bed at the end of the night. Then when it's all said and done, you'll only hit and run, all the way back to your lonely little wife."

"Poetic justice," Ramon replied. "I do wanna hit it. You're right about that. But, I also wanna get to know you." He released his hold.

"Do you know that I have the stamina of three women?"

"You're young."

"And you're old," Jayde retorted. "I'll tell you what. Be waiting in Suite 306 after midnight. You'll get your chance to show me you still got it."

Jayde spun around and led her crew inside the hotel. Carl, from the governor's office, was sitting in the lobby, waiting for Francine. He jumped up when he saw the four of them walk in.

"Hey, ladies," Carl shouted. "I've been calling you all week, Francine. Where have you been?"

Ramon patted him on the shoulder as he walked past.

"Mr. Delay, don't forget we're doing eighteen holes this weekend," Carl reminded him.

"I won't. I'ma practice shooting a few holes myself, tonight."

"Good, good," Carl murmured, then gave Francine his undivided attention.

Francine asked, "You bring some money?"

Carl reached for his wallet. "Yeah ... I ..."

"Good. Let's go upstairs.

# # # #

Just before midnight, Ramon stood at the front desk, inside the lobby, barking at the clerk about being rude to the guests. While he did so, Jayde walked past and slipped him a note.

Ramon pointed a long finger at Gabby, the desk clerk.

"One more time, Gabby. One more time, and you won't have a job." He stormed off.

He waited until he was on the elevator before he read the note.

It read:

Don't forget Suite 306 after midnight.

When he stepped off the elevator to his office, he tossed the note in the trashcan. Inside, he found Snug and a white woman that he knew as Faye fondling each other out on the terrace.

"Snug," Ramon called. He started taking off his clothes. Snug left the girl outside, and rushed to his aide.

"Yeah?" He saw that Ramon was getting undressed. "Whoa. We can't share this one, playa."

Ramon sneered. "I don't want none of that stankin'-ass white bitch. Here." He tossed him his key ring. "Keep an eye on my hotel. I got some business to tend to."

Asshole naked, he walked to the shower.

Snug toyed with the keys while glaring at Ramon's back. "My hotel." Those words puzzled Snug.

Ramon inserted his master key into Suite 306 and slipped into the room. All the lights were out. Usher's *"Seduction"* played from someplace in the room. He let his eyes adjust to the darkness before he took another step.

"Lay down on the bed," Jayde's voice said. "It's five steps forward, and four to the right."

Ramon did exactly as he was told.

The lights came on a bit, but were still dim. Out of the shadows came Jayde holding onto a leash. Lashay, Francine and Roberta all had chain-linked collars around their necks. They crawled on all fours in front of Jayde as if she was their master.

"Like I said before, boss. I have the stamina of three women. Conquer this obstacle, then maybe I'll give you a taste."

Jayde unleashed them. "Sic 'em."

They all stood up naked and crawled onto the bed. Ramon couldn't believe his luck. Roughly, they began pulling off his clothes.

Jayde only watched.

# # # #

Yawni lay in bed, unsatisfied, after previously having a two-minute sexual encounter with Murphy. He was snoring on his side while she let thoughts of Ramon and Jayde hover inside her head.

All of her nights were spent the same. Sleepless. Because she couldn't stand the idea of having to leave Ramon at the hotel with Jayde. Yawni wasn't hating on the younger woman. She was just plain old jealous.

She peered at the clock on the wall and saw that it was just after midnight. She smiled at the thought of arriving at Ramon's office wearing nothing but a fur coat and heels. Yawni snatched up her robe and ran to the shower. She was excited because she had been wanting to do that ever since she saw it done on TV, years ago.

After she tapped Murphy a few times to make sure he was asleep, she left the apartment.

# # # #

Lashay and Roberta playfully fought over Ramon's dick with their lips. One would get a few licks, then nudge the other to the side like two kittens fighting over a toy. They decided to split up, with one taking the balls while the other sucked him off. Then they would switch.

Francine squatted over his face. She growled loudly as he gripped her ass and munched on her clit.

Jayde stood at the edge of the bed, watching with an expressionless face.

Francine climbed off of Ramon's face and walked over to the table where she picked up a joint. She lit it, but did not inhale. Ramon was lost in the zone when she crawled back onto the bed. She took a long drag, then pressed her lips up against his, blowing the smoke into his lungs.

Ramon sat up coughing and gagging. Lashay patted his back. Then she took a puff, and blew the smoke into his mouth as well. Roberta followed suit.

He took a deep breath as he lay back, experiencing the greatest head rush he had ever felt. It was so intriguing, he could not figure out why he felt that way.

He felt lips, tongues, titties and teeth gnawing at his body. When his eyes fluttered open, he saw Lashay bouncing up and down on his joint. Her eyes rolled back in her head as she humped herself into an orgasm. When she finished, Francine straddled him backward, then held on for the ride. Roberta lay between his legs and started sucking his balls while she restlessly awaited her turn.

All of a sudden, the glorious high that he felt disappeared just as quickly as it came. Ramon sat up on his elbows. "More! More!" he hollered. "Give me more!"

Lashay relit the joint, puffed on it, and blew it into his lungs while holding his nostrils closed. Roberta sucked on his balls, causing him to explode inside of Francine. She climbed off thinking that he was done.

Ramon flipped Roberta over in the doggy style position. He planted himself deep inside her velvety walls. Her back arched deeply as she felt that painful yet pleasurable feeling shoot through her body.

"Harder!" she begged.

"Uhh! Uhh!" He lost control of himself as he started pounding into her viciously, as if he was trying to inflict bodily harm.

Roberta begged for him to kill it. She gripped the sheets while he clamped her small waist, forcing her backward. Francine smacked Roberta's ass. Lashay slid up under her and started sucking her titties.

# # # #

Yawni pulled up outside at the valet. She made her face up in the mirror before exiting her car.

She wore a chinchilla coat and high-heeled stilettos. No clothes or underwear were on underneath. She had smoked a joint on the way so she was feeling pretty good.

Upon entering the hotel, she observed guests lingering about in the lobby. Loud music was blaring from the club around back. Some people were running around in bathing suits, heading for the pool area.

Yawni had the desk clerk call Ramon's office to see if he was in. He wasn't. That disappointed her, but she knew he was somewhere near, because his Cadillac was parked outside.

She hopped on the elevator to The Den. As soon as the doors parted, she stepped out into a whole new atmosphere. People were gambling, laughing loud and drinking. Some were even dancing. The cocktail waitresses were running around in skimpy little outfits taking orders and being hit on.

Suited men were lounging on the sofas chatting perversely with women while sipping expensive champagne. Yawni thought that it might be more females in there than inside the club. All of them were chasing the almighty dollar.

Yawni's jewelry glittered with the many lights as she swayed around the room, hunting for Ramon. Every suited black man with a baldhead she encountered wasn't him.

She was about to get discouraged until she spotted Snug at the bar, surrounded by four white women. They were all smiles while they were being entertained by the small man.

Yawni walked up to him and tapped him on the shoulder. Snug automatically reached for his gun as he spun around. He was at ease after he saw Yawni standing there, smiling.

"What the hell is wrong with you, Yawni?" Snug said. "You know you can't be sneaking up on me like that. Niggas want my head. I can't get caught slipping."

Though he was right, Yawni ignored him.

"Have you seen Ramon?"

Snug noticed how good and young she looked. Had they not been partners, he would have made a pass at her a long time ago. Somehow, Ramon had slid in and up in her.

"Yeah," Snug answered. "He's upstairs in his office."

# # # #

A little ways down, toward the end of the bar, a medium-sized Italian man with dark hair sat next to a tall, white man with a red mustache. The shorter of the two was Detective Molina and the tall one was his partner, Detective Lawton. They were eavesdropping on Snug's conversation while having a few beers.

They watched carefully as Yawni marched away from Snug back to the elevator. Then Snug resumed his conversation with the beautiful women. Bobby was over at the crap table, losing a shitload of money. Chico was upstairs in a suite entertaining two under-aged girls.

Molina turned around on his stool and faced the crowd.

"Well, they've done it," Molina spat. "Finally

made the big time. They've gotten away with enough capers to open a fuckin' casino in my goddamn town." He raised his beer mug. "Here's to Snug fuckin' Brim." He took a big gulp.

Lawton glared at Bobby. He was standing between two chicks screaming at the dice.

"Believe me, Mo, these guys won't stop here. I mean, there's too many fingers in this pot for them to turn much of a profit." He took a sip. "Besides, stealing is in a nigger's blood. It's just a matter of time before they make their next move. You'll see."

Molina tossed some bills onto the bar. "I hope you're right." He surveyed the place one last time. "Let's go."

Outside, Molina handed the valet his ticket. He lit a cigarette while he waited on his car. After glancing to his right, he saw Ramon's Cadillac in the "Reserved For Owner" spot.

"Lawton?" Molina asked. "I thought you said this place is owned by several investors."

"It is. Residue Entertainment. Why?"

Molina pointed at the Cadillac XLR as he approached it. He took out a small notepad and wrote down the license plate number.

"This sign here says reserved for owner. Not owners." He flipped it closed, then stuck it back inside his jacket pocket. "Something fishy is going on here. And we're gonna get to the bottom of it."

# # # #

Yawni stepped off the elevator and saw Jayde scurrying across the hall and into Ramon's suite. *What is she doing coming out of Ramon's office?* she thought. She was just about to grab the door handle when she heard laughter behind her.

She saw Jayde, Roberta, Lashay and Francine exiting Suite 306. The group of women stopped when they saw her. They were half dressed, looking like they had just finished banging one another.

Jayde smirked. "Hey, Yawni. If you're looking for the boss," she nodded toward the room, "he's in there taking a shower."

They walked away, giggling to themselves. Francine purposely dropped her underwear on the floor.

"Excuse me." She smiled as she picked them up.

Yawni saw steam coming from the shower when she entered the room. With anger in her eyes, she stepped into the doorway.

Ramon heard heels tapping against the marble floor. He ignorantly mistook her for one of the girls.

"One of y'all get in with me. I think I can get him up one more time." He laughed.

Yawni slid the door open. Ramon's smile disappeared when he saw her standing there naked. For a moment, he didn't know what to say or what to think. She stepped inside the shower. Beads of hot water attacked her honey-colored body. She stared up at him seductively as she cupped his hands, then placed them on her breasts.

"What's the matter?" she asked in a husky voice. "You can't get him back up for me? Hm?" She reached down between his legs, clutching his limp organ. "That's funny. You were able to get it up when you thought I was one of those freaks."

Yawni faced the opposite direction, held onto the wall and arched her back. Reaching back, she spread one of her butt cheeks.

"C'mon, Mr. Delay, don't you still find me attractive?" Ramon said nothing. "I know what you want."

Yawni dropped to her knees and attempted to kiss his dick.

"Yawni, stop!" he yelled as he pushed her back. She fell against the tile wall. "What the fuck is wrong with you?" He shut off the water before he stepped out. He snatched a towel off the rack on his way to the other room. Yawni followed.

Ramon slipped on his robe, then lit a cigarette.

"I'm not pretty to you anymore?" Yawni stood in front of him.

When he didn't respond, she snatched the cigarette from his mouth and threw it. "Answer me, damnit!"

"Bitch, you better calm down." He tried to step around her, but she stepped in his way. "Move, Yawni. You gon' fuck around and get the shit slapped out of you."

Yawni placed her hands on her hips. "Here I am. Slap me, muthafucka! What, you're mad cause I caught you —"

Wack!

He slapped her onto the floor.

"You're too tough for your own fuckin' good, bitch," he hollered as he glared down at her. "You ain't no damn man. You a bitch. And you better start learning how to stay in a bitch's place, real quick."

She held her hand up to her face while pretending to still be woozy. As soon as he came in reach, she kicked him in the balls.

"Aaah!" he cried as he fell to his knees.

Yawni picked up her stiletto as she stood up. She shot daggers at him while she circled him.

"You've got the wrong bitch, Ramon." Yawni plucked him on top of the head with the heel of her shoe. His face fell toward the bed.

"You bitch," he murmured.

"Aw, yeah?" Yawni kicked him in the stomach. Then the back. Then the ass.

When she finished, he lay curled up on the floor in pain. He tried to get to his feet, but her punch to his nose sent him back down.

"Lie there and think, bitch," Yawni spat. "Cause you just lost the best thing that ever happened to your arrogant ass."

Yawni put her shoes and coat back on, then left the room. She bumped into Snug on her way out.

"You alright, Yawni?" Snug inquired.

Yawni peered back at the doorway, then down at Snug.

"No, I'm not alright. My feelings have been hurt."

She strutted to the elevator.

Ramon crawled to the doorway, yelling, "Stop that bitch, Snug!"

He tried to get up and run, but tripped into Snug. Yawni waved at him teasingly as the elevator doors closed.

"Ramon, grab a hold of yourself," Snug said. "Man, that's Yawni!"

"I know who the fuck it is." He snatched Snug's jacket open and reached for his gun.

"Unt unh." Snug pushed him away. "Pull yourself together and tell me what happened."

Ramon started toward his office. "Unlock this goddamn door."

Snug fumbled with the keys until he found the right one. Ramon barged in, running straight for the balcony. He peered down in time to catch Yawni getting into her car.

"I'ma have your ass erased, you fuckin' bitch!" he yelled. Spittle surrounded his lips. "Yo' ass won't live another night."

"Try it you cocksucker," Yawni retorted. "You's a big-headed nigga. You wouldn't be shit if it weren't for us."

Snug tried to grab him, but he snatched away.

Ramon leaned over the iron railing, shouting, "I did this, bitch! I put all this together. I negotiated the deals. Me, me, me!"

Yawni smirked while she gazed up at him making a fool of himself. His robe blew open, exposing his naked body. A small crowd began to gather down below.

"You hear that, Snug? He did everything by his goddamn self. We couldn't have had nothing to do with it." Shaking her head, Yawni got into her car and drove away.

Ramon turned around and stormed toward the bathroom, bumping into Snug along the way.

"I want that bitch hit, Snug. You hear me? Dead before the devil finds out what's going on." He slammed the bathroom door.

Snug sighed while he gazed up at the star-filled night sky. Ramon was getting out of control and Snug had no idea what to do to stop him.

chapter

12

Ding ... ding ... ding ... ding ...

"Aaah!" the lady exclaimed. "I won! I won! Aah! I just won $10,000!" She jumped for joy as the coins flowed out of the machine and into her bucket.

Two guards rushed to her aid to offer her protection until she left the casino.

Jayde scanned the entire room from the sofa. Francine was at the bar watching as well. Roberta was on the dance floor, but she was still well aware of her surroundings. Lashay was at the craps table, rolling the dice for some hustler.

Two armored-car guards walked in, one carrying two bags, the other holding onto a pistol. They walked through the room, almost unnoticeable, and into the count room on the far west side of The Den.

Jayde could only catch a quick glimpse of the room before the door swung closed. No one was allowed inside the count room with the exception of the counters and armed guards.

The guards spent exactly 10 minutes inside the

room, according to the time that all four of the women kept. Then they snuck back out of the casino.

All four women looked at one another and nodded.

# # # #

Ramon sat with his vest open on his large sofa, drinking champagne in front of his giant TV screen. His two Dobermans sat on either side of the couch.

Robert De Niro was on TV in the movie "*Casino*." Ramon was taking notes on him. He had already watched it four times that week.

The ears on both dogs stood erect as vicious growls escaped their mouths. Ramon hurriedly picked up the remote and punched up the security monitors on the screen.

He saw Snug's Cadillac DeVille parked at the front gate. Ramon pushed a button that opened it. Minutes later, Snug walked through the front door. He examined the spacious, luxurious living room of the house. The high, angled ceilings, Italian furniture, the cozy stone fireplace. One would have thought that Ramon had lived that way all his life. That was, if they didn't know any better.

Ramon sat picking his teeth while he glared at the TV screen. Snug removed his suit jacket, then took a seat in the chair next to the sofa.

"Snug, you take care of Yawni?" His eyes never left the TV.

Snug dropped his head. "Nope."

Again, Ramon picked at his teeth.

Snug said, "I haven't summed up —"

"Nevermind," Ramon interrupted. "I've got something else planned."

"I'm listening." Snug fired up a cigarette.

Ramon gestured toward an alligator-skinned briefcase that rested on the table in front of Snug. Snug opened it up. It was a photograph of a blond man in an expensive suit.

"What's this?"

"Fredrick Bewig the fourth. He's an associate of Murphy's. Said to keep a black notebook in a wall safe inside his home office."

"So?"

"So, I want it," Ramon stated before he finished the rest of his drink. "Murphy wants it, and he's willing to pay a pretty penny for it."

Snug gazed at Ramon with greedy eyes. "How much?"

Ramon sighed. "A million dollars."

Snug asked, "Any help on this one?"

"Yeah. He'll be at the Shamrock Golf Club until six o'clock, Thursday evening. Drives a chauffer-driven Lincoln."

"Who is he?"

"Some guy who owns a company that Murphy wants to take over. The book contains his personal strategies and whatnot."

The phone rang.

Snug got up to answer it.

"Hello. Un hunh, just a moment." Snug handed the phone to Ramon.

"Hello."

"It's Murphy. Have you talked to him?" He sounded anxious.

"Just a minute." Ramon peered at Snug curiously. Snug nodded. "It's all good, man."

"Thank you, brother," Murphy replied with satisfaction.

"You'll thank me enough after I get my money." Ramon hung up and gave the phone back to Snug.

"You comin' along?" Snug asked as he returned the phone back to the charger.

"Nope. I'll be on the golf course with Bewig. I'll call and inform you when he's departing."

The dogs growled again.

Ramon punched up the security screens. Jayde's Camaro was at the gate. Ramon's blood started pumping as he jumped up.

"Make yourself scarce, Snug. I got company." He hit the button that opened the gate. Then disappeared into the other room.

Jayde was getting out of her car when Snug came out of the house. He gazed at her slim figure candidly.

She smirked as she passed him, leaving behind her sweet fragrance for him to feast on. He couldn't help but peep the gold underwear she wore under her transparent skirt. Her stilettos tapped a beat against the concrete as she swayed up to the door.

Snug tossed his cigarette down and got into his car. A black Volvo that wasn't there when he first arrived sparked his attention. It was parked across the street. He stopped his car next to it and peered in the window. He saw no one. So he drove away thinking nothing of it.

# # # #

After Snug pulled away, a woman's head popped up. She watched Ramon give Jayde a hug in the doorway. He had changed over the years. His body appeared to be solid from the distance. The dreadlocks that he once wore were shaved, leaving an oval-shaped gleaming baldhead. But yet and still, even after all those years and all that drama he took her through, the man still turned her on. She had to admit that.

When Jayde and Ramon disappeared inside the huge house, the lady skipped across the street and dropped a note inside his mailbox.

# # # #

"I got your note," Jayde said. She sat her purse on the table.

Ramon walked toward her with two champagne glasses. He handed one to her.

"Obviously. You showed up." He shut the TV off. "Let's go out back."

Jayde followed him through the luxurious home

to the kitchen and out the back doors. There was a statue and a fountain surrounded by a stone patio. Manicured shrubs, plants and flowers decorated the entire yard. Across the way, Jayde could see a small guest house. Off to the right was a three-car garage. To the left was a polished gray stone platform that housed a Jacuzzi.

Ramon led her over to one of the benches where they both sat. For a while they drank in silence.

Jayde finally spoke up. "So, why did you ask me to come here?" The look in her eyes intimidated Ramon.

He looked away. "Because I passed your stamina test. Now it's time for you to put out."

"Put out?"

Ramon peered down at the huge princess cut diamond on her finger, pondering what to say next.

Jayde smirked. "Age has made you insecure, you know that? I watched you and Yawni. She's very pretty but you handle her like she belongs to you. Like you're in control of yawl's situation." She giggled as she slid over close to him. "But for some strange reason, when you're in the presence of a young ... fine ...tender like me, you clam up."

She put her face up close to his. Ramon leaned in for a kiss but she backed away.

"Did I say kiss me?"

"No, but ..."

"But nothing. If you want to lay with me, you have to admit one thing." She grabbed his cheeks with her hand. "And that is ..."

"You're in control," he said in a low whisper.

Jayde stood up, gazing down on him. Before he knew it, she had let her skirt fall to the ground. Her huge round implants demanded his attention.

She placed her foot up on the bench and parked it between his legs. "Kiss my foot." He did. "Now, remove my shoe and suck my toes." Her facial expression had turned into that of a slave master.

Ramon did as he was told. He poured champagne on her knee and let it run down to her toes. He heard a soft moan escape her lips. Slowly, he brought her foot up to his mouth and gently sucked each one of her little toes.

Jayde let her head fall back, with her eyes closed, enjoying the feeling. He tongue-fucked her toes so well that her natural juices soaked her panties.

The cool night breeze and the cold champagne on her legs gave her goose bumps.

"I'm cold," she stated.

He stood, scooped her up and carried her inside to his bedroom. He stepped up on the two-step platform that sat next to his bed, then gently laid her down.

Ramon crawled on top of her and started sucking her breasts. Jayde caressed his baldhead. For the moment, she seemed to be in total submission. She reached inside his pajamas and stroked his organ.

Using his free hand, Ramon pulled his pants down over his butt. Jayde was jerking him off.

Carefully, he eased her panties down and over her feet, then tossed them. A completely shaved, dripping wet pussy stared him in the face. He bent her legs back to where her toes were damn near touching the headboard.

Her wet crevice glistened. He thought about tasting that young nectar first, but he was too eager to get inside of her velvety walls.

Just as Ramon was about to enter her, she screamed, "No! Stop!"

"Huh?" he asked confusingly.

"Get up! Get up!"

The second he released her, she jumped up, grabbed her panties and left the room. Ramon didn't know what to make of the situation. He stood, pulling up his pants.

He was walking out of the room when Jayde shot past him with her skirt and heels in her hand. She left out the front door.

"Jayde, wait!" he called after her.

She got into her car and fired the engine up. Ramon hit the button that opened the gate for fear that she was about to drive through it. Besides, it was no use trying to force her into doing something that she didn't want to do. For all he knew, she would end up shouting rape. He figured that she would give herself to him when the time was right.

The flag on his mailbox was standing. Just to be doing something, he walked out to the front gate, opened the box and took out a letter. There was no writing on it.

He glanced at his surroundings to see if anyone was there. Cars drove up and down the busy street. Other than that, all was well.

Ramon closed the box, then jogged back inside. He plopped down on the sofa and opened the envelope. It was a letter and a stack of photographs. Each picture was what appeared to be a young lady's face. Only there were no clear shots of her whole face. They were only close-ups of her swollen lips, a bruised eye and a broken nose. She was reminding him of who she was, and what he had done to her. Only problem was, Ramon had beaten so many women in his past that it was hard to pinpoint which woman this was.

He sat the pictures down and unfolded the letter.

Dear Ramon,
As I remember, you used to possess a natural instinct that alerted you of danger.
How come you can't see it now?

13

The tour bus of actor-comedian Dion Chapel pulled into the parking lot of the Resthaven Hotel & Casino. He would be performing three shows for three nights. The after-parties would be held at the club, After 7.

Jayde and her girls were standing outside the bus to greet the star and his entourage. They all looked stunning and sexy in high-heeled boots and skirts. Dion took one look at the selection of women, all from different ethnic backgrounds, and knew that he had chosen the right spot.

"I'm fuckin' all four of y'all," he said to them after he stepped off the bus.

Francine and Lashay gave him a look of approval. They escorted him inside. Ramon adjusted his tie and cuffs as he stood in the lobby waiting to greet the man. Snug stood to the right of him. Security men from both the hotel and Dion's entourage were everywhere.

"Mr. Chapel," Ramon said with a smile. They

shook hands. "I see you've met my ladies. They'll be more than happy to assist you with all your personal needs and desires. And thank you for choosing the Resthaven for your stay."

Dion nodded. "Make sure me and my crew get a whole floor to ourselves. 'Cause we come to kick it and fuck some of y'all Kansas City freaks. So we gon' be very ... very noisy."

"Your manager already took care of your reservations in advance." He faced Francine. "Would you show them up to their floor, please?"

"Certainly, Mr. Delay," Francine say gaily. "Right this way."

The group walked toward the elevators. Jayde lagged behind taking up the rear, holding the hand of Dion's tour manager. She winked at Ramon as they strolled past.

Ramon felt a jolt go through his scrotum. He wanted her so bad, he would do almost anything to get it. Even marry her if he had to.

Snug nudged Ramon. "What happened between you two last night? I know that young, hot ass is sweet."

"Nothing happened," he said regretfully. "That bitch played me like I was in high school. I got the little bitch butt-naked, on my bed, with her legs pinned back. As soon as my dick came within an inch of her, she jumped up, grabbed her clothes ... and left."

"No fuckin' way."

"I couldn't believe that shit. I'm damn near forty-two years old."

Snug laughed at him. "Man, let's go get a drink. We got some shit to discuss."

"Do me a favor and keep that between me and you. That shit gets out, all these bitches will be trying to play me for a damned fool."

# # # #

"Fuck that, man!" a drunk white man yelled. He was inside the casino, stumbling away from the Black Jack table. "I just lost my whole income tax refund." He burped. The Absolut Vodka was working on him.

His friend was walking beside him trying to hold him up.

"Four fuckin' thousand dollars I lost tonight." He pushed his friend away from him. "Get off me, you dumb fuck. I can't go home like this." He rested his elbows on the bar. "My wife's gonna fuckin' kill me."

The bartender gazed at him from across the bar.

"Hey, baby," she said in an attempt to calm him down. "Why don't you just go home and get it over with." She patted his shoulder.

Beavis jerked away from her. "Don't try to comfort me, Suzie. I'm not a goddamn baby."

Suzie pushed her hair out of her face. "Go home, Beavis, okay?"

"It ain't okay!" Beavis yelled. He was big, about

6′ 3″ and 270 pounds. "I want my fuckin' money back."

Ramon and Snug walked into The Den while Beavis was going off. They heard the commotion going on to their right. The big drunk man stumbled over to the card table. Joyce, the card dealer, looked terrified.

"Give me ... my fuckin' money back, bitch," Beavis demanded. He picked up the drink of the man sitting next to him and downed it. His face and nose wrinkled as the bitter-tasting hot liquid traveled down to his stomach.

"What the fuck is that, piss?" Beavis threw the empty glass at Joyce.

Joyce called for security.

The little, brittle old man, whose drink Beavis took, frowned up. He was an ex-boxer from the 70s. It had been a heck of a long time since he used his once powerful over-hand right hook. He had been wanting to use it again for almost 30 years, and he finally had the chance.

Jesse "Thunder Bird" Littleton saw security coming. He knew if his jab wasn't effective, then they were gonna step in and intervene anyway, so, he went for it.

He drew back with all the strength he could muster and hit Beavis in the nose. The punch had no effect. Beavis stood there glaring at the man as if nothing happened. That's when security rushed him. Jesse stepped out of their way, holding his sore fist.

Without even thinking, Beavis hit a guard in the face and kicked another. Then two more guards attacked him.

Beavis' big country ass started slinging people everywhere. He accidentally hit himself upside the head.

"C'mon you black motherfuckers!" he challenged.

The guards all attacked him simultaneously, seizing his arms and feet. They lifted him in the air.

"Take this piece of shit out back and flush it," Ramon commanded. "Snug, you go with 'em." The guards rammed Beavis' head against the exit door to open it. Snug followed them out.

While everybody was concentrating on the scene Beavis was making, his friend was busy swiping chips from the tables.

Ramon tried to get the crowd back in order. "Everything's okay, people. Please go back to gambling." He left The Den.

Out back, the guards slammed Beavis down on the ground. So many feet started kicking him that he couldn't count them if he tried. Snug pulled out his gun, then grabbed him by the hair.

"Aaah!" Beavis hollered.

"I don't ever wanna see your fat ass near this place again, you hear me?"

"Yes."

"Huh?"

"Yeess."

Snug raised the gun, then brought it down on Beavis' forehead.

Wack! Wack!

Beavis sprawled out on the pavement.

"Ever again, you piece of shit." Snug put his gun away as he followed the guards back inside.

# # # #

Ramon was called upstairs to the camera room to review the tape. The cameras had caught Beavis' friend stealing chips while everybody was preoccupied with the diversion.

"Where is he now? Did he get out?" Ramon inquired.

"No. He's staying in room 209. He's in there now."

Ramon got on the radio and called Snug.

"Yeah," Snug answered.

"We got a thief in room 209. Why don't you go up there and check it out."

"Will do."

Snug alerted two backup security guards and led them upstairs. He stood back while one of them knocked on the door.

"This is hotel security. Open up."

Anderson sat on the edge of the bed counting up the chips. When he heard knocking at the door, he damn near panicked. He took off his shirt and raked the chips off the bed into it.

Knock! Knock!

Anderson quickly glanced around the room for a hiding place. His eyes settled on the bathroom. He dashed inside and snatched the lid off the back of the toilet.

Boom!

The guards kicked the door open. They rushed in looking around the room for him. Snug spotted Anderson's hairy back through a crack in the bathroom door.

"Get that sonofabitch," he commanded.

The two guards rushed him before he could get the lid closed. They clutched his arms, then dragged him into the other room.

"Wait a goddamn minute!" Anderson yelled. "What's going on?"

They threw him to the floor. Snug casually removed his jacket and laid it over the back of the chair.

"I'ma show you how we deal with thieves at the Resthaven Hotel. Pick'em up."

The guards held him in an upright position while Snug went to work on him.

# # # #

Ramon walked into his office, placed his jacket on the rack and sat behind his desk. Out of his drawer, he removed some important papers.

"Mr. Delay," his night secretary said through the phone.

He hit the button. "Yes?"

"A Detective Molina is on the phone for you."

This late at night? It can't be about nothing good, he thought.

"Ah, tell him to call me tomorrow. And remember, I'm not the boss. I work in the entertainment department."

"Yes, sir."

Ramon sat back in his chair trying to imagine what the detective wanted with him. He froze when he saw a silhouette out of the corner of his eye. Quickly, he reached for the gun that was clamped under his desk.

"Don't bother," Yawni said as she stepped out of the shadows. Tears were in her eyes.

He relaxed after he saw who it was.

Her hands fidgeted when she approached his desk. She noticed how powerful and distinguished he looked in his suit.

"I've been thinking." She placed her hands on his desk, unable to give him eye contact. "I'm sorry."

"You're sorry?" Ramon snickered. "Is that all you have to say to me?"

"I shouldn't have hit you." She finally looked at him. "Ramon, I've been in love with you for years."

"Step around here." He was stone faced. Yawni slowly walked around his desk and kneeled before him. Ramon slipped his foot out of his shoes. "Take my sock off and kiss my foot."

Yawni saw the serious look in his eyes. Gently,

she removed his sock, then placed a soft kiss on his foot.

"Now stand up ... then remove your clothes."

Yawni stood and shucked her dress down to the floor. She wore no bra underneath. She bent over and pulled off her stockings and panties. While she was doing so, he thought about what Jayde told him. She said he controlled Yawni, and she, Jayde, had control over him.

Yawni started on him. She undid his pants and pulled them down to his thighs. After stroking his dick hard, she straddled him.

# # # #

Jayde stepped off the elevator carrying a bottle of champagne and two glasses. Yawni's loud cries of pleasure could be heard out in the hallway. Jayde stopped for a second to listen.

"Ah! Ssss! Oooh!"

Suddenly, Jayde began to back away. It seemed like it took forever for the elevator to return. In the meantime, she stood there with her ears tormented by Yawni's moans of pleasure.

She rode the elevator to the main lobby, clocked out and walked to her car. The tires on her car squealed as she bolted out into the street. Jayde popped the bottle of champagne, then turned it up to her lips. She pulled to a stop at the intersection of 87th and Blue Ridge. A police patrol car was traveling north on Blue Ridge.

Jayde hit the bottle one good time, then tossed it out on the street. Pieces of broken glass scattered on the road. The cop driving the patrol car slowed to a stop after he saw the bottle come flying out of the Camaro.

The top on Jayde's car began to retract. She put on her driving shades, revved the engine, then hit the gas. Her rear spun sideways as she made a sharp right turn onto Blue Ridge. At first it looked as if she might lose it, until the car straightened and proceeded.

The police activated his sirens, and got in pursuit. Jayde watched the speedometer accelerate at a quick pace. She looked in the mirror and saw that two more cars had joined the chase.

She sped past cars and through red lights. When she shifted gears, the Camaro's ass dropped and fire spit out of the exhaust. Her head bobbed to the imaginary music inside her head. A patrol car parked at the Longview intersection. The driver jumped out and laid down the tire spikes.

When she neared the intersection, she swerved over in the opposite lane, then made a sharp left. She was rolling now, with the wind blowing through her hair. The thrill of being chased did something to her body that she was unable to explain.

After she made a right on Food Lane, which was a straightaway, the policemen watched her tail lights disappear before their eyes.

That should do it, Jayde told herself. Just before she hit Main Street, she brought the car to a screeching halt. She took the time to light a cigarette while she waited on them to catch up. Soon, she was surrounded by patrol cars. Policemen leapt from their cars with guns pointed at her. She spit out the cigarette while she lifted her hands toward the sky.

"Step out of the car, now!" one of them ordered.

# # # #

Yawni held her palms firmly against Ramon's desk while he pumped her from behind.

"Haaa! Haaa! Uhh!" Yawni was left gasping for breath when he pulled out of her.

Ramon collapsed in his chair, dick still standing. His tank top was soaked with sweat. Yawni put on his button-up shirt and went to the bathroom. Seconds later, the shower came on.

After a while, she returned with his robe in her hand.

"C'mon. Let me clean you up," she said. He stood and walked over to her.

Yawni gazed up at him. When he peered into her beautiful eyes, he saw love and passion. Yes, she really loved him. To her, he was more than just a fling, he was her world.

Ramon kissed her. "Tell me you love me."

"I love you, old man."

His hands traveled down to her butt. "I think I'm

ready to go another round."

"Ooh, you must've have popped a Viagra tonight."

"I think you gon' need one."

"Unt unh, I'm not even forty yet," she reminded him. He popped her on the ass as he took off for the shower.

The phone rang.

He prayed that it wasn't that detective calling for him again.

"Hello."

"It's me, Jayde."

Ramon peered at the bathroom door. "Un hunh?"

"I'm in jail. Can you come get me?" He didn't responded quick enough. "I can just spend the night at your house, if you don't mind. I need to get out of these filthy jail-smelling clothes."

Damn, he thought. "Uhh, ye ... yeah. Where are you?"

"On Hickman Mills." Her voice was a childlike plea.

"I'll be there in a minute."

Jayde made a hissing sound into the phone. Ramon slowly placed it back on the base.

"Ba-by," Yawni called. "Hurry up before I get cold."

Ramon ignored her and sat in his chair to think. What was he going to tell Yawni? If he didn't come up with a good lie in a hurry, they were gonna break up just as quick as they made up. He had to ask himself, was Jayde worth losing her?

Ramon put his pants and shoes back on. He stopped at the bathroom door, contemplating going in and doing it the right way. But why? He thought. He didn't have to explain himself to no one.

The shower door slid open. Yawni stuck her soapy face out.

"Ramon? Ramon?"

She rinsed the soap off her body, then stepped out. Yawni grabbed a towel and wrapped it around her.

"Ramon?" She glanced around the empty office, baffled.

The phone rang.

Yawni pulled her wet hair back into a ponytail on her way to answer it. "Hello. Manager's office."

"Has Ramon left yet?" Jayde asked, well aware of what she was doing.

Yawni placed her hand on her hip. "Who is this?"

"This is Jayde. He was supposed to be on his way to pick me up."

Yawni was afraid to speak, knowing that Jayde would hear her voice crack. So in order to save face, she just hung up.

chapter
14

Jayde was already sitting on the steps at the police station when Ramon drove up. When he saw her, he wondered how she got out without him. Had it all been a hoax to get him to come?

He honked the horn at her. Jayde picked up the brown paper bag that held her things and got into the car.

"How did you get out?" Ramon inquired.

"My bondsman sprung me. He's a friend of mine." She fished her cigarettes out of her sack.

"Then why did you call me?"

Jayde sneered. She didn't like the rise in his tone. "I called your office and some woman told me that you were busy. That's why I had to get out myself."

Yawni. Oh my God, Ramon thought as he pulled out the lot. He wouldn't be able to lie his way out of this one if he wanted to. He dug into his jacket pocket, taking out his cigarettes. Jayde sat back, relaxing on the leather seat, enjoying the cool nighttime breeze.

She looked over at Ramon, examining him. He saw her but kept his eyes forward. He was angry with her for making him ditch Yawni for no reason. Jayde would definitely have to come off some pussy in order to make that up.

Ramon stopped at the local 7-Eleven to pick up a bottle of Armadale Vodka, a bottle of orange juice and two cups of ice. Then he hit the highway headed for the lookout point down by Washington Street.

"Where're we going?" Jayde asked.

Ramon smiled. "Someplace romantic."

Jayde returned his smile with a warm smirk. "That's cool with me."

The lookout point was almost empty, with the exception of one van parked in the middle of the circular parking area. It was occupied by two teenagers who were sharing a bottle of E&J, trying to work up the nerves to screw. When they saw the other car pull up, they jumped in the back.

Ramon backed in about three spaces from them and popped the trunk. Jayde grabbed the liquor while he put in a Delfonics CD to set the mood. It was chilly, so he took a couple of blankets out the trunk.

"What are we listening to?" Jayde joked.

"The Delfonics." He seemed baffled. "Don't tell me you're too young to appreciate good music?"

"I'm a music fanatic. I was just joking with you. You're too self-conscious about your age."

"Sheeit, you would be too if you spent the majority of your young life behind bars."

They found a nice spot on the grass overlooking the downtown area. He helped her wrap the blanket around her, then poured two warm cups of vodka to help heat up their blood.

Jayde tasted hers while he wrapped himself. "Whew! Needs some juice."

"I thought you were the baddest bitch?" He opened the bottle of juice and poured some into her cup.

"I am. But I like to watch what I put inside my body." She tasted the mixed drink. "That's better. So tell me about Ramon Delay." She gazed at him, studying his handsome face.

"Like what?"

Jayde shrugged. "Tell me how you ended up in prison. What did you go through while you were in there? Things of that nature."

Ramon took a big gulp, then sat his cup down. "It's a long story. I shot and killed my baby's mama's brother in front of her. She called the police and had me locked up." He stared out into space. "You know, when they found me guilty, I looked back at her and could've sworn … that I saw a smile on her face."

"What about your baby?"

Ramon finished up the drink, then poured another before he answered. "Never saw her again. She's grown now and probably in school, or pregnant. I did some fucked up shit to her."

"Wanna talk about it?" Her voice was comforting.

"Her brother stole some money from me. He was young, probably about 17, I don't know. I shot him in cold blood, right in front of her and my child. I also threatened to kill my girl, and kid, if he didn't return my money."

"Would you have done it?" She watched him intently.

Ramon pondered the question. "Back then ... I might have, just to show him that I meant business." He took another gulp. "Back then, I just didn't give a fuck. I loved the sound of my gun going off. Someone could wave at me, and I would instantly become angry. Then I would lash out at them. My little girl saw enough in six years of living with me to be a cold-hearted something. Plus, it's in her blood."

"Sounds to me like you miss her."

Ramon sighed. "I did, while I was locked up. It can get lonely on the inside. In jail, you miss things as little as walking barefoot on carpet. Isn't that ironic?"

Jayde stood and got inside of the blanket with him in front. Then she wrapped her long legs and arms around him. He relaxed under her tender touch.

She giggled. "I probably smell like that funky jail, don't I?"

"Baby, it wouldn't matter to me if you smelled

like an outhouse right now. I just wanna be with you. I wanna marry you. I wanna ... wake up to you every morning."

"There's a lot that comes along with me."

Ramon shook his head slowly. "It don't matter. The road I'm traveling on now is headed north, and I can't lose. Everything you need and want will be handed to you."

He pressed his lips up against hers. At first, she was hesitant to open her mouth, but due to the intimate moment they had shared, she eventually gave in.

For the next hour or so, they sat quietly, holding each other, keeping each other warm. They drank out of the bottle of vodka until it was gone. Then they got up and danced to the smooth grooves of The Gap Band. When it got too cold to keep up with the rhythm, they sat and talked some more.

Finally, some time around four o'clock in the morning, the liquor started to catch up with Ramon. His speech turned into a slur.

Jayde helped him into the passenger seat of his car. Across the lot sat a Volvo facing their direction with the lights out. The woman that occupied it went unnoticed as she watched them.

Ramon stood up in the seat. "The world is mine. All mine!" he yelled.

Jayde urged him to sit before they both ended up in jail this time around. She pulled him down and locked him in the seatbelt.

"Let's see what this baby can do," Jayde said. The brand new engine purred when she started it.

Ramon held on while she cut corners until she got on the highway. She then went for 90 mph. Cautiously, she weaved in and out of traffic lanes, just barely avoiding collisions.

Jayde glanced over at Ramon to see how he was handling her reckless driving. He looked like he was about to puke at any given moment. She smirked as usual, but didn't slow down any.

The tires squealed when Jayde turned onto Ramon's street. She hit the button that opened the gate. After she parked, she helped him inside. He was sluggish and heavy.

"Lights," Ramon barked upon entering the house.

All the lights came on. Jayde helped him to the bedroom. His heavy body fell onto the bed, shaking up his stomach.

"OHH!" he moaned. Reaching up, he pulled her down on top of him.

Jayde giggled as she straddled him. She began kissing his neck and face. His body relaxed while she removed his clothing.

He was so drunk that he was near unconsciousness. Jayde gazed into his eyes hypnotically.

"Wha's wrong?" Ramon asked curiously.

Jayde got up, then went to the living room. She returned a minute later with a joint inside her hand. She climbed up on the bed next to him, fired it up, then passed it to him.

"Is this the same shit as last time?" Jayde nodded. Ramon accepted it.

He took a long puff, holding the smoke inside his lungs as long as he could. Jayde sat back and watched him through mischievous eyes.

"Hit it again, baby," she urged him.

Ramon did as he was told. The smoke hit his lungs so hard that it made him gag. He lay back on the pillow with his eyes closed, unable to move his lips. Jayde removed the joint from between his fingers, laughing silently.

# # # #

Lawton snapped pictures of Ramon's car and home from the passenger seat of Molina's vice car parked across the street.

He got a couple of shots of Jayde helping Ramon into the house. They had been watching his every move since earlier that day. So far, the investigation came up blank. They had learned nothing other than he was a killer and an ex-con who had done time in prison.

"Get a few shots of the dogs, too," Molina said. "They can go down with him."

Lawton got two shots of the dogs while they were resting next to Ramon's Cadillac.

"What do you think of that hot piece of hot ass he's got with him?" Lawton asked. "I'll bet she cost a mint, huh Mo?"

"Yeah, I'll bet." Molina sucked his teeth. "Criminals. They have all the fun, don't they? The guy gets out of prison just a couple of years ago, and is secretly heading a multi-million dollar business. A gambling business at that." He shook his head.

Lawton shifted in his seat. "I don't know, Mo. I mean ... maybe we're jumping the gun, here. Maybe the man is head of the entertainment department like he says he is."

Molina peered over at him through suspicious eyes. "You switch sides or something?"

The stare that Molina gave him made Lawton shift in his seat. "No, Mo. I'm just saying, everything ain't always as bad as it seems."

"Of course it is. That's why we're here. Don't you forget that."

Lawton sat the camera down and opened his door.

"Where are you going?" Molina inquired.

"I need to call the Missus."

"What, you don't want me to hear what you're saying?"

"It's private," Lawton said with a smile. "Give me a minute, okay?"

Molina peered at Ramon's window. "I'm gonna get you, you slick fuck."

# chapter 15

Ramon stood in a golfer's stance while gripping his putter. He measured up for the shot. Fredrick Bewig and his personal caddy stood five feet away, looking.

"You might wanna tighten your butt cheeks just a little bit, Delay," Fredrick joked, hoping that he would miss the putt.

"Thousand bucks says I sink it," Ramon said.

"You're on." Just as Ramon was about to hit the ball, Fredrick yelled out, "Fore!"

Ramon hit the ball too hard causing it to veer too far to the left. He glared over at Fredrick, who had his gloved hand over his mouth, snickering.

"What kinda shit you on, man?" Ramon asked hotly.

"You have to holler 'fore' before you hit the ball, Ramon," he chuckled. "I thought you knew that."

Ramon pulled out a wad of bills and counted out ten hundred-dollar bills. He held the money up, then dropped it on the ground by his feet.

Fredrick didn't take offense to it. Instead he snapped his fingers, ordering his caddy to get it. The man pulled his slacks up at the knees, bent over and picked up the money.

A huge grin was glued to Fredrick's face when he accepted the money. "A fool and his money will soon part."

It didn't take long for Ramon to remember where he had heard that saying before. It was written on that mysterious letter he received.

Gripping his club tight, Ramon asked, "You say that a lot?"

Fredrick took a break from counting his winnings to look up. "Say what?"

"That thing about a fool and his money."

"Yeah. It's something that my old man used to tell me when I was a kid. Why?"

"Not important." Ramon relaxed. He laughed inside thinking how true that statement was. Only Fredrick didn't know that he was speaking to himself.

Fredrick sunk his putt. "Ha ha, I win again."

"Give me a little time, Fred."

They loaded themselves onto Fredrick's golf cart and rode back to the club. He ordered his caddy to take care of his things.

Fredrick glanced at his Rolex watch. "Ooh, it's getting late, Delay. I have to fly to Hong Kong early tomorrow." They shook hands. "A pleasure playing with you. Have your people call my people so we can do this again."

The arrogant businessman strutted out the door, dialing numbers on his cell phone. His limo was parked out front. Ramon peered out the front door at the Buick Century parked on the north end of the lot.

When Fredrick's limo drove away, the Buick followed. To kill some time, Ramon took a shower, then sat inside the steam room for a while.

# # # #

Tulu was behind the wheel of the '05 Buick Century. Snug rode in the back seat behind him, while Bobby rode shotgun.

Snug had yet to start trusting Tulu. Every time they were around one another, Snug kept a close eye on the slick looking man. He talked too much, and told too many lies.

Snug would feel more relaxed if the man would just shut the fuck up, sometimes. He had to smoke a cigarette to calm his nerves.

"Like I said, we oughta run up in there and cut that cracka's throat wide open," Tulu suggested. "In the joint, I woulda cut his asshole open and hide all my knives and dope in it. Make that bitch carry it around with him, like a ... a fuckin' human stash spot."

Bobby and Snug looked at each other. They both burst out laughing.

"Where did you get this guy, Snug?" Bobby

asked.

Snug had to regain his composure before he could answer.

"Man, I don't know. Ramon found this crazy-ass fool in the joint, I guess."

Tulu's eyes shifted from Bobby to Snug's reflection in the mirror. "What the fuck's so funny?"

"You," Snug said. "Yo' crazy ass belong in the nut house some damn where."

Bobby pointed out the window. "He's pulling into the gas station."

Snug got on his cell phone. "Do it here?"

"Do what?" Yawni asked. She was about half a block behind them.

"I don't know. Improvise."

She let out a long, frustrated sigh. "Okay."

While the limo driver filled up, Fredrick walked inside the store. He talked away on his cell phone on the way to the cooler.

The bell on the door jingled when Yawni walked through it. Her eyes searched the area for Fredrick. She found him bent over, reaching inside the cooler. She headed in his direction.

Frederick found the drink that he was searching for. Just as he was about to straighten up, he felt something, or someone, bump into him. When he turned around with a frown on his face, the first thing he saw was a long, smooth set of legs. He thought he smelled her fragrance, but the cold air coming from the inside of the cooler smothered it.

His eyes traveled up her legs to her thighs, over the hills of her breasts, then rested on her smiling face.

"Excuse me," she said in her most cheerful voice. "How clumsy of me. I didn't see your cute little butt sticking out of there."

Fredrick flipped his phone closed, hanging up on whoever he was talking to.

"If you think my butt is cute," he said, "you oughta see the rest of me."

Yawni pretended to be offended. "I don't think so. Excuse me."

When she attempted to walk away, he grabbed her arm. She peered down at his hand.

"I'm sorry," he apologized as he released his grip. "I just didn't want you to walk away angry at me." He offered his hand. "Fredrick Bewig."

"Not the same Fredrick Bewig who owns Bewig toy company?"

He put on a cocky smirk. "That would be me." He gestured toward the window at the limo waiting outside. "I'm shocked that you know of me. How so?"

After running her fingers through her hair, she said, "I used to work for you."

"Used to?"

"Yes. Unfortunately women who work for your company seem to have a hard time climbing the corporate ladder, no matter how qualified they are."

His handsome face softened. "I'm sorry to hear that, Mrs. ..."

"Miss," she corrected him. "Just call me Margo."

They shook hands. He caressed hers and she pulled away.

"Well, Margo," he said, "you do know that in this day and age, there are various ways for a woman to get into an executive position. It doesn't always boil down to what she knows, or how many degrees she has. Sometimes it's as simple as ... uh ... a one night stand that keeps them from escalating." He shot her a knowing look. "Need I say more?"

Yawni pretended to be contemplating an answer. She nervously looked to the left, then to the right. Finally her mouth opened. "Your place or mine?"

He smiled. "Mine's nearby. You can follow my limo there."

She nodded.

The limo driver looked constipated as he held the door open for his boss to get into the back. Fredrick was gonna say something, but quickly disregarded it when images of Yawni lying naked across the bed flooded his brain.

"To my estate, please."

The driver nodded without saying a word before he closed the door.

Yawni followed the limo inside the gated driveway. Fredrick hopped out, talking on his cell phone. His two Akitas rushed him.

"Down! Down!" he shouted. "Jesus! You're gonna ruin my pants. Yeah, Murphy, I'm here." He motioned for Yawni to follow him inside.

The driver took his position to the right of Fredrick. Yawni walked past them into the house. While Murphy was yapping in his ear, Fredrick was visualizing Yawni's big lips wrapped around his massive white cock.

Fredrick covered the phone and whispered to the driver, "After I'm finished with her, come up with an excuse for me to kick her out."

"Like what?"

He shrugged. "Doesn't matter. I gotta get some sleep before my flight tomorrow."

"Sure, boss."

Fredrick disappeared inside.

Tulu was hiding in the front seat of the limo. When he saw Fredrick go inside, he stepped out of the car. The driver was scared half to death.

"Good job," Tulu said. "I didn't wanna have to step out of that car firing."

"What now?"

"Open the gates so my friends can get through."

The driver did as he was told.

Meanwhile, Fredrick stood behind his bar, mixing two drinks, with his back to the security monitors. Yawni could see them. She saw the Buick driving through the gates.

"Why don't we cut to the chase and go straight to your bedroom," Yawni said, distracting him.

He immediately stopped what he was doing. "What, no appetizer?"

Yawni shook her head. "I'm ready for the main course."

Fredrick felt his nature rising in his pants. He sat the mixed drink down, walked around the bar, gazed down at Yawni sitting on the barstool and stuck his tongue inside her mouth.

"Mm," he grunted. "You're such a whore, you know that?"

"Yes." Yawni tugged at his pants. *He likes to talk dirty,* she thought. "And you're such a stud, baby. Let me see it."

"Whip it out, you slut." Mock anger was in his eyes.

Yawni undid his pants, then reached in, pulling out one of the biggest dicks she had ever seen. The swollen pink organ dangled in front of her. The sight of it shot spasms through her crotch, almost making her forget the plot. Her ambitiousness and female lust made her want to test her skills by seeing if she could swallow it all. Then she remembered that she was not a whore, and this was only an act.

Snug, Tulu and Bobby followed the driver through the house.

"Where is he?" Snug inquired.

The driver started to cry. Tulu slapped him across the face.

"Where is he?" Snug asked again.

He nodded toward the stairs.

They all took out masks and pulled them over

their faces.

"Take care of him, Tulu," Snug commanded. He looked at Bobby. "C'mon." They took the stairs.

The driver peered at Tulu with terror in his eyes. "What's gonna happen to me?" His lips and hands were trembling.

"Sheeit, what you think? Yo' ass is fitna die," Tulu said coldly, staring at him through his bug eyes. "Hell is in your future."

Tulu stabbed the driver to death, then caught up with his crew at the top of the circular staircase. They heard the music, but couldn't figure out which room it was coming from. It seemed to be echoing throughout the entire mansion.

# # # #

Fredrick and Yawni had shucked out of their clothes and jumped into his jet stream hot tub. His head lay back on the cushion, while Yawni strad-dled him, kissing his hairy chest. Jazz played through the speakers on the wall.

Fredrick reached for his glass. The water on his fingers caused it to slip out of his hands. The broken glass scattered across the floor.

"Damnit!" he cursed.

Snug wheeled to the left after he heard the glass break. "This way."

They stood outside the bathroom door. Snug put his ear flush up to it, but only heard the saxophone playing. He placed his gloved hand around the knob, and turned.

"I'll get it, baby," Yawni said, referring to the broken glass.

"No, no! You just relax. I'll get it."

Fredrick stepped out of the tub naked. Snug could see the pink side of his ass and balls while he was bent over picking up the shards of glass.

Fredrick got the feeling that someone other than Yawni was watching him. He peered back between his legs and saw a masked Snug glaring at him.

"Shit!" Fredrick tried to run to the other door. He heard Yawni screaming for help. "Gomez!" he yelled.

When he reached out for the door, he slipped and fell. Snug grabbed him under his left arm. Bobby grabbed him under his right. Tulu came up from behind, landing vicious jabs to his kidneys. Fredrick yelled and screamed, but it was no use. By the time Tulu was done beating him, the man was barely conscious.

Yawni grabbed her clothes and made a run for it.

"Stop her!" Snug ordered.

"I got that bitch," Tulu said. He took off out the door behind her.

Snug looked down at the bloody man lying on the floor beneath his feet. "Now that you know how serious this is, I trust you'll tell us where that safe is."

Tulu came running back into the bathroom, out of breath.

"I couldn't catch the bitch," he said, panting.

Snug said, "Well, we gotta move fast."

They dragged Fredrick all the way to his bedroom. "Please!" he cried.

Tulu yelled, "Shut the fuck up!"

Snug and Bobby slammed him on the thick carpeted floor in front of his bed. Tulu kneeled down, glaring at him with his bug eyes wide open.

"You scared as a muthafucka right now, ain't you, honky? Yeah, you scared." Tulu slapped him across the face. "Look at me when I talk to you."

Fredrick's chest was heaving rapidly. He looked up at Tulu's masked face with terror in his eyes. He wanted to cower away but didn't want to get struck again.

"My wallet is on the dresser," Fredrick offered. "Take it and leave. Please!" He was straining to talk.

Tulu smacked him again. "You know goddamn well we didn't come for no fucking ... get up!" He snatched Fredrick up, then pushed him toward the door. "Take us to the money."

Fredrick spit out a clot of blood. "I keep my money in a bank. There's not much here."

Snug peered at Bobby, then nodded his head. Bobby left the room to search the house.

Tulu walked over to the closet and found a crocodile-skinned belt. He wrapped it around his hand, on his way back over to Fredrick.

With a sneer on his face, Tulu said to Fredrick, "I'm about to whoop you like you a useless-ass dog."

"Owwww!" Fredrick screamed after he received the first lash across his back.

Snug fired up a cigarette and admired the artwork on the walls while Tulu punished the man.

Bobby ran down the stairs, searching, until he found Fredrick's office. It was furnished like it belonged to a college professor. A massive collection of books covered the entire south side wall.

First, he scanned the painting along the walls, coming up blank. Then he moved over to the bookshelf. Dead smack in the middle, he found what he was searching for. He took out the book *Huckleberry Finn* and the surrounding books.

He stuck his hand inside the empty space and felt the metal exterior of the safe's door. Then, he felt the knob. After he jumped to his feet, he pulled out his Nextel to hit Snug.

"I found it," Bobby informed. "I'm downstairs, second door on your right."

"Okay."

Tulu stopped beating Fredrick. "You lying muthafucka, you." He reached down and snatched him up. "Get up! And get yo' ass downstairs and open that ..." he hit him again, "goddamn safe."

Whips and bruises covered Fredrick's back and ass. His body was in pain as he limped into the hallway, then down the steps. It seemed like it took him forever to get to the bottom. To him, it was no longer about the money, he just wanted to get Tulu away from him.

He hoped that the girl had called the police and that they would arrive before they escaped. Stalling was the furthest thing from his mind. There was no telling what Tulu would do next.

Fredrick led them inside his office. Snot and tears covered his once handsome face. The powerful businessman looked more like a wounded boxer than a corporate executive.

Bobby stood in front of the bookshelf with books scattered around his feet. He waved them over. Tulu put his hand on the back of Fredrick's head, pushing him toward Bobby. Frederick fell to his knees.

"Hey!" Snug shouted at Tulu. "Calm the fuck down, man." Snug grabbed a sports jacket off the back of the office chair. He tossed it at Fredrick. "Put that on. I don't want to keep looking at your naked ass."

Tulu said, "Yo, man. Don't ever holler at me again."

Slowly, Snug turned his head in Tulu's direction. "What?"

"I didn't stutter, nigga. I said ..."

Snug took a step toward him.

"Hey! Hey! Hey!" Bobby shouted as he stepped between them. "Knock it off!"

That's exactly what Fredrick wanted them to do. *Take your time. Keep fucking around. Eventually the police will come, and it would be all over, you black bastards*, he thought.

When Bobby was satisfied that both had calmed down, he went back over to Fredrick.

"Now, open the safe."

After Fredrick put on the jacket, he turned the knob. When the door opened, Tulu pushed him away.

Bobby peered inside. There were a few stacks of cash, some jewelry, files and of course, the black book. Bobby tossed the cash to Tulu, then stuck the jewelry in his pocket.

Fredrick was exhausted, but he watched carefully, hoping that they didn't take his black book. Bobby didn't want him to see him take it. As far as Fredrick knew, it was supposed to be just a random robbery.

Tulu peered at Fredrick. "What the fuck're you looking at, peckerwood?" he yelled. He was frustrated because he had to let Snug get away with talking to him like that. He walked up on Fredrick with the gun pointed at his forehead. "Close yo' fuckin' eyes."

Fredrick closed them, and squeezed them tight.

"Take the money. Just please don't kill me," he begged.

Bobby swiftly tucked the book away in his pants, then closed the safe. "Let's go."

Snug snapped his finger at Tulu, signaling him to come on before he left the room.

"Be there in a minute. Up on your fuckin' knees." Tulu held the gun on him while he did as he was told. "I want your pretty, rich, white ass to remember this every time you go to thinking that you have control over the black man. You hear me?"

Fredrick nodded.

"Alright." Tulu brought the gun down on top of his head, knocking him out.

chapter

16

"I call," **Ramon stated**. He pushed another $2,000 worth of chips toward the dealer.

Several businessmen surrounded the table dressed in suits, all on the same mission – to beat the house. Two of the players folded their hands. The last man stuck around the see who really had the best hand.

"What're you gonna do?" Ramon asked.

The man slid another thousand dollars worth of chips into the pot. "Raising another grand."

Ramon smiled. "I'll see your measly grand." He slid in some more chips. "And raise you another five."

The onlookers whistled out loud.

The man regarded Ramon curiously. "You're bluffin'."

Ramon shrugged. "You gonna bet or tuck your fuckin' tail?"

The man peered at his hand again. They were playing Low Ball and he had a 7 high. There was a good chance that Ramon had a 5 or a 6, which would beat his 7.

"Uhh!" the man sighed and wiped his forehead. "I think I'll fold," he announced regretfully, then threw in his cards. "Let me see your hand."

Ramon flipped the cards over. He had a pair of 9s, which was a losing hand.

"I bluffed you," Ramon said. "Scared men can't win."

The crowd couldn't believe it. And the man sitting across from him was pissed off.

"Sonofabitch!"

A waitress walked over and whispered something into Ramon's ear. He nodded. She returned seconds later with a cordless phone in her hand.

"Hello."

"We have the black book." It was Snug.

"Good. Just for good measure, photocopy every page, then bring it to me."

"You got it."

"Hey. How's Tulu holding up?"

"I don't know where you got that clown."

Ramon chuckled. "Lighten up. He's a handful but I trust him." He hung up. "Deal me in. I just made 2 million dollars."

The waitress interrupted him again by tapping him on the shoulder.

"What is it, now?" he said with frustration. "Can't you see I'm gambling?"

She whispered into his ear again. Ramon

peered over her shoulder toward the lounge. Jayde was sitting on a sofa with her legs crossed, looking elegant in a red wraparound dress. She held up two glasses of Brandy, motioning for him to come join her.

"Your bet, Mr. Delay," the dealer informed him.

"Uhhh ... why don't you just cash me out, Jewel." Ramon slid his rack of chips to her and rose from his seat. "I'll pick my money up later."

A handsome white man, about 30 years of age, was sitting next to Jayde when Ramon arrived. Ramon grunted but the gentleman ignored him.

Ramon tapped him on the shoulder. "She's with me."

The guy took offense. "And just who the fuck are you?"

Fiddling with his cufflinks, Ramon smirked as he said, "You got about 10 seconds to move your ass before you get fucked up."

The man jumped up with anger in his face. Ramon grabbed the collar of his jacket and slung him over the glass table, next to theirs. Drinks spattered on the floor as security rushed to his aid.

"I'm okay." He gazed down at the man getting up on his knees. "Go over to the bar and get yourself another drink. On me."

He sat down next to Jayde. "You rang?"

Jayde finished sipping from her brandy glass. She seemed unimpressed by his heroic act of violence. "I did."

"Why?"

"Because, I wanted to have a drink with you."

Ramon picked up his glass and sniffed the rim. "Mm, Moesha Brandy."

"You know your stuff. I was thinking a thug like you might say it was something cheap, like ... Christian Brothers."

"A thug like me?" He peered down at his shirt and tie. "You know this suit I'm wearing is by John Varvatos? Custom-made cufflinks." He took off his shoe and showed her the inside.

"Specially made for Ramon Delay," Jayde read. "Cute."

"Cute hell. That's class." Ramon put his shoe back on. "I left that thug shit back in the joint."

"I bet your daughter would be proud." Jayde sipped her drink. While she let her eyes roam The Den, Ramon stared at the side of her head.

"Well, I can see where this conversation is going." He stood. "Excuse me."

Jayde clutched his hand, pulling him back down onto the sofa. She wrapped her leg around him and kissed him on the lips.

Seconds later, she came up for air. "Let's get out of here, baby," she whispered seductively. She stood up, still holding his hand. "Let's go."

"Okay. Let's stop and get some of that weed you like to smoke," he said.

As they passed the bar, Ramon spotted a familiar-looking woman sitting at the end of the bar.

She was looking straight ahead, ignoring the drink in front of her. Though he could only see the side of her face, he was sure that he knew her from somewhere.

Subconsciously, he started for the bar, but Jayde intervened by tugging his arm the other way. Seeing Jayde from the rear cleared his mind of the woman. He happily followed her out the exit.

The woman finally turned her head when he was gone. She smiled to herself before taking a drink.

# # # #

Hours later, Ramon awoke in his bedroom. He looked next to him, but Jayde wasn't there. His lips were chapped and his throat was dry, just like the last time. And as usual with Jayde, he didn't remember a thing that happened the night before.

He rolled over, sitting up on the edge of the bed. After wiping the sleep from his eyes, he saw what was left of the joint he and Jayde smoked sitting in the ashtray.

Curiously, he picked it up, examining the wrapping. It seemed to be wrapped in regular rolling paper. He had to be sure that it was weed he was smoking. Slowly, he began to unravel it.

A shadow came over him. Ramon turned his head to find Jayde standing there. She had her mouth twisted up in a wicked sneer and held a butcher's knife in her hand.

"Being a bit too nosy for your own good," she growled, then raised the knife.

"Jayde, no!" Ramon screamed. He raised his hands to try to block the knife.

Then he woke up panting in a cold sweat.

Ramon peered to the left, then to the right while he tried to collect himself. When he realized that it was just a dream, he reached for his cigarettes on the nightstand.

Quickly, he retracted his hand after he saw the butt of the joint sitting in the ashtray. This time it was for real. He looked down at Jayde, who was sleeping soundly, with her face under the pillow.

Ramon contemplated searching the guts of the joint, but the thought alone sent a chill down his spine.

The buzzer to the front gate went off.

Ramon got up and slipped into his robe and slippers on the way to the living room. He punched the security screens up on the TV. He saw Snug's face and buzzed him in.

Snug walked to the kitchen. Ramon was standing by the counter fixing a pot of coffee while he watched the news on TV. Snug dropped the mail on the table.

"How many?" Ramon asked. He poured two cups of coffee. Snug held up three fingers. Ramon dropped three cubes of sugar into his cup, then sat it on the table in front of him.

Ramon took a seat at the table next to Snug.

Snug slid him the black book and the photocopies. He scanned the pages. They were filled with a lot of business garb that he didn't understand. After about ten minutes, he shook his head.

"Murphy's a slick bastard." He rose from the table.

He led Snug back to his office and opened up a cabinet, revealing a safe. After he opened it, he took out a briefcase and handed it to Snug.

"That's 600,000 dollars in cash," Ramon explained. "You, Tulu's and Bobby's half of the million split. I'll pay Yawni myself." Ramon took a seat in his office chair. "How is she anyway?"

Jayde crept into the kitchen. Her eyes locked on the black book sitting on the table. She glanced in both directions before she tiptoed over to the table.

After careful examination, she realized that the book was of no interest to her. She left the room. Outside Ramon's office door, she heard voices.

Snug was saying, "She misses you, and is waiting on you to call her with some kind of explanation for what happened that night you just up and left her."

Ramon's elbows rested on the arms of his chair while he clasped his fingers together. "I'ma have my secretary schedule us a trip somewhere to make it up to her. I love Yawni. We were just friends for so long that I kinda overlook her. You know what I'm saying."

"No," Snug said plainly. "While we're just talking, when are me, Yawni, Bobby and Chico gonna start seeing some revenue from this hotel?"

Ramon's gaze shifted to the floor. "I've been meaning to talk to y'all about that."

That did not sound good to Snug. "I'm listening."

Ramon took a deep breath. "I'ma buy the whole crew out except for you."

Snug's eyebrows shot up. "For how much?"

Ramon shrugged. "Say ... a million each."

"And if they refuse?"

"They won't have a choice." He reclined in his chair.

"And me?"

Ramon looked him in the eye. "You'd assume the position as my right-hand man. Same as the old days."

Snug scowled. "What?" He jumped up, planted his hands on the desk and leaned forward. "Is that what you think of me? As your fuckin' right-hand man? A little buddy?"

"Calm down."

"No, you calm down. I'm fuckin 39-years-old. We ain't kids no more." Snug's eyes narrowed as he shook his index finger at Ramon. "You're a fuckin' no good piece of shit, you know that?"

"Look who's tal —"

"Sixteen years ago, I would have went for that bullshit, but now ... I'm smart enough to see that

163

Ramon Delay is all about Ramon Delay. And everybody else comes after." He snatched his briefcase up and stormed to the door. He stopped suddenly and turned around. "By the way, you can cash me out too. I ain't like you. I'm not selling out my fuckin' friends."

"Like AJ? He was your friend, wasn't he? You killed him because he was late," Ramon shouted.

"He knew the rules."

"Yeah, he knew the rules. And you knew mine." Ramon fired up a cigarette.

"I guess there's nothing else to be said."

Ramon shrugged. Snug walked out the door.

Jayde ducked into the next room, just missing Snug storm out of Ramon's office.

Ramon stood, unfazed by what had just taken place. He walked back to the kitchen, sat at the table, sipped his coffee and sorted through the mail.

He came across another letter addressed to him with no return address. After taking a short breath, he opened it. Inside was a picture of a little girl. She had two long ponytails on either side of her head, and her wide smile revealed two missing front teeth. From the looks of her attire and the scenery, she was either going to or coming from church.

On the back was his daughter's name, Trishay, and her age, 9. A smirk crept on his face. He traced the photo with his finger. Jayde watched him from the doorway. He closed his eyes, imagining what she would look like as a grown woman. Probably in college somewhere, or she had kids and was on welfare, living on Section 8. If she was, he was to blame because of the bad example he set as a father.

His mind traveled back to that familiar woman he saw sitting at the bar. Now that he thought about it, he had seen her out in the parking lot earlier that day. She was sitting in a black Volvo, just staring at him.

Could it be ... no, it couldn't. The woman was too old, way too old to be his daughter. *Then who is it?* he thought.

When Ramon finally opened his eyes, he saw Jayde standing beside him. Concern was all over her face.

"Who's that?" Jayde asked. She took the photo from his hand. "Pretty. Looks kinda like you."

"My daughter. Her name is Trishay." His voice was low.

Jayde sat. "When did you ..."

Ramon got up and walked away.

Minutes later, Jayde heard Ramon playing the piano in the living room. While he played, he sang Ray Charles' *"Drown in My Own Tears."* Jayde stared at the picture of the little girl and wondered what was going through Ramon's mind when he threatened to kill her.

After Ramon told her what happened years ago,

that night he was arrested, she really didn't know what to think of him. Was he a gruesome murderer who would've killed his own seed over some money? Or was he just a man stuck, trying to be somebody fearsome and scarcely respected?

"Your past is who you are," she said to herself.

Ramon was deep into the song when Jayde entered the living room. He was singing toward the window but his eyes were closed. Slowly she crept up behind him and placed her hands on his shoulders. He opened his eyes, but didn't stop playing. Music soothed his soul and at the moment, his soul was aching.

Jayde whispered something in his ear that he didn't understand.

"What?" he asked.

This time, Jayde yelled, "Will ... you ... marry ... meee?"

Immediately, he stopped playing the piano. When he stood and faced her, he wore the biggest smile was on his face.

"What did you say?"

Jayde peered down at the floor, then back up at him. "I said, will you marry me?"

"Yes!"

"Do you promise to take care of me? To beat me when I've been bad? To shower me with exotic gifts? Do you vow to love me no matter how bad I've been or how many times I mess up with you? Huh, Mr. Delay?"

Ramon held both of her hands. "I promise."

"Then it shall happen. In return, you shall have," she turned around, showcasing herself, "all of this at your disposal."

Ramon was so excited he leapt over the bench, took her down to the floor and started kissing her.

Jayde spoke. "Your first thing on the 'to do' list is to inform Yawni about our engagement, then go out and buy me the biggest diamond you can find."

chapter

17

"Why am I down here?" Fredrick asked. "I already told your fellow officers everything I know."

Molina sat at the table inside the police station across from Fredrick. "I know, Mr. Bewig. We just wanna go over a few things for our investigation. Maybe show you a few photographs."

"I didn't see their faces."

"We know that. We were just trying to see if we ... you could try and match a voice or two with some faces, you know ... kinda help us get on the right track. Are we clear on that?"

Fredrick swallowed. "Yes."

"Good." He shuffled through some papers. "You say there were three suspects?"

"Yes."

"All male?"

"Yes ... well ..."

"Well what? Were the attackers all male or not, Mr. Bewig?"

Fredrick seemed unsure. "Yes, it was three

males."

"You're sure?"

"Yes, I'm sure."

"You're not holding back or leaving anything out?"

"No."

"Now, with all of your cameras and security gates, how did they get in?"

"Like I said before, they took Gomez, my driver, hostage."

Molina removed his glasses. "They took your driver hostage without you seeing them? See, that's what gets me. Tell me," he licked his lips, "how was that possible?"

Fredrick sighed. "It must have happened when I went in the store."

"Where you met the woman?"

"Yes."

"Tell me about her." He smacked his gum.

"Nothing to tell. I picked her up ... no wait ... she followed me home."

"Your idea or hers."

Fredrick shrugged. "I don't know. Anyway, I took her to my house. Next thing I know, we're about to make love and then these punks came bustin' in."

"And she gets away?"

"Yes."

Molina smiled. "She did call us, Mr. Bewig. At least some woman did. She phoned us from a near-by pay phone." He shifted in his seat. "The problem is, we think whoever this mystery lady is, she was in on it. She set you up ... and you went for it."

Fredrick looked surprised.

"See, you were too out of it to remember when or what time all this took place, but if you could, I'd bet we'd find that it took her enough time for them to clear out before she phoned us." He shook his head and smacked his gum, while staring at Fredrick.

The door opened. In stepped a young, balding, army-built policeman. He carried a file in his hand.

"What is it, Boyd?" Molina inquired.

"I got the file you wanted, sir." He placed the folder on the table in front of Molina.

Molina examined the file on Snug's crew carefully. He was halfway through it before he reached something that should not have been there.

"Mr. Boyd," Molina said slowly. "I thought we didn't have a file on the woman."

"I never said that."

"Then who ..." Molina caught himself. The answer to his own question popped up in his head. He looked over the complete file of Yawni Rantala. She had been busted for several misdemeanors and domestic violence. There were other things on paper about her, but nothing of interest to Molina. There was also a photograph.

Molina examined it, then passed it to Fredrick. "Was that the woman you took home with you?"

Fredrick's angry facial expression said it all

before he even answered the question. "Yes, it's her."

"I thought so. Ms. Yawni Rantala," he said to himself.

"You gonna go pick her up? They stole some very valuable information from me."

Molina rubbed his face. "Unfortunately, that's all we can do is pick her up and put some pressure on her. But she won't confess, because she's good at what she does." He looked over at Boyd. "Show Mr. Bewig here to the door, will you? And send Lawton in, please."

Fredrick stood. "That's all?"

"For now." Molina stood and shook his hand.

When Fredrick left, he rolled up his sleeves and loosened his tie. The second Lawton walked through the door, Molina grabbed him and slung him over the table. Paperwork flew everywhere. Lawton covered his head as he fell to the floor.

"Jesus, Mo!" Lawton hollered.

"Get up! Get up, you piece of shit." Molina lifted him by his shirt, then pushed him into the wall. He clutched his face with his hand. "Look at me! Why did you lie to me?"

"I didn't." His voice was weak. "What're you —"

"You didn't? You didn't tell me that we didn't have a file on the girl in Snug's crew?" He yanked his shirt. "Look at me and tell me you didn't say that."

"Yeah, yeah, I said it, Mo." Lawton looked afraid.

"Why?" Molina yelled. "Why did you tell me that, when I just got finished going over a complete file on her?"

"I promise, Mo. I searched the entire file and did-n't see anything on the girl. Somebody messed up, but it wasn't me."

Molina stared into his eyes and saw sincerity. This was his longtime friend, and he didn't want to believe that he would lie to him.

"Somebody did." Molina released him, then turned, heading for the door. "C'mon. Let's see if we can find this broad."

# # # #

"May I help you?"

Yawni was sitting on the terrace of the hotel's restaurant, staring out at I-435. She was deep in thought until the waitress appeared and interrupted her.

"Excuse me?" Yawni asked.

"Can I get you something while you wait?"

"Yes. I'm sorry. Umm ... I'll have a margarita. And could you bring me *The Call* paper, please. Thanks."

Ramon walked through the restaurant at a fast pace. He was supposed to meet Yawni there 15 minutes ago, but unfortunately, he had gotten tied up in a meeting with his investors.

He spotted her sitting on the terrace looking down at the highway. Her hair blew with the wind.

He stopped short of her, admiring her from the distance.

She wore a dress, stilettos and a pair of dark shades. Every so often, she would take a sip from her drink, then politely sit it back down.

Now there's a woman, Ramon thought to himself. Tender, feminine and submissive. Nothing like Jayde. She was completely the opposite. Jayde was a wildcat that teased just for the thrill of the chase. That's what turned him on about her. When it came to the tug-of-war between Jayde and Yawni, Jayde always won.

Yawni was reading her newspaper when she heard Ramon grunting. She peered up and saw him standing over her.

"Well, hello," she said with a pleasant smile. She removed her shades. "Have a seat."

Ramon sat his briefcase in one of the four chairs, then took the seat across from her. He motioned for the waitress, then ordered a cup of coffee.

Yawni touched his hand. "You know ... the last time we were together, we had just had some great make-up sex. Then ... I went to the shower. Then ... I returned to find you gone."

"I can —"

"Before you do, there's more." Her face turned angry. "Then I answered your office phone and some tramp asked me had you left yet." She smirked embarrassingly as she held back tears. "Can you imagine how that made me feel, Ramon?

I mean, can you really imagine it? I loved you!"

"Loved?"

Yawni nodded her head. "You know, I was fool-ish enough to think that jail had changed you. But it didn't. You're the same old piece of shit that left in the 80s. Only you're not as young." Yawni fired up a cigarette. "Why are we here?"

Ramon hesitated. What he was about to say was going to make all the things she just said about him seem true.

The waitress brought his coffee. "Here you go, Mr. Delay."

"Thank you, Rana." He blew at the hot liquid before he took a sip, allowing enough time for Yawni to calm down.

"So?" she asked impatiently.

Ramon opened the briefcase, took out a cashier's check for $1 million and slid it to her. Yawni picked it up and read it.

Yawni's eyebrows shot up. "What's this?"

Ramon sat his cup down. "I'm cashing you out. You're no longer a part of the hotel business," he calmly stated, as if what he was doing didn't faze him.

She put the check inside her bag. "You want it all for yourself, don't you, Ramon?" She forced a smile as she shook her head in disgust. "What is it with you, man? Are you so stuck on yourself that you feel like you have to always have total control over everything?"

"Listen, Yawni. You, Snug, Bobby and Chico are still in the business of stealing. Me, I got to separate myself from y'all, and whatever y'all are doing. I got plans, big plans, and legitimate plans. And I don't need y'all fuckin' it up by bringing the heat around me." He sat back in his seat. "There it is. I said it. You, Snug or anybody don't like it, I don't give a fuck."

"You're right, you said it, you arrogant bastard!" She hollered as she stood and gathered her things. "And you've done it, 'cause I've had it with your black ass." She leaned over the table and said, "Hell hath no fury like a woman scorned."

After she straightened her dress, she started walking away.

"One more thing," Ramon said. Yawni stopped but did not turn around. "I'm getting married to Jayde."

Yawni stood erect for a moment, clutching her bag tightly, holding back her words. After she calmed down a bit, she politely walked away.

Ramon giggled quietly, knowing that he had stabbed a dagger right through the center of her heart. Then he drank his coffee.

Rana showed up carrying a cordless phone on her tray. "You have a phone call, Mr. Delay," she announced. "It's from Mr. Bewig."

# # # #

Yawni stormed outside to her truck. She fumbled

through everything in her purse, looking for her car keys. While she was doing so, Molina whipped the Crown Victoria into the lot.

Lawton pointed in her direction. "There!"

Molina brought the car to an abrupt stop in front of hers, then the two of them jumped out.

Yawni froze after she saw them walking toward her, flashing badges.

"Evening, Miss Rantala," Molina said with a smile. "I'm Detective Howard Molina," he looked back at Lawton, "and this lug here is my partner, Detective Robert Lawton."

"Un huh." Yawni hoped they couldn't see the fear in her eyes through her glasses.

"Well, Miss Rantala, we had a forced entry that occurred a few days ago, and your name came up."

"Really."

"That's right," he sang. "Anyway, the victim told us that he was with you when it happened."

She stared at him for a moment, wondering how they identified her.

"Miss Rantala?"

"Yes. Um, yes, I was there," she admitted.

"And you were the mysterious woman who called us, I presume?"

"Yes, I was."

"Good." He grabbed her arm. "We'd like to ask you a few questions, downtown."

Yawni sighed. "I don't need this shit."

"Yeah, neither do we," Molina replied. "But

somebody's gotta do it. C'mon, you can ride with us."

Yawni glanced up at Ramon's office window before she was placed in the backseat of the car. They were pulling out of the lot when Ramon walked out the front door.

# # # #

Ramon jumped in his Cadillac and burned rubber out of the parking lot. Northbound, he hit the highway on his way to the park. Some of the people jogged, some power-walked around the huge track. But for the most part, the park was empty. It was windy out, not cold, but not particularly warm either.

Ramon circled the area until he found Bewig's Benz. He parked beside it. There was a sign on Bewig's windshield that read: *By the swings.*

He buttoned his jacket, then took the long stroll around the track until he reached the swings. Fredrick was laughing while he stood next to his daughter, who was flying a kite. His son was only a few feet away, teaching their German Shepherd how to catch a tennis ball.

Fredrick heard leaves crackling and looked around. Instead of interrupting their fun, Ramon nodded, then took a seat on a nearby bench.

"Sammy," Fredrick called his son. "Come over here and help your sister."

Sammy frowned. "Ah, dad," he pouted.

"Now, mister!"

"O-kay."

Fredrick, with his hands in the pockets of his slacks, walked over and sat next to Ramon. Two squirrels were fighting over an acorn, and had Ramon's full attention. He liked to see a good squabble.

"What do you know about a woman named Yawni Rantala?" Fredrick asked.

Ramon tried to read Fredrick's blank facial expression to see where he was coming from.

"Why?"

Fredrick lit a cigarette, smoked about half of it, then tossed it into the grass.

"My home was robbed the other day," Fredrick explained, "for some very important information. Now, as far as I know, it was a bunch of hoods who don't have a clue as to what they have." He shrugged. "What I'm trying to say is, I need that book back." His tone was serious.

"What can I do?"

"Ask around. Put some people on the streets. Use your clout, spread some cash around. Whatever it takes, just please try to locate it for me."

"How much is it worth to you? Assuming that I located it. And need I remind, Freddy, that you're not talking to a child here, so don't hold back on me."

Fredrick gazed at his two happy children. Sammy had tackled his sister, and the dog had tackled him.

"Seven figures."

"I'll see what I can do."

That was enough to put Fredrick's mind temporarily at ease. He stood, then went back to join his family.

"Hey, Fred," Ramon called out. Fredrick stopped and turned around. "You think that I was involved somehow, don't you?"

"Truthfully?" Fredrick looked down at the grass for a second, then back to Ramon. "Yes." Then he walked away.

Ramon could hear little Sammy ask his dad if the scars on his face hurt. For some reason, Ramon thought that he should have felt pity for the family, the businessman, but for some reason, he didn't.

# # # #

The sun was setting. A collage of yellow, orange and blue colors covered the sky. It was cool outside. The evening air chilled Ramon's dome.

He zipped up I-435 on his way to a meeting with Murphy. Girls were riding by him honking their horns, waving and checking out his expensive car. On another day he would have been enticed by all the attention, but at the moment, his head was in another place.

Where did Fredrick learn Yawni's name? Ramon wondered. More importantly, was she also one of the suspects that Fredrick was thinking of? Ramon had come up with a lot of great schemes in the past, but this time he believed he might have screwed up. He should not have involved Yawni. Not only could Fredrick identify her, but she could also be linked to him.

Ramon jumped into the right lane and got off on the Gregory Boulevard exit. From the highway, he could see Murphy's Lincoln parked under the bridge with its flashers on. He pulled alongside the road behind Murphy's car.

Murphy got out and ran to Ramon's car. "Where is it?" he said nervously.

Ramon showed it to him. When he went to reach for it, Ramon snatched it back.

"Not so fast," Ramon said.

A look of confusion came over Murphy's face. "What's the problem, brother?"

Ramon grunted. "Brother, huh? White people always want to act like family when they're trying to beat a nigga."

Murphy was baffled. "Ramon, I don't understand."

"Understand this. The price just went up."

Through suspicious eyes, Murphy watched him. "Who've you been talking to about this?"

Ramon gazed out the window at the passing cars.

"Bewig offered me 2 million dollars to buy it back," he lied.

Murphy's mouth fell open. "Jesus! He knows?"

"No. Just wants me to put my ear to the streets and see what I can find out."

Murphy began rubbing the gold ring on his finger. "I can probably go as high as 2.5 million, but that's it."

"I was thinking more like three." Ramon opened his door. "I'ma take a piss while you think it over."

Murphy noticed that Ramon had left the black book on the seat. He gazed at it with greed in his eyes. *If I only had a gun, I would ...*

Ramon opened the door. "Forgot something." He picked the book up then left again.

"Conniving black bastard," Murphy spat.

By the time Ramon got back inside the car, Murphy had made up his mind.

"Okay, you win, 3 million. But it'll take me about a week to get the money."

"Fine by me. Long as I get it." Ramon wiped the book down with his handkerchief before he handed it over.

chapter

18

A month later, Ramon and Jayde were married on a secluded island in Port Antonio, Jamaica. Ramon rented an 8-bedroom beachfront home that lodged all 20 of his guests and an 8-man staff to wait on them, hand and foot.

Ginuwine sang at the reception while the happy couple danced for the first time. After the vows were exchanged, Ramon led his new bride to the front of the home, where two brand new Porsche 996 Turbos were parked. One was fire-engine red and the other was platinum gray.

Jayde kicked off her shoes and straddled the front seat of the red one. Ramon got into the gray one. The two raced around the beautiful coast enjoying the scenery as well as the ride. Jayde was shocked to see all of the goats and chickens running wild, like regular pets.

While the exotic island was fascinating her, Ramon zoomed right past Jayde. She took the challenge and shifted gears. Dust blew out from under her tires.

Ramon held the lead around the bend, hogging both lanes so Jayde could not pass. Dirt covered her front windshield, forcing her to slow down. By the time she caught back up, Ramon had parked, gotten out and was peering out at the ocean waters. Six white women in bikinis were enjoying a game of volleyball. People were scattered about trying to catch an authentic tan. Others played in the water.

Jayde's dress blew sideways as she walked up to him. Ramon turned to face her. For what seemed like an eternity, they stared into each other's eyes. Then they shared a long, passionate kiss.

"It's beautiful, isn't it?" Ramon said. He leaned up against the car while Jayde stood in between his legs.

"It sure is." She smiled. "I've dreamed of seeing places like this since I was a child."

The sweet scent on Jayde's neck soothed Ramon's nostrils. Gently, he caressed her neck with his nose. She closed her eyes and cocked her head back, enjoying the feeling.

Before she knew it, Ramon had unwrapped her dress and let it blow away. She stood there wearing nothing but her bra, thong and garter belt.

Jayde faced him and giggled shyly. "Baby, what're you doing?"

"Let's go at it right here in front of everybody,"

Ramon dared her.

Jayde leaned in and kissed his nose. "Let's save the kinky stuff for tonight, okay?" She faced the beach. "Right now, I just wanna enjoy the moment."

They both fell silent, each in their own thoughts.

Ramon wrapped his arms around her shoulders. "From now on, I'm gonna take care of you. Daddy's gonna buy you a mockingbird if you want it."

Jayde kissed his hand. "All I want out of life is what I got coming. Nothing more, nothing less."

Out of the front seat, Ramon picked up a bottle of champagne and two glasses. Jayde held the glasses while he popped the cork. The liquid erupted all over the hood of the car. She shook the hair out of her face while Ramon filled the glasses.

"I'd like to propose a toast," he announced, holding his glass out in front of him. "From rags to riches. May our lives be filled with joy while we make bittersweet memories. Cheers."

After they tapped their glasses together, they downed the chilled liquid, then tossed the glasses out onto the road.

"Let's go," Ramon said. "Last one back don't get no head tonight."

"Bet." Jayde started her engine. "Ramon!" she yelled through the open window.

"What?"

"Watch out for the glass in front of your tire." She laughed as she burned rubber, making her tires spray dust all over his windshield.

Ramon looked down at the broken glass near his tires. Jayde had done him again. He could do nothing but shake his head.

# # # #

That night, Ramon chartered a 156-foot yacht. Among the guests were Jayde's crew, Carl Peterson from the governor's office, Tulu, and of course, the host himself.

While countless bottles of bubbly were being popped, the girls pranced around in bathing suits that left little to the imagination. Carl was high off blow and hyper as a 16-year-old boy. Tulu grinded behind Jayde in the middle of the deck, dancing to the music.

Jayde was drunk and seemed to have forgotten that Tulu wasn't Ramon. She allowed his hands to violate her body like he was the rightful owner.

Ramon stood on the upper deck in his robe with a champagne glass in his hand, staring out at the ocean. Life was truly great for a change. Never once while he was locked up did he imagine that he would go this far in life. Especially as old as he was.

He was enjoying his drink when Roberta walked up behind him. She placed her hands on his shoulders, massaging them gently.

"Guess who?"

He could smell the alcohol on her breath.

"I know it's not my baby," he replied.

Roberta reached around him, into his robe, and grabbed his dick. Ramon removed her hand as he spun around.

"Damn, girl. It's my wedding night. Show some respect."

"It's not like I haven't already fucked you," she reminded him. "Don't worry. Jayde won't get upset. I promise."

She placed her hands on his chest, opening his robe. He rested against the railing while her tongue tickled his nipples. Slowly, she fell down to her knees.

Ramon's leg trembled nervously when she reached her cold hand inside his boxers, pulling out his dick. Roberta sucked on it for about ten seconds before he pushed her face back and stepped away.

Roberta wiped slobber from around her lips with the back of her hand, then glared up at him. "This is a party. What the hell is wrong with you?" She got up from her knees.

"My wife is down there, Roberta," he said while pointing toward the stairs leading to the lower level.

"Let me show you something." Roberta took his hand and led him quietly down the small stairwell and onto the main deck. She pointed to a glass-encased cabin, where another party of sorts was going on. As they walked into the cabin, the lights were dimmed, and seductive music played as they both witnessed Tulu leaning up against the wet bar, while Jayde danced exotically before his eyes. Her bra had been removed. Carl was stretched out on a plush off-white lounge chair while Francine performed a lap dance. His tie was wrapped around his neck like a noose.

Lashay walked around with her camera, filming it all. When she spotted Roberta's face in the camera, she saw Roberta signaling for her to come.

"This is how we get down, Ramon," Roberta explained while she waited for Lashay. "You're gonna have to get with the program."

Jayde removed her panties and bent over, jiggling her ass in Tulu's face. Tulu ran his tongue up her ass crack. Ramon had seen enough. His anger had gotten the best of him. He took a step in their direction but Roberta held him back.

"Unt unh. Let her be. I promise they won't do any more than what they're doing now. Okay?" She nodded toward the chaise sitting in the corner. "Go over there and make yourself comfortable. Lashay and I will join you shortly."

Ramon glared at Jayde who seemed to be enjoying herself. *Fuck it*, he thought. *I'll play their little games.*

When he turned and headed for the chaise, Jayde cut her eyes at him and smirked.

Ramon slipped into the bathroom and fished around the pocket of his robe until he located what he was looking for. The little purple pill he had gotten a hookup on. He swallowed a couple handfuls of water to wash it down. He had heard that Viagra worked, and he was going to put it to the test.

When he came out, Roberta was laying on the chaise with her legs agape while Lashay lay next to her, three fingers deep inside her pussy.

Roberta enjoyed playing with her own nipples while watching Lashay penetrate her. Ramon stood at the head of the chaise, his dick sticking up.

"Who's first?"

Roberta smiled. "Me." She positioned herself on all fours and waited on him to enter her. "Stick it in my *culo*."

Lashay spit slobber down Roberta's ass crack, then smeared it around her booty hole. Ramon spread her cheeks wide, then ever so gently, entered her.

"Uhh! Uhh!" Roberta moaned as she gripped the cherry wood of the chaise. "Hit it good ... *papi*!"

Ramon clutched her tiny waist, bringing her body back hard against his. Roberta reached back between her legs, rubbing her own clit while he continuously stabbed her.

Lashay eased away and picked up the camera. She stood behind Ramon filming his ass muscles tighten with each stroke.

"Ooh, spank me!" Roberta begged. "Call me Jayde."

Ramon smacked her on the ass. "Oww!" she screamed. He clutched the back of her neck, choking her. "Please! Please! Don't hurt me, please! Stop it, daddy!"

He stopped. "You alright?"

Roberta peered back at him through wild eyes like he was stupid. "Don't pay any attention to my speech. Now hit it and talk to me like a bitch."

Ramon started stroking her again. "You like that, bitch? Huh, Jayde? You triflin' whore."

"I'm sorry! I'm sorry! Stop it! Stop it!"

Lashay had filmed enough. Her pussy juice started oozing down her thigh. Watching Roberta get abused like that got her aroused. Her anus was throbbing and aching to be plugged. She sat the camera down, then took position next to Roberta. "Help me out, Roberta."

Roberta licked her fingers and rubbed them across Lashay's asshole.

Ramon withdrew himself from Roberta and entered Lashay. She screamed out as every inch of him slowly dug into her insides. She closed her eyes and bit down on her bottom lip. She let out a loud howl when he hit the bottom.

"Owww! Pull it out! Pull it out!"

Ramon continued ramming her unmercifully. For about 45 minutes, he went back and forth, from girl to girl, splitting their asses like logs and busting nuts.

When he collapsed on the bed, panting, Lashay showed up with a joint. He had been craving some of that weed all month. She inhaled and hit him with three shotgun blasts, nearly busting his chest.

That intense feeling came back to him again. He was so high that he thought he had reached the limit. Then, like a thief in the night, the high vanished just as quick as it came.

Sweat rolled down his forehead while he sat up on the chaise between the two girls. Though his eyes were barely open, he thought he saw Jayde bent over the bar while Tulu long-dicked her.

Ramon shook it off thinking that it was just the drugs and liquor that had him paranoid, and he was not seeing his wife over there getting knocked by his goon.

"Gimme some more of that shit," he begged. Lashay lit another one. This time, he snatched it from her and smoked it himself. Several minutes later, his head started bobbing around. It leaned to the left, then to the right.

Ramon glanced up and saw Jayde standing before him, naked. She had a wicked smirk on her face. He smiled at her then his face fell forward into the chaise.

The girls offered to let Tulu hit the joint but he declined, saying, "I don't smoke nothing that I did-n't see get rolled up. I been in the joint, and I know better than to accept everything that's offered to me."

Lashay stood over him naked with her hands on her hips. "What're you saying, Tulu?"

Tulu snorted. "It's really self-explanatory. Everythang that glitters ain't gold. Young funky cock hoes can't make me do shit that I don't want to do."

Lashay looked over at Roberta who was standing next to her. "Booty bandit?"

Shaking her head, Roberta said, "Being locked up for so long. Yes, I would say so."

Lashay, using her index finger said, "C'mere, Tulu."

Thirty minutes and a shot of butt later, Tulu was knocked out on the floor. A victim of the same joint that put Ramon on his ass.

# # # #

The unsettled waves rocking the yacht awakened Ramon. He blinked his eyes repeatedly and looked around. He was now in another cabin and in a bed. He looked over to his left and saw Jayde, sound asleep. As he got up to retrieve his robe, the constant motion made his stomach uneasy.

As he walked out of the cabin and onto the main deck, he saw Tulu asleep on the chaise lounge, where he, Roberta and Lashay were just hours earlier. What was interesting was that everything was as clean as a whistle, but his head was pounding like he had been partying all night.

Female chatter could be heard coming from the deck above. He gingerly walked up the stairs and saw Lashay and Roberta sitting at the table eating breakfast. Roberta had on the captain's personal hat.

"Mornin' sleepy head," Lashay said.

"Mornin' *papi*."

Ramon waved. He was about to ask about Carl until he looked overboard and saw him swimming in the ocean with Francine. Naked.

It was something peculiar about the way the girls were staring at him. It alerted him that something wild had gone on the night before, but he couldn't remember a damned thing.

chapter

19

"The cops brought me in for questioning a month ago," Yawni said. She was pacing round Snug's living room floor with her shoes off. "Did you know that?"

Snug nodded. He was slouched on the couch, still groggy from being awake so early. Half a cup of coffee was sitting on the table in front of him waiting to be finished. After about two of them, he would be ready to begin his day.

Yawni's eyes narrowed on him. "You knew and didn't bother to see what happened?"

Snug cleared his throat. "Honestly, I panicked, Yawni. When I found out that you had been brought in, I got the hell outta dodge and hopped on the first plane to Belize."

"Belize?!"

"Yeah. It's nice over there. You should see it. They have these —"

"Okay, okay," she interrupted with frustration. "They don't know who you three are, and they don't have nothing on me, other than I was there. They were just fishing, hoping that I'd crack under pressure."

"That wasn't supposed to happen. What happened to —"

Yawni raised her hand, shushing him. "Let me handle that. I'll talk to him."

Snug thought momentarily. "You know Ramon bought me out."

"That's just like that pig. Bastard gave me a check for a million dollars, then sent me on my way. Right before he told me that he was engaged." She stared out the window.

Yawni felt Snug's body heat when he crept up behind her. His nose barely came to her shoulder. She remained still while he inhaled her scent.

Her body tensed up when she felt his hand caress her butt.

"Snug?"

"Huh?" He continued fondling her.

"What're you doing?"

"Honestly." He kissed her shoulders. "Tryin' to fuck."

Yawni's body unintentionally relaxed as her eyes closed while he kissed the back of her neck. "Why ... mmm ... are ... you ... tryin' to fu ...ck me? Huh?"

He removed the belt from her dress and pulled it down to her ankles. Snug had to take a step back to admire her natural beauty for a brief moment. She posed with her hands on her hips, flossing her peach-colored fishnet panty set. Her curly pubic hairs protruded through the holes.

Snug shucked off his robe. Yawni gazed down at the little man standing there with his dick straining to bust out his briefs. She had to smile.

"Snug, I'll break your little body in half. Look at me." She ran her hands over her body. "I'm a lot of woman."

He pulled down his drawers. His long 10-inch dick sprang up, then started bobbing like a diving board.

The look on her face showed that she was impressed by the size of his sex weapon.

"I'm a whole lot of man," Snug bragged.

Yawni shrugged. "To the bat cave."

# # # #

After Yawni removed her clothing, she relaxed in his soft bed. Snug climbed on top. When she spread her creamy thighs, Snug caught an eyeful of her pink vulva. He shot nut all over her legs and stomach.

"Unt unh," Yawni hollered angrily. "Get up! Get the fuck up!"

"Wait a minute," Snug pleaded.

"Nah, see I knew this wouldn't work." Yawni jumped up, racing to the bathroom.

Snug hit the mattress, angry at himself for blowing a once-in-a-lifetime chance.

When Yawni returned from the bathroom, Snug was standing out on the front porch smoking a cigarette. He heard her step out the front door.

"Was it good for you as it was for me?" he said jokingly.

Yawni couldn't help but laugh. Snug joined her. Now that it was over, the shit was funny to both of them.

"I can't believe you shot cum all over me before you got to get inside," she said.

"Me neither." After the laughter died down, he passed her the cigarette, and became serious. "What are we gonna do about our old buddy Ramon?"

Yawni tossed the cigarette as she turned to face him. "Relieve him of his money. Bring his big-headed ass back down to earth." She offered him her hand. "You down?"

He shook it. "Retaliation is a must where we come from."

# # # #

Lawton continuously snapped photographs of Snug and Yawni on the porch. They were shaking hands.

"Can you read their lips?" Molina asked.

"Ahh, whatever she just said, it looks like he just agreed to it."

"Um hm. They're planning something. I can feel it." He inhaled his cigarette. "The question is, what?"

Lawton shrugged. "It's probably nothing."

"Maybe it's everything," Molina retorted in full disagreement with his partner. "First, she's in cahoots with Murphy. Profits at his hotel go down then she introduces him to Ramon. They set up the bank robberies, now they're in business together. Trouble is, Delay is a greedy bastard. He breaks the deal by probably forcing them to cash out. Now these two are fucking each other, and no doubt plotting revenge."

"How you figure all that, Mo?"

"Because I'm a seasoned veteran. I've been around and interrogated a lot of snitches. These kinds of thoughts come natural. I'm telling you, Ramon's living the glamorous life and smoking cigars with the big fish. Now he don't want to school with the sardines no more."

Yawni planted a kiss on Snug's lips.

"Get a shot of that."

# # # #

Yawni kissed him gently, then held his cheeks with her hands. "Still friends?"

"I guess so."

Yawni chuckled. "Call me later."

While she was walking to her truck, Snug yelled out, "You missed out on a great lay."

# # # #

"Ah ha," Lawton blurted out.

"What? What?"

"I just read his lips." He sat the camera down in the seat.

"What'd he say?"

"I made out the words, 'you a great lay'."

Molina smiled triumphantly, showing nicotine-stained teeth. He took a deep breath. "You smell that?"

"What? You farted?"

"No. Deceit, my friend. Deceit." Molina started the car. "Let's get outta here."

# # # #

Carl Peterson, Ramon, Murphy and three representatives from the Save the Kids Foundation all held a mock check for $50,000, donated by the Resthaven Hotel & Casino. They smiled for the cameras. Ramon held a false smile while the bulbs flashed.

So this is how the politicians do it, he thought to himself. *Feed the public a bunch of charity bullshit and they love you for it.*

The crowd in the dining room cheered when Murphy announced Ramon Delay as the great humanitarian of Kansas City. Ramon raised his hand in acknowledgement as the crowd applauded him. Murphy invited him to the podium.

Ramon stepped behind it, shaking Murphy's hand in the process. He mouthed the words "thank you" before Murphy left him alone. The crowd quieted down when he spoke into the microphone.

"Thank you. The children are our future. So, I'm gonna do my part to help make sure they get what's coming to them. Higher learning. That means we have to start putting money to the side to invest in schools, books, computers and scholarship funds. Because one day, they are gonna inherit this place we call earth. And I, for one, don't want to leave it in the hands of a bunch of uneducated minds."

The crowd rose to its feet clapping and cheering. As Ramon enjoyed the respect, his eyes scanned the dining room until they fell upon a hole in the crowd. The light held a glare in his eyes. He had to squint to see the face of the only protester in the room.

When she saw him looking, she stood so he could get a good look. It was Hershey, 16 years older. She was frail, her hair looked like a bad weave and bags were under her eyes, but she was dressed accordingly. The years hadn't been good to her and somehow he knew that she blamed him for her fuck ups.

Hershey waited for the applause to die down before she opened her mouth to speak.

"Excuse me, Mr. Delay. I have a question," Hershey shouted.

Ramon licked his lips. Before he had a chance to decline, Murphy said, "Go right ahead, miss. Mr. Delay has all the time in the world to address the public."

Hershey took three steps forward. "I would just like to know why you are so concerned about every kid in the city's future except for your own?"

The cameramen took shots of her and the reporters broke out their pads and pencils. Jayde sat at a table next to the stage regarding Hershey.

Ramon put on a false smile. "Ah, miss, I'm sorry but I don't know what you're talking about. Uh, security, could you please show this insane woman to the door, please?"

Within seconds, several members of the security team jumped down on Hershey, seizing both her arms.

"Tell these people who Ramon Delay really is!" Hershey shouted. "Tell 'em how you threatened to kill your own daughter over some money!"

"Get her outta here!" Ramon yelled angrily.

The guards scooped her off her feet and hauled her out the door. Ramon peered down at Jayde who returned his stare. Then, she stood and left the room as well.

Ramon exited the stage leaving Murphy to close the ceremony. Murphy was so baffled that all he could say to the crowd was, "Thank you."

After Ramon stormed into his office, he snatched off his jacket then flung it across the room. He stepped outside, gazing down at the security guards escorting Hershey off the property.

An idea hit him. Quietly, he went back inside, picked up the phone and called Tulu's cell.

"Hello," Tulu answered.

"Where are you?"

"Down in The Den gambling. Man, it's some freaks down here and I'm all over 'em. What's up?"

"Security just escorted a woman out of the building. Stop what you're doing and find out where she's going."

"What? Man, didn't you just hear me say it's some freaks down here?"

"Now, Tulu!" Ramon hung up the phone. Next, he called Jayde but didn't receive an answer.

Murphy stormed into Ramon's office while he was setting the phone back down.

"What the hell was that?" Murphy demanded.

"Did you just walk into my office, Murphy?"

Murphy stopped short of Ramon's desk. "Right now, there is a group of reporters downstairs waiting for you to come down."

Ignoring him, Ramon pointed at the door. "Did you ... just walk in my fuckin' office ... without knocking?"

Murphy scowled. "So what? You wouldn't have this office if it weren't for me." Murphy pointed a finger at him. "Don't get big headed with me, boy. I'll hang you with the same goddamn rope I'm feeding you."

"Boy?" Ramon came from behind his desk. "Who the fuck you callin' boy? Is that what you think of me? I'm one of your fuckin' kids?" Ramon looked very intimidating all up in Murphy's face, glaring down at him.

Murphy spread his arms wide. "What are you doing? This is for me and you. Bitch comes in and airs your dirty laundry to the public and you take it out on a friend?"

"You're no friend of mine," Ramon stated bluntly.

The statement took Murphy by surprise. He was at a loss for words as his feelings were hurt.

"I guess there's nothing left to be said." Murphy walked over to the door and opened it. "If you want to apologize, I'll be down in the club having a drink. If you don't," he shrugged, "then I'll be insulted. And I don't take insults kindly, Delay." With that said, he closed the door behind him.

# # # #

Music blared inside the club. Exotic dancers stood on circular platforms 7 feet off the ground, dancing. The music was hip-hop, and the crowd was too immature for Murphy, but the scenery was worthwhile.

Young black, white and Hispanic females were in the club getting tipsy and buck wild. Disco lights flashed throughout the room, and big-boobed waitresses served the drinks.

Murphy saw a group of black guys occupying the pool tables. He had a pretty good stick. He contemplated walking over there and shooting a few games, but he wanted to wait for Ramon to come down. He hoped he did, because Murphy would hate to have something done to him.

He took a seat at the bar across from the dance floor. He received a few winks and smiles from some of the women. They could tell by his expensive suit that he was a wealthy man.

The waitress placed a napkin before him. "Can I get you something to drink?"

"Yeah. Let me get a dry martini and a glass of whatever it is Mr. Delay drinks." Murphy took out his cigarettes while he waited.

# # # #

The phone rang.

Ramon snatched it up. "Hello."

Rap music played in the background. "It's me, Tulu. Yeah, I found the bitch, man. Hold on a minute." Tulu spoke to the woman sitting next to him. "Girl, don't you spill none of that shit on my leather seats. I'ma kick you and that drank's ass the fuck up outta here. Think I'm playing if —"

"Tulu?"

"Yeah, I'm here. The bitch is staying at the Relax Inn on Blue Parkway. You want me to go in and knock that bitch's head off or what? You know I'm a killer." The woman next to him stared at him. Tulu regarded her. "What? Yea, I said it, ho. You don't even know who you in the car with, do you?"

Ramon hung up on him.

"Hello. Hello," Tulu said into the phone. He hung

up. "Damnit, bitch! You don' got me in trouble with the boss."

Ramon's intentions were to go downstairs and have a drink with Murphy, but the news that he had just received distracted him.

He showered, shaved his head and face, then put on a blue pinstriped suit. He looked over his handsome reflection in the mirror to make sure he was up to par.

"Yeah," he said in regard to his looks. He adjusted the ring on his finger, and shut the lights off as he walked out the door.

# # # #

Murphy grew tired of waiting on Ramon to show up. After twenty minutes of waiting and two drinks, he made his way to the pool table where the black guys were hanging.

He was in the middle of his third game when the waitress walked up on him.

"Mr. Murphy?" the waitress said.

Murphy completed the shot before he faced her. The fine black woman standing before him sent a jolt though his scrotum.

"Yes?"

The waitress handed him a martini off her tray. "Complements of the young lady over there." She nodded toward Jayde, who was sitting at a booth against the wall.

Murphy was confused and didn't know what to

make of it. He raised his glass in acceptance. Jayde patted the seat next to her and motioned for him to come over.

"Gentlemen, if you'd excuse me for a moment," Murphy said. He sat the stick down on his way over to her.

He made his way through the crowd and over to where Jayde sat. She patted the seat again. Murphy complied. He jacked his slacks and took a seat. Jayde slid over until their bodies touched.

"Hi, Murphy," Jayde said in a husky voice.

"Hello." She placed her hand on his leg. "Aren't you Ramon's new, young, and I must say, very attractive bride?"

"Yes." Jayde shrugged. "So? You got a problem with getting to know me ... intimately ... just because I'm married? If so, then I made a bad decision. Sorry." Jayde stood as if she were about to leave.

Murphy grabbed her wrist. "Wait ...wait. Have a seat. We're both mature adults. I think we can have a few drinks and enjoy each other's company."

Jayde sat and crossed her leg over his. "Okay."

Murphy's phone vibrated. He dug it out of his inside pocket and checked the LCD screen. Yawni's number showed up.

"That the old lady?" Jayde sipped her drink.

"Yeah," he answered grimly.

Jayde gently pried the phone from his fingers, then hit the power button, shutting it off. "You're with me tonight, baby." She then dropped it inside her glass.

# # # #

Ramon drove his Porsche into the Relax Inn parking lot. He parked in front of Hershey's room. To be on the safe side, he took his 9mm along with him.

Voices could be heard through the room door. Ramon knocked but didn't receive an answer. After he glanced around and saw that no one was watching, he kicked the door in.

He didn't see anyone. The TV was turned up, loud, which explained where the voices came from. Ramon entered with caution. First, he checked the bathroom. Nothing. He lifted the mattress. A Polaroid picture was laying flat on its face.

Ramon picked it up and looked at it. What he saw was a picture of Hershey laying in a hospital bed. Her lips were chapped and she looked to be about 80 pounds.

Ramon sighed. He stashed the photo inside his pocket, then left.

chapter
20

It was 2:21 in the morning and Jayde still hadn't made it home. Ramon had been calling her cell phone all night. No answer.

Full of rage and anger, he threw the TV remote at his new parrot's birdcage. The huge bird flapped his wings desperately as he jumped from side to side. Ramon called him Petey, short for "repeat."

"Fuckin' bitch!" Ramon spat.

"Ock, bitch," the parrot mimicked.

"Shut up."

"Shut up. Ock! Shut up."

Ramon paced the floor in his robe and slippers while drinking vodka straight out of the bottle. Fifteen minutes later, he found himself calling the police stations and hospitals. None of them had heard of her.

Vodka dribbled out of the corner of his mouth. He desperately needed something to smoke. Earlier that night, he had gone out and bought three different kinds of weed. None of it had brought him to the level the stuff with Jayde had brought him to.

Ramon picked up the phone again. To his surprise, somebody was already on the line.

"Hello."

"Hi, Ramon. This is Roberta."

"Roberta?"

"Yes. I was just calling to see what you were doing all alone inside that big house."

"How did you know I was alone?" he asked suspiciously. "Where's Jayde?"

"She left here hours ago with some rich guy," Roberta said truthfully. "Look, I get off soon. I'm coming over to keep you company."

Ramon did not respond. He was looking at his wedding ring.

"Ramon?"

"Yeah. Bring some of that smoke with you. Bye."

He let the phone fall to the floor. Shit was fucked up. He hadn't been married a month and already he was being cheated on. The bad thing about it was that he had really fallen for her. His heart was aching like it never had before.

When Roberta showed up, she found herself looking at a pathetic figure. Ramon's eyes were bloodshot, he only had on one house shoe and he reeked of vodka.

Roberta helped him to the bathroom where she bathed him. Then she helped him into a fresh pair of underclothes. He stretched out across the bed.

Wearing one of Jayde's many sleep outfits,

Roberta sat next to him on the bed and lit a joint. Ramon sat up, anxiously awaiting his turn.

She hit it a few good times before passing it to him. Ramon took a good hit. Then another. Then another. Suddenly, he felt himself floating like a butterfly on cloud nine. He soared for about four minutes before he came in for a landing.

A little while later, he was feenin' for more. Roberta removed her panties and lay back on the bed.

"Eat me while I take a hit, baby," she said.

Ramon noticed that she was perspiring badly, and her eyes were bulged. She was on her back, legs spread eagle, while he played Pac Man on her pussy lips.

After a minute, he came up for air. "Give me some."

Roberta inhaled deeply, then pressed her lips up against his. The smoke traveled down his throat, filling his lungs. He had to back away after he began to choke.

She sat up on her elbows with her head tilted back, enjoying her high. Ramon's head cocked to the left as if he heard something. He jumped up.

"What's that?" he asked.

"I didn't hear anything."

His head cocked to the right. "There it is again."

Roberta sat up laughing. "There you go trippin'. You know what it is baby? You're spooked. Paranoid. D-boys call it geekin'." She fell back, laughing.

"Fuck you talking 'bout geekin', bitch? I'm not no fuckin..." Ramon glared down at the ashtray. He unraveled the butts, but they were all burned up.

He growled, "Get up!" He grabbed her roughly by her arm. She continued to laugh. "What the fuck is so funny, bitch?"

Roberta stopped laughing long enough to say, "You."

Ramon picked her up and threw her over his shoulder. She palmed his booty while he carried her through the living room.

"C'mon, Ramon, baby. Let's party, *papi*," Roberta begged. "Don't throw me out."

Ramon sat her on the front porch.

"You too high, Roberta. Go the fuck home."

He stood while she picked herself up. She slipped and almost busted her ass. Before Roberta had a chance to fully recover, he went back inside. Seconds later, he returned with her purse, and shoes and clothes. He threw them at her, then retreated back inside.

Rushing to the bathroom, he hit the light switch on his way to the sink. Gazing at his own reflection in the mirror, he repeatedly told himself that Roberta was only kidding, until he started feenin' for some more.

Then he started believing her.

# # # #

Jayde came home at 6:30 in the morning. She carried her shoes in her hand when she walked into the bedroom. Ramon was wrapped up in the covers, snoring loudly.

Her eyes were on him while she slipped out of her dress and underwear. She went into the adjacent bathroom and turned on the shower. Standing in front of the mirror, she pulled back her hair and noticed a hickey on her neck.

"He's a horny fat bastard," she said. Jayde peered down at the faucet and cut on the water. When her eyes shifted back to the mirror, Ramon was standing behind her. "Whoo!" she gasped.

"Why're you taking a shower?"

"Because I been fucking." She opened the shower door. "Now, would you excuse me so I can wash his scent off and go to bed?"

Ramon took a step closer to her. "Would you mind repeating yourself, 'cause I couldn't have heard you right."

"I said, I been fu —"

Wack!

Ramon hit her so hard she fell backward into the tub, under the hot shower water. She screamed, squirming to get up. He reached in, clutched her throat and snatched her out. Terror was in her eyes.

"You got the wrong man, honey." He smacked her again while he held her throat. Blood ran from her lips.

Jayde kicked at his legs, trying desperately to get

loose. Ramon pushed her violently out the door and onto the floor. She grabbed her throat, gasping for air.

"I'ma teach yo' hot ass some respect," Ramon warned. He took a leather belt out of the closet.

Jayde stood her naked body up, trying to break for the door. Ramon caught her by the waist, then slammed her on the bed.

"Ramon, please!" she begged. "Don't hit me with … owww … owww! Ouch!"

He viciously brought the strap down across her back, chest and legs repeatedly. Jayde scooted over the entire bed trying to dodge the heavy lashes. She fell over the side of the bed and scurried to the bathroom.

By the time he got over there, she had kicked the door closed and locked it. He banged on the outside.

"Go away!" Jayde screamed. Her flesh was on fire.

"You'd better lock yourself in, bitch," Ramon yelled through the door. "You got me fucked up."

"I hate you!" Jayde screamed. "I'm leaving you."

Ramon jiggled the knob. "Bitch, you lucky this door is too fuckin' expensive to break down."

Jayde sat on the floor in front of the locked door with her knees up to her chest, crying. Ramon dropped the belt, then went and sat on the bed.

He glanced at the roaches that were still in the ashtray. They were calling for him to smoke them. He swore he could actually hear little voices inside his head chanting, *"Smoke me. Smoke me, damnit!"*

Against his better judgment, he picked up a roach and set fire to it. It was enough to take him to Lala Land and back. Before the sun rose, he had finished off every joint in the tray.

The dope had him too geeked up to sleep. Instead, he paced every floor of the house peeping out every window along the way. He could have sworn he saw the devil sitting on his front gate, swinging his legs, staring up at him. Ramon ducked out of the way. He wasn't sure what kind of sign that was. Had Lucifer himself come for him? Was he set to die tonight? When he looked again, the devil was no longer there.

He was more than happy when it came time for him to leave for work. Jayde did not come out of hiding until he left.

# # # #

After Jayde left Murphy's hideaway, Murphy showered, changed clothes and locked up. He hopped in his Lincoln and hit the highway. It was shocking to him that Yawni had not called to see where he was. Now he was left to wonder what she was doing that had her so busy.

He smiled to himself as he fired up a cigarette. *Boy, that young, sweet Jayde was a great lay,* he thought. Man did he love the texture of a black woman's pussy. It was more psychological than reality, because in reality, they all felt the same.

Some pussies were just tighter than others.

Murphy picked up the phone and dialed 10 numbers.

"Hello."

"Yeah, this is Murph. Can we meet?"

"I'm with my family."

"It's important."

The guy on the other line sighed. "Yeah, why not. Ahh … where?"

"How about the Waffle House on Main Street. I could use some breakfast."

"Okay."

When Murphy arrived at the restaurant, he ordered breakfast and a paper. He was reading the "Money" section when he saw his associate's car pull into the parking lot. He folded his paper and sipped on the hot coffee.

The guy walked through the door. Mrs. Kastening, the manager, smiled at him.

"Hi Howard," she said with a smile. "How's things out in the field?"

Detective Molina inhaled. "Well, Janice, they don't make criminals like they used to." He peered at Murphy. "Yep, these days, there's a rat amongst every crew."

She laughed as she walked away.

Molina ordered a large coffee before he joined Murphy at his table. He stared into Murphy's eyes while smacking his gum.

"Mornin'."

Murphy nodded.

Molina looked out the window. "Look, Murph, I know that you and this fellow, Delay, were both in on the bank robberies. You were his inside connection. I know that because now all of a sudden, you guys are in business together, parading around town like the best of friends."

"All you know is what I tell you."

Molina shrugged. "Maybe so, Murph, but I'm not a dummy either." He accepted his cup of coffee from the waitress. He tasted it. "Coffee's a little strong this morning. So what's up? You wanted to see me, you rat motherfucker? What's so important that you dragged me out of the house before my shift starts?"

Murphy smirked. "You asshole. You used to work for me, making sure the law stayed off my ass. Now that you got a promotion and we swap a little information here and there, now I'm a rat motherfucker?"

"Sure you are, Murph," he stated calmly. "You get your hands dirty right along with an accomplice to obtain businesses. Then, when business reaches its max, you decide to take it all by yourself, by ratting your business partners out to the cops." He leaned in close. "Tell me something, do you take care of them while they're on the inside?"

Murphy looked him in the eyes. "I only betray them after they betray me."

"So you say." They stared at each other. "What do you want from me?"

"I want Delay gone."

"How? If we take him in for these robberies, we'd have to take you. I'm covering the fact that those security tapes of yours did not show clear pictures of the suspects. So give me something else."

Murphy rubbed his chin. "I'll come up with something."

"Well, don't take long. I want this guy bad. It'll make me look good. If you don't come up with something quick, then I'll just have to take both of you down." He stood and picked a piece of sausage off Murphy's plate.

Murphy glared at him. "You seem to have forgotten who helped pay the mortgage on your house."

"I forgot that after I made the last payment five years ago. And not one cent of that money can be traced. Look, we go way back, Murph, but I got a job to do." He took two steps, stopped and turned around. "By the way, I wanna pay my wife's car off too ... this month. You think you can help me?"

"After I'm satisfied, you'll get taken care of."

"Fair enough." He left.

# # # #

Ramon returned home around eight o'clock that night, way earlier than usual. When he walked into the house, he smelled the seasoned aroma of good food cooking. The house was spotless, the table in the dining room was set for one and there were candles lit.

Jayde came jogging out of the kitchen with an

apron on. She wore a big smile on her face when she approached him. First there was a kiss, then she removed his jacket and pulled out the chair for him.

"Have a seat and kick off your shoes. Dinner will be ready in a minute."

Ramon saw that she wore plenty of makeup. Possibly to shield the bruises on her face.

"Cut the shit, Jayde. What's up?" Ramon asked suspiciously.

Jayde massaged his shoulders. "It's just my way of saying that I'm sorry. I love you, daddy. I'm supposed to be punished after I've been bad. I just hope that you find it in your heart to forgive me."

She watched as he stood and planted a kiss on her lips. She broke the embrace. "Relax yourself, Ramon. Let me do all the work."

Jayde left and returned with a sirloin and baked potatoes. While he ate she massaged his feet. After he finished eating, she washed him up like she was his servant. When she finished, she took off her clothes and rested in his arms. He wrapped his arms around her.

"Mm, this feels good, daddy," Jayde said softly. Her eyes were closed. "I love being in your arms."

"I'm sorry for hitting you." He kissed her head.

She laughed it off. "I deserved it. I don't mind a good ass whoopin' when I've been bad. You see how that belt put me in my place, don't you?"

Ramon smiled. "I wasn't gonna say nothing, but I did notice a change in your attitude."

"Daddy?"

"Yeah?"

"I wanna go shopping in the ATL this weekend at the underground mall. Maybe kick it at a club or two. I've never been there."

Ramon circled her nipple with his finger. "Anything else?"

"Yes." She turned around and kissed his chest. "I love you, daddy."

"You too."

"I want you to spoil me like a child. Make me feel good. I promise I'ma make you proud."

# # # #

Ramon and Jayde, along with Tulu and his broad, flew down to Atlanta on a chartered flight for the weekend. They enjoyed a nice walk around the zoo, looking at the animals while sharing a drink. That afternoon, Ramon took Jayde to buy up the mall. The night ended at dinner at Justin's where they dined on Puffy Shrimp.

By the end of the night, they were so exhausted that they spent the night cuddled up in their hotel room, watching movies.

Saturday, they want to Six Flags. Ramon tried his best to win Jayde a stuffed toy, but luck wasn't on his side that day. He ended up having to buy her one. Though it wasn't the same as winning one, Jayde appreciated the effort.

Age must have taken a toll on Ramon, because

the roller coasters were getting the best of him. He'd thrown up twice. On the second go-round, Jayde had to ride with a young man who she met at the park. Ramon waited at the gate, eating funnel cake.

That night, they dressed for the club. Ramon surprised her with the platinum and diamond bracelet set he'd purchased earlier and had delivered.

# # # #

The woman was the first to climb over the wall behind Ramon's house, then the man followed her lead. The two vicious Dobermans came running from the front of the house. Their barking grew louder as they came near.

Roof! Roof!

The two thieves stood still. For a moment, it seemed like the dogs were going to attack them. The woman pulled up her mask. The dogs stopped immediately. She held out her hand so they could smell her scent.

While she occupied them, the man walked ahead. He found the circuit box on the side of the house. The tiny flashlight showed him what he needed to see. He clipped the hotwire that powered the alarm. Then he whistled for the woman to come on.

The woman held a black leather bag. Inside, she removed a small crowbar that he used to pop the screen door. Then she went to work on the deadbolt. A minute later they walked inside the house.

Quickly but quietly, they moved through the house on their way to his office. Behind his desk was a small file cabinet secured by a combination lock. She opened up her bag again. The man took out a small torch, set fire to it, then went to work. With the skills of a trained thief, he cut a near-perfect circle around the lock. When it fell off, the girl stuck a screwdriver through the hole and turned until she heard a click.

The man opened the drawer, searching until he found what they were looking for. When he found it, they left back out the way they came.

# # # #

They all rode to the club in a chauffeured, stretched Navigator. The line to get into the club was about a mile long, but Ramon thought too highly of himself to wait in line. He escorted Jayde up to the front. It took only a brief moment and a hundred dollars to persuade the doorman to let them inside, ahead of everybody else.

Inside the club, they got their drink and their dance on. Jayde was a bit too fast for the old dog at first, but after his second wind kicked in, he was shaking a tail feather.

Ramon left Jayde to go to the restroom, and while he was away, the guy that Jayde had met at Six Flags spotted her sitting alone. She was bobbing her head, looking at the dancers on the floor.

The guy ordered himself a drink from the bar and

strutted over to her table. He was already sitting before Jayde even noticed him.

Jayde smiled. "Hi, Tracy." She pushed her hair out of her face.

"Hey. What're you doing here alone, girl? What happened to your old man?"

"Umm," she glanced around the room, "he's in the restroom."

"If he's in there doin' the number 2, then we have time for one dance."

"Okay."

Tracy swallowed a big gulp of his drink before he led her out on the floor. Jayde turned her back to him, dancing slowly and seductively, grinding her ass up against his crotch. He was smooth with it. His hands held onto her small waist while both their hips swayed from left to right to the rhythm of the beat.

His thin fingers felt like tickling feathers as they traveled up and down her body.

"Let's get outta here," Tracy whispered in her ear.

Jayde peered in the direction of the restroom. She didn't see Ramon. "Let me grab my purse."

Ramon came out of the restroom wiping his hands on a paper towel. He spoke to several young ladies on his way back to his table. Jayde's drink and an odd drink were resting on the table when he arrived. His wife was nowhere to be found. He scanned the room. The waitress started picking up the glasses.

"You seen the lady I came in with?" Ramon inquired.

"Um hm," she answered. "She left a minute ago with Tracy."

"Tracy?" Ramon mistakenly took the name for a female.

"Um hm."

Ramon raced for the exit. Tulu was sitting at the table with his girl when he saw Ramon take off. He immediately rose from his seat. "Be right back, baby."

Ramon reached the front of the club. He looked around the entire lot for any sign of his wife. Girls coming and going hissed and gawked at him. Tulu came up behind him. "What's going on man?"

"This bitch don' …" He spotted Jayde getting into the passenger side of a Honda Accord. "Follow me."

Tracy slipped his tongue inside Jayde's mouth as he eased his hand up under her skirt. She let the seat back so he could get a good feel.

Jayde giggled while Tracy freaked her. Her eyes popped open when she heard the car door snatch open. Tulu reached in, snatching Tracy out of the car.

"Hey!" Tracy hollered. "Ahh!"

Tulu hit him in the stomach. Tracy fell to the ground. Ramon kicked him repeatedly until blood drained from his mouth.

Tulu said to Jayde, "Bitch, didn't OJ teach you bitches about cheating on a rich nigga with a broke nigga?"

Ramon pulled her out of the car by her neck, forcing her to look down at Tracy.

"Look at 'em!" Ramon demanded. "Next time I catch you fuckin' around with one of these young niggas, that's what's gonna happen to you. Ya hear me, bitch?" A large crowd started to gather. "C'mon." He held her arm tight while he spoke to Tulu. "Catch a cab back to the hotel and take care of this."

"Okay."

Ramon literally dragged Jayde to the Navigator and shoved her inside. He got in and slammed the door.

"What the fuck is wrong with you?" he asked angrily as the car began to move. "Every time I ..."

"You had no right to do what you did!" Jayde yelled. "I'm a grown goddamn woman and if I want to fuck around, I'ma fuck a —"

Ramon punched her in the eye, causing her head to slam into the window. She held her hand up to her eye while purring sounds escaped her lips.

"Urgggh! You pussy!" she shouted as the truck slowly turned the corner. "Don't put your fuckin' hands on me again." She opened the door of the moving vehicle, but Ramon reached around her and slammed it shut.

"Driver, let me out!" she hollered.

"I can't do that. Girl, you might get lost down here."

"I'd rather be lost in Atlanta than dead in the back

of this truck."

While she screamed at the driver, she reached into her purse and fished out her pocketknife. Ramon heard the clicking sound of the knife opening a second too late.

"Owww!" he screamed when he felt the knife entering his right arm.

"Get out!" Jayde screamed, twisting the knife, digging deeper.

Ramon fumbled for the door handle until he found it and pulled it. The light came on when the door opened. The driver instantly pulled over on Peachtree. An oncoming car hit its brakes when Ramon fell out of the truck and onto the street, holding his arm. Jayde got out and stood over him, clutching the knife tightly in her hand.

Carefully, Ramon removed his jacket and shirt. It was only a small wound but still he almost fainted when he saw the fat meat hanging out of it.

"Bitch, you tried to kill me!" he shouted. "I swear to God, I'ma fuck you up."

A black BMW pulled over and stopped. The driver stepped out to make sure that they were alright. Southern hospitality. Jayde ran over to him and persuaded him to take her away from the scene.

The limo driver helped Ramon up. He spat on the window of the BMW as it sped past.

"Don't bring yo' ass back!" he yelled. "Bitch ruined my fuckin' jacket."

# # # #

That night, back at the hotel, Ramon sat out on the balcony jonesing for Jayde and something to smoke besides cigarettes. He did not want to admit it but he was beginning to feel as if he had taken on a habit that he didn't need.

Just to be sure, he caught a cab down to the projects and copped a quarter bag of green and a fifty-dollar piece of crack. As instructed by the junkie cabby, he copped a used glass pipe for $50.

Back inside the hotel room, he laced three joints with sprinkles of crack. Then he stripped himself naked and climbed into a tub of hot water.

Ramon, what the fuck are you about to do? he heard himself say inside his head. *Don't do it man.*

He fired up one of the joints. He locked the smoke inside his lungs for a long as he could. Then he released a thick white cloud of smoke into the air.

"Goddamn," he said as a smile grew on his face.

He had found it. The high he was looking for, other than Jayde. And it indeed was crack cocaine. If someone would have told him 16 years ago that would be a crack head, he would have shot them dead.

An hour later, all three of the joints were gone and so was the high. The bath water had grown cold. He was ready to quit, but the monkey dancing on his back wasn't finished just yet.

He was still craving that high.

His head rolled to the right, letting his eyes lock on the crack pipe sitting next to the tub. Licking his dry lips, he reached for the glass. His hand cupped it. He hesitated for a second to think about what he was doing. He knew that once he turned down that road, there was a great chance that he would never return. Ever.

"I'm stronger than that," he told himself. "One last time. I promise I won't get hooked."

Ramon picked up the glass, stuffed it with crack, struck a match and sealed their union. The drug hit him so hard, his heart nearly exploded. When the pipe dropped to the floor, his head fell backward.

Thump! Thump!

"What's that?" He jumped out of the tub.

He thought he heard the front door opening. He sprung out of the bathroom. From under the mattress, he pulled out his 9mm and drew it. No one was there.

Thump! Thump!

Ramon's heart also began to thump while his eyes darted around the room. The thumping grew louder.

Thump! Thump!

Ramon whirled around, shot the couch twice and ran out the door butt naked. He chartered a plane back home without Jayde, Tulu or his girl.

chapter
21

Ramon sat around the conference table surrounded by members of the gaming commission, investment bankers, the mayor and Murphy. His eyes were blood red and he appeared to have been up for days. The suit that he sat slumped in was not as crisp as usual. His hands fidgeted.

Murphy shot daggers across the room at him. Not because they had gotten into it the last time they spoke, but because Jayde had talked a bunch of bullshit in his ear. She had told Murphy a bunch of dirty things about Ramon, and as they spoke, Jayde was asleep in one of Murphy's apartments.

Ramon didn't hear one word that was spoken. He was too busy trying to figure out who would break into his home and steal copies of the black book. It could have been some of Fredrick's people but the fact that the intruders went right to the cabinet said it was an inside job. And that could have been Snug or Jayde. Or maybe they were in it together. But at what gain? Maybe they were planning to sell it back to Bewig.

Whatever the case, Fredrick was gonna have to die. Ramon couldn't take the chance of his name getting mixed up in that. There was too much at stake.

Before the meeting was adjourned, Ramon stood and said that he wanted to say something.

"Ah, I want to," he stopped to clear this throat. "I think that it would be a good idea if we invest in and build a treatment center for drug addicts as well as battered women. Uh, not only would it be good for business, but publicity as well for you, Mr. Mayor."

They all nodded in agreement. "Good idea, Mr. Delay," the mayor complimented. "I nominate that to be the next thing on our agenda. All in favor?"

"I."

"I."

"I."

"I."

Ramon nodded and took a seat.

"Ladies and gentlemen, this meeting is adjourned," the chairman announced.

"Uh, excuse me," Murphy said. "If you gentlemen would for a minute, please listen to what I have to say." He stood, placing one hand in his pocket. "I vote that we remove Ramon Delay from the board."

"Why?" the chairman asked.

"Well, first, because he's an ex-felon."

Everybody focused their attention on Ramon after they heard the word "ex-felon." Ramon's chin dropped.

"Secondly," Murphy continued. "Because right now, he's being investigated for a string of robberies. And last, I have good reason to believe that he's a drug addict and he should be ordered to submit a urine sample to be tested for narcotics."

Ramon fought hard to remain in control of himself. He could not believe what Murphy had done to him. Putting his business out on the table like that.

Murphy knew that it wouldn't do Ramon any good to involve him in the bank robbery conspiracy, because his tracks were covered and he had the law backing him.

The board faced Ramon. The chairman asked, "Mr. Delay? What do you have to say about these accusations?"

Ramon ran his hand over his face. "Well, Mr. Chairman, I don't know where Mr. Murphy here gets his information, but I can assure you that it's false."

The mayor addressed the chairman. "I'll look into it. You have my word on that. And Ramon, if these accusations are confirmed, consider yourself fired, and you will be brought up on charges."

"I understand, Mr. Mayor."

The chairman said, "Ramon, you will remain manager of this casino until the matter is resolved. After the New Year, however, you'll be placed on paid leave until the conclusion of a thorough investigation. Is that clear, Mr. Delay?"

Ramon nodded. "Perfectly."

"Alright. Once again, this meeting is adjourned."

All of the men stood, gathered their things and whispered to the person next to them as they filed out of the room. Ramon remained seated. Murphy stood and looked out of the window. They waited until everybody left.

"You shouldn't have disrespected me in your office that night, Ramon. On top of that, you stood me up at the bar."

Ramon stood slowly. "You wanna end my career over some bullshit like that? A fuckin' argument?"

"It may have been just an argument to you, Ramon!" Murphy yelled. "But to me, it was about respect. Hell, I'm the goddamn reason you're living the way you're living, boy. Then you go and talk to me like some fuckin' nigger? Fuck you! Your tough ass is going down!"

Ramon grabbed Murphy by his throat and slammed him down on the table. He snatched the telephone cord out of the wall and wrapped it tightly around his neck. Murphy's face and neck turned red as a tomato. He kicked and squirmed under the pressure. After a few seconds, Ramon released him. While Ramon walked away, Murphy stood up, gagging and holding his throat.

"You're a dead mother fucker! You don't have to worry about getting removed," he threatened. "I'm taking you out. You think that monkey's on your goddamn back, I'm gonna be up your ass like a shitty thong."

Ramon slammed the door behind him, breaking the glass window.

# # # #

Ramon jumped into his Porsche and got on the phone.

"Hello."

"Tulu. I need you to holla at Bewig for me."

"Holla at him for what?"

"No, I mean, holla at him. See if he was involved in what happened to my house the other night. I want him silenced. I don't need my name mixed up in no bullshit. Especially right now. And I'm thinking … never mind."

"A'ight. I'll get on it."

"Thanks."

Ramon hung up. What he was also thinking was that Jayde and Murphy might somehow be involved with each other. They had to be. How else could Murphy be so sure of his drug usage?

Jayde wasn't home when Ramon arrived. He put on some sweats and a T-shirt to get comfortable. Something had to be done. By tomorrow, the mayor would know his whole background by placing one phone call. And that would be the end of Ramon Delay.

At least he had 3 million dollars worth of the hotel's stock, but Ramon couldn't let it end like that. Not just yet. After all the money he had been spend-

ing on his house, cars, wedding, jewelry and dona-
tions, his cash level wasn't that high. His credit was
long, but that would go with his job.

He had to think of something. As stressed out as
he was, Ramon wondered how he could think at all.
He needed something to help calm his nerves.
Something neither the weed or drink could handle.
He needed that almighty feeling that could only be
obtained by crack.

"This'll be my last time," he promised to himself
as he reached for his car keys.

He drove down to his old neighborhood. It was a
little after one in the morning. The corner hustlers
were probably in for the night, but it was worth a
try.

A young man of about 19 was standing on the
corner of 57th Street along with a crack head runner
of his. He saw the Porsche coming down the block.
He thought how there were only two types of people who would be driving a car like that through the
hood — a baller or some rich white man looking to
get high.

"See who that is, Smiley," he ordered the crack
head. "Ask him do he want to rent out his car."

"Okay." Smiley walked up to the Porsche when it
pulled over.

Ramon let the window down. "Anybody
holdin'?" He couldn't believe what he had just said.

Smiley peered at his face real good. "You the
police?"

"C'mon man. I'm driving a fuckin' Porsche. Now what's up? I'm not trying to get busted here."

"What you tryna get?"

"Gimme something for a hundred."

"Hold on." Smiley left to talk to the hustler.

While he was doing that, Ramon searched his pockets for his wallet. That's when he realized he had left it in his suit jacket.

Damn!

He wouldn't be able to get credit here and the monkey was calling him. Ramon refused to leave empty handed. He was too good of a thief. What he couldn't buy, either he stole or robbed.

Smiley walked back over to the car clutching a chunk of crack in his hands.

"What you got?" Ramon inquired nervously. He didn't have a gun either.

"Where's the money?"

Ramon smiled. "C'mon man, I'm rich. I'm not tryna fuck you. Let me see what I'm paying for."

Smiley stuck the dope in the window. Ramon eyed it as it sat in Smiley's hand. With the quickness of a striking snake, Ramon hit Smiley's hand, forcing the dope to fall in the car, then hit the gas.

Ramon almost reached the corner when he heard gunshots.

Boc! Boc! Boc! One of the bullets went through his back window. He ducked without letting up off the gas.

He made it all the way out to Tower Park where

he parked at a shelter house. He dug the piece out from between the door and seat. Then he took the pipe out of his pocket. After he loaded a piece onto it, he took a blast.

For two hours he sat in the car getting spooked, until half of the chunk was gone. Around 3:30 that morning, he drove off. As he drove up Troost Avenue, he peered in his rearview mirror and saw what he thought was the devil sitting in his backseat.

"Ahhh!" he screamed, opening his door. He leapt out, rolling across the street.

Cars came to a screeching halt, trying to prevent collisions. The Porsche veered off the road, jumped the curb and was stopped by a light pole. Ramon was unconscious when the ambulance arrived to pick him up.

He woke up alone, in a hospital room. A quick check of his fingers, toes and a turn of his neck told him that he was all right. He suffered from a few scratches and bruises and a terrible headache. Other than that, he seemed to be fine. The shocking thing was there weren't any newspaper representatives there trying to get a story.

Ramon picked up the phone and dialed Yawni's number. He was feeling lonely and needed someone to reach out to. The phone rang only once before the answering machine picked up. Patiently, he waited for the recording to end before he started speaking.

"Yawni, this is Ramon."

# # # #

Yawni pulled her tongue out of Snug's mouth and looked over at the phone. Snug was on top of her, deep up in her crevice. She reached for the phone.

Snug grabbed her arm. "Wait. I wanna hear this."

"I'm sorry for the way I treated you," Ramon continued. "Man, I feel so alone and ... and I wish that I had my friend to talk to."

Snug chuckled. "Listen to him. He's begging. His big head has gotten too heavy for him to hold up."

"Yawni?" Ramon called.

Snug reached over and pulled the phone cord out of the wall. Then he placed himself back inside of her and went back to humping. Yawni held onto his back, even moaned, while he handled his business. Physically, she was there, but her mind was on Ramon. She thought of how they had violated him by robbing his house.

Fredrick had contacted her by phone and offered her a million dollars for his black book. After consulting with Snug who knew about it, and where the copies were, she offered to sell Fredrick the copies. It was the best that she could do. Fredrick agreed to purchase the copied version for $750,000, but she did not leak to Fredrick where she obtained the copies. She wouldn't stoop that low.

Snug must have sensed that Ramon was on her

mind and not the dick he was giving her. He dug in deep, hitting bottom. Yawni let out an uncontrollable howl that could have very well awakened the neighbors. Suddenly, she cleared Ramon from her thoughts and focused on the meat that filled her insides. Right now, she would focus on reaching an orgasm. Ramon would come after.

# # # #

Ramon slowly placed the phone back on its base. Then he lay back in bed. Fatigue settled in on him. His eyes fluttered shut. Someone busted into the room and his eyes popped back open.

"Oh, my God!" Jayde said. "Baby, what happened?" She sat down on the bed next to him.

"Had an accident."

"The doctor said that you suffered a mild concussion. They also said that you were lucky you weren't killed."

Ramon shot her a cold look. "Where you been?"

She looked away. "I needed to be alone for a minute. You know?" She massaged her hands. "After I stabbed you, I got scared."

"Scared of what?"

"Of everything. Of being tied down, of losing my youth." She stood and started fiddling with things. "I wasn't sure if I wanted to be married."

"Yeah, well, I'm not so sure now, either."

"What is that supposed to mean?"

"You know exactly what I'm saying. Tell me

something ... how does Murphy know so much about my drug habit?"

"Murphy?" she said in a low voice as if she couldn't remember who he was. "I ... I ... don't know ..."

"Bitch, don't lie to me now."

"Baby, don't let this bullshit get your blood pressure up." Her tone was serious. "Now, I said I don't know, so let's leave it at that. I have no reason to lie to you."

She kneeled down next to the bed and cupped his face in her hands. "I realize that I'm wrong for treating you like I do, but I love you, and wouldn't betray you." She suddenly stopped. "Drug habit?"

"Yes, drug habit. Or don't you know nothing about that?"

Jayde stared at her feet.

Ramon bit his bottom lip. "I'm a crack head now. All because I'm in love, drunk and sprung off of young pussy."

"I'm an addict too, Ramon," she stated softly. "And I guess I wanted us both to experience the same thing. I thought that maybe ... just maybe you and I could kick this thing. I don't know 'bout you, but I can't do it alone." She got down on her knees, and held his hand. "Please, let's start over. I love you."

That was all game coming from her lips, and Ramon knew it, but it worked. He peered at her sneaky-looking pretty face and wanted so bad to throw her out, but something else inside of him wanted to help her. If he could save her by helping her get on the right track, then it would help improve their relationship.

"We don't need no doctors," Jayde said. "Together, with our love alone, we can kick the habit. That's why I done it. That was the only for sure way that I could get help."

The mayor barged into the room unannounced. He stopped at the foot of Ramon's bed with his hands on his hips and glared down at him. Ramon could read his body language.

"Jayde, could you excuse us for a moment," Ramon said.

"Sure." Jayde kissed him on his cheek, then whispered, "Am I forgiven?"

Ramon painfully nodded his head.

The mayor gazed back over his shoulder until Jayde was gone. He sighed heavily.

"The doctors did some blood work on you. And do you know what they found?"

Ramon lowered his head. "Cocaine."

"Cocaine. Can you imagine how disappointed I was when I found that out?" Ramon did not respond. "You can thank me that the reporters are not in here jamming microphones up your sorry ass."

"Thank you," Ramon responded humbly. "I am grateful."

"You're gonna be more than grateful. See, politics are exactly like you see on TV and everything you've ever heard. It's dirty, and it costs to play in our game."

Ramon poured himself a cup of water and drank it all. "How much?"

"Twenty-five thousand, cash. To be paid immediately." The mayor walked to the door and turned around. "And if you want that background of yours to disappear before the investigation starts, it's gonna cost you another twenty-five grand. And, we never had this conversation."

"I'll have," Ramon coughed, "Tulu get you the money by tomorrow evening."

"I don't trust drug addicts, but just this one time, I'ma take a chance." The mayor left.

"You ain't got no fuckin' choice, you fuckin' cocksucker," Ramon said to himself.

chapter

22

The armored truck made several stops before it came to the Resthaven Hotel & Casino. Snug and Bobby had been tailing the truck all day. The security guards walked into the hotel at approximately 7:47 pm and walked out, ten minutes later, carrying black bags.

"We're gonna take 'em at the grocery store," Snug said to Bobby.

The two were parked a little ways behind the truck. They now had all the information they needed and a plan to enter and exit the hotel with the money. If things went the way they planned, the whole thing would go smoothly.

Bobby took several photographs of the guards.

"Get a shot of the gun holes on the truck," Snug suggested.

Bobby snapped a few more shots. "Got 'em." He peered over at Snug. "Don't it feel weird plotting to rob Ramon?"

Snug placed a cigarette between his lips. "Of

course not. The man snaked us out, Bobby." He put the car in drive. "Besides, a lot of that money goes to taxes, investors and so forth. So, in reality, we're robbing the goddamn state. It's all insured anyway. He'd be proud of us knowing that we are able to plan and pull off a heist like this one." Snug drove away.

"Assuming that we pull it off," Bobby whispered to himself.

# # # #

Meanwhile, Yawni was walking along the plaza. She had on a flashy dress, a full-length mink coat and dark shades. She stopped suddenly to look inside the window of a clothing store. Only she wasn't admiring the clothing. Yawni was look-ing into the glass at the reflection of the man across the street who was staring at her.

Molina moved swiftly though the crowd of Christmas shoppers trying to catch up to Lawton, who was standing in front of a building looking across the street at Yawni.

She dipped inside the store for a little while.

"What's happening?" Molina asked, finally catching up.

"Nothing yet. Browsing through a few store windows."

Molina scanned the area with his eyes. "She's up to something. You can believe that."

Suddenly, Yawni burst out of the store's door,

moving at a fast pace.

"Let's go," Molina said.

Yawni walked west to the corner, made a right, then another right. She came upon a jewelry store. After staring up at the sign for a minute, she walked in.

Molina and Lawton stopped running and tried to catch their breath.

"How did you get onto her?" Molina asked.

"An informant of mine sent me a message saying something about a robbery on the plaza. I was hoping that it might be them. So I came down here and drove around for a little while, you know, just to see what was down here that's worth robbing. That's when I spotted her."

Molina looked at the jewelry store, then peered around at the only semi-secluded area on the plaza. That's when it hit him.

"This is the place."

"What place?"

"Where it's all gonna go down. First, they'll take down the jewelry store, then we'll take them down."

Lawton could see Yawni inside the store chatting with the clerk. She had a platinum ring in her hand, with a huge diamond on it.

"I think you're right, Mo."

"Of course I'm right."

A gray Cadillac pulled up in front of the store. Yawni casually walked out of the store with nothing in her hands and climbed into the backseat. The car bolted away.

Molina walked out into the middle of the street as the car made a sharp right and disappeared.

"Get on the phone and get me an around-the-clock surveillance team set up in this area. Not only are they watching the store, but also this entire perimeter." He smacked his gum. "I'ma enjoy taking that slick bitch down."

"What about Delay?"

"He's in it with 'em. Though he might not physically take part in the actual heist, you bet the hair on your ass he's in on it. I have good faith that we'll have enough to nail his ass too."

# # # #

"They take the bait?" Snug asked over his shoulder.

Yawni took out her cigarettes and fired one up before she answered. "We'll know later, won't we?"

Bobby turned around, peering over the seat at Yawni. His eyes traveled down into her coat and his stare landed on her cleavage.

"You know, you have some really big tits, Yawni."

"You're not snorting nothing off of them, Bobby. But thanks for the compliment."

Bobby frowned as he turned back around. "She ended that before it even got started, but that's okay. I know she wants to fuck me. I saw how—"

"C'mere Bobby," Snug said, interrupting him.

"Huh?"

"C'mere for a second."

Bobby leaned toward him.

Smack!

"Hey!" Bobby held his jaw. "What the hell—"

"You talk too fuckin' much. Now sit yo' ass back and shut the fuck up!"

While they were arguing, Yawni sat back and began daydreaming about Ramon. He was supposed to be her soul mate, yet she wasn't wanted by him. When he called and left that message, she recorded it and replayed it 20 times. It only proved that she still had feelings for him.

She returned the call that night after Snug left, but there was no answer. What kind of games was he playing? Her feelings were all mixed up about what she should do. He had dogged her for a younger woman. That was understandable because that was just life, but when he called the other night, Yawni took it as a cry for help. His new young bride wasn't all she was cracked up to be.

Yawni made up her mind. The cat was not gonna keep chasing the dog. If he called her before the New Year, then she would try to call off the heist. If he didn't, things would go as planned. And she would have no remorse.

# # # #

Ramon stood behind his office desk turning the dial on his safe. When it opened, he took out $50,000 and placed it on his desk. He heard the toilet in his restroom flush.

Tulu came out, buttoning up his pants. He nodded toward the money on the desk. "That it?"

Ramon said, "Yes. Run it over to the mayor's office. Pull around back. He'll have someone come out and get it." He took a seat.

Tulu put the money in a bag. "Be back in a few."

"Any word on Bewig?"

"Man, I been lookin' all over that muhfuh. Can't find him, but don't worry, I will."

"Good. The sooner the better."

Once Ramon was alone, he started going over some paperwork. Then, the monkey called him again. He tried to ignore it and concentrate on what he was doing. Before long, his started scratching his arms and his body started twitching.

"No," he told himself. But the monkey wouldn't let up.

Ramon knew he would not survive the hour without a hit. So he devised a plan. Each time, he would take a smaller hit until he weaned himself off the narcotic. It wouldn't work, because deep down, he loved the high.

He called downstairs and had Roberta sent up. She arrived minutes later, looking nervous.

"Am I fired?" Her hands fidgeted.

"Not yet," Ramon replied. "You got any stuff on

you? I know you do, so cut the bullshit."

Roberta put her purse on the desk, then pulled one of the chairs up to it. She emptied out a pipe, lighter and a plastic bag.

"Let's go in the bathroom," Roberta suggested.

"Let's do some here first. I'm achin' like a muthafucka."

Ramon waited anxiously for her to break the rock down and load the pipe. She took the first blast, then passed it to him. The longer he hit it, the larger his eyes swelled. It took a while for the high to kick in. The batch wasn't as good as usual. When it finally did kick in, he became instantly spooked.

His head slowly turned in Roberta's direction. "Who are you? How did you get onto me?"

Roberta regarded him like he was crazy. "What? C'mon, don't start wiggin' out on me. You're gonna blow my high."

"Who sent you?" Ramon leapt from his seat and slapped Roberta across the face. He clutched her shoulders, shaking her violently. "Who ... sent ... you?"

Roberta started crying. Blood dripped from her lip. "No one."

"Get the fuck outta here!" He threw her to the floor. "Get!"

"My purse."

Ramon flung it at her. Roberta stumbled out. He walked back to the desk and just as he was about to take another blast, someone knocked at the door.

"Who is it?" He pulled on the pipe.

"Your wife."

Ramon snatched open the desk drawer and scraped everything into it. *Bitch ain't gettin' none of this,* he thought. "Come in."

Jayde strutted in wearing her work uniform—boy shorts, a sports bra and knee-high boots.

"Hi, husband." She seemed cheerful.

He allowed her a peck on the cheek before he hurried to the bathroom. He brushed and rinsed away the awful crack smell from his breath.

Jayde beat on the door. "Ba-by."

Ramon opened it. She jumped into his arms, kissing his cheeks. He winced from the pain in his aching bones. He still hadn't fully recovered from the accident. They fell onto the couch, kissing.

"I love you, daddy," Jayde said with a smile.

His high had vanished. He caressed her cheek.

"You feel awfully thin. What have you been eating?" she inquired.

Ramon thought about her question. He hadn't really eaten since they were in Atlanta. The dope had stripped him of his appetite.

"I think it's the shit," he admitted. "I haven't been hungry since I tried the glass."

"I'm sorry." She looked at him sincerely. "Baby, after the New Year, I'ma sign us both up for rehab, okay?"

Ramon rubbed his head. The thought of living in a rehab center didn't sit well with him. *That's for bums and crack heads. Wait a minute ... I am a crack head.*

Jayde said, "On New Year's Eve, while the fight is going on, let's me and you get a suite and enjoy each other's company. What do you say?"

He nudged his nose against hers. "Okay. Sounds fun." He stared into her pretty eyes and almost lost his breath. Looking at her, he now knew what it was about her that had his nose wide open.

Her youth.

Chasing and fighting with Jayde made him feel young again. Like he was living out the life he had lost behind bars. Yawni made him feel like the middle-aged man he was, but that wasn't who he wanted to be. That's why he so easily took on the drug habit. It took him away for a moment, not caring if he was old. Crack took away every aching pain in his body and lifted his spirits as high as the heavens.

"You were right, you know that?" Ramon admitted.

"About what?"

"You're in control. You've caught me, hook, line and sinker. I can't control you like I can't control it. Ever since you came in my life ... it has changed dramatically. Really for the worse, but at the same time, for the better."

"Well." Jayde looked down at her lap. "I'ma do my best to make it all for the better this time around."

"How?" Ramon inquired.

"By being a good wife, as well as your friend. Okay?"

Ramon nodded.

# # # #

Tulu got off on the downtown exit and drove to City Hall. He pulled up in front looking for the mayor's aide. A tall, white man wearing a black trench coat and dark shades walked down the steps. Tulu let him in.

"Pull away from here," the man instructed him.

Tulu became angry. "Look man, I thought you was suppose to grab the money and go."

"There's been a change of plans. Turn left at the corner."

Tulu made the left, then another left, then drove until the man told him to pull into an alley behind a building.

"Man, where the fuck is you taking me? I got a bitch waiting on me back at the hotel." He looked at his phone to see if he had any missed calls.

"Don't worry about it," the man said. "You're not gonna make your appointment."

"Wha ..."

"Stop the fuckin' car!" he ordered, and pulled a gun.

Tulu stopped and put the car in park. He heard the back door open but didn't take his eyes off the man who held him at gunpoint. The first chance he got he had to make a move. Someone got into the back seat.

The man in the front seat looked toward the back and said, "Whe ..."

In one swift motion, Tulu grabbed the gun and pushed it toward the ceiling. Two shots went through the roof. While he was tussling with the man, the second man wrapped a piece of wire around Tulu's neck, pulling Tulu toward him.

"Urggh!" Tulu lost his wind, but didn't give up. His hands still remained on the gun.

Tulu lifted his leg and knocked the gear out of park with his knee, then hit the gas.

"Nooo!"

The car crashed into the building. Two front seat airbags deployed, striking both Tulu and the other man in the face. The man in the back seat struck his head hard on the headrest. He released the wire.

One hand still remaining on the gun, Tulu used his other to slide his out of his waist. Though the airbag was in the way, it wouldn't stop the bullet from getting to its target. He fired.

Boc! Boc!

Blood squirted out of the man's chest all over the front seat. The light came on when the back door opened. Tulu pointed the gun over the seat at the man's already-bloody face.

"Where the fuck you think you goin'?"

"I ... I ..."

"I tried to tell them niggas I was a cold-blooded killer."

The man tried to flee.

Boc! Boc! Boc!

The man's head fell backward, his eyes staring at the ceiling while blood seeped from the three holes across his forehead.

# # # #

Yawni pulled into the lot of the Blue Bird Motel on Highway 40. She touched up her makeup in the mirror, then went to knock on the door.

Detective Lawton answered, wearing his work shirt, boxers and black socks. She kissed him on the lips as she kicked the door closed.

"Mm, did they buy it, baby?" she asked.

"Yep. They think y'all are plotting to rob the jewelry store."

"Good." She kissed him. "You did good, baby."

After the bank robberies occurred, Lawton found Yawni's file and decided to use her to get paid. He started by dropping notes in her mailbox until they finally met up at The Cheesecake Factory. Lawton showed her pictures of his son, Andrew, and explained that he needed $125,000 for an operation that his insurance refused to cover. He had been turned down after applying for several loans and he was down to his last option.

Yawni agreed to get in cahoots with him. To be sure it wasn't a trap, she used her pussy as a weapon to open his nose. Once she got him hooked, she gave him his first assignment—to keep the cops off their tail while they took down the casino. So far, he had done a good job.

"So, when do I get my money?" he asked eagerly. "Andrew is running out of time."

Yawni fiddled with her skirt. "Like I told you. Half now," it fell to the floor, "half later."

# chapter 23

The next morning, Ramon sat at his computer inside his home office e-mailing the mayor. He was trying to find out if he had received his package. A hot cup of cappuccino kept him company while he waited for a response.

Jayde walked in wearing oversized pajamas, carrying a cup of coffee in her hand. She sat down Indian-style on the sofa.

"Mornin', daddy," Jayde said cheerfully. "You didn't get much sleep last night."

Ramon sat his cup down. "Did I wake you?"

Jayde shrugged. "Doesn't matter. I love you no matter what. You can be a sleepwalker for all I care."

She stood and strolled over to the bookshelves and ran her hand along the rows of books until she found one that sparked her interest.

"*Den of Thieves*," she read out loud. "Nice title."

Ramon peered at the book in her hand. "True story. Those white boys got rich running scams on the stock market. America didn't know what hit 'em."

Jayde smirked. "The element of surprise. That's what makes a great thief."

Leaning back in his comfortable leather chair with his legs crossed, he kept his eyes locked on her while she thumbed through the book. She seemed to be genuinely infatuated with it.

"Thievery fascinates you?" Ramon asked.

Jayde placed the book back on the shelf. "Very much."

"I used to steal for a living," he told her. "That's how I got where I am today." Ramon took a sip of the hot liquid. "I stole to enrich my life, not to define it."

"For some people, it's exactly the opposite," Jayde replied in a serious tone. "Breakfast?"

"Yes," he replied slowly. His eyes remained on her as she exited the room.

It was chilly outside when Ramon stepped onto the porch. He fastened his robe, then blew hot air into his hands on his way to the mailbox. After he sorted through the mail, he stood there browsing through the latest edition of *FHM Magazine*.

# # # #

Hershey watched Ramon from where she stood. He looked nothing like Trishay, yet he was so handsome and athletically built. She hated to have to do to him what had to be done, but he owed a debt to her.

# # # #

The sounds of tires squealing on concrete caused Ramon to turn around. Tulu's Cadillac was pulling up at the gate. Ramon checked his watch, thinking that it was kind of early for him to be there. Something was up.

Tulu stepped out of the car holding his gun at this side, watching over his shoulder. Ramon regarded him curiously.

"Mornin'," Ramon greeted him.

"Mornin' hell. We got niggas out here looking to take our heads clean the fuck off. Literally." Tulu showed him the bruise around his neck.

It left a frown plastered to Ramon's face. "What happened?"

"I showed up at City Hall and met the man, like you said. Unlike what you said, them honkies made me drive to an alley and tried to off my ass. But I reversed it, you see, 'cause I'm a muthafuckin' trained killa, nigga." He pointed the gun at Ramon. "We got to find out what happened and get they ass today. Not tomorrow nigga, today."

"Be cool, Tulu."

"Fuck cool!" Tulu walked away, then came back. "Nigga, they tried to kill me!"

"Alright then, Tulu. Let's go." Ramon started toward the car. "Wait a minute. Where're we goin? Huh?"

"I don't give a fuck. I'll knock the mayor's and the governor's heads clean off, then lay down and do my time the right way." He paused for a brief moment. "On medication."

Ramon just stared at him, shaking his head.

# # # #

Ramon didn't go to the hotel that night. Instead, he shook Jayde and rented himself a cheap motel room. For the entire night, he sat on the bed, smoking rock after rock and drinking vodka. One thing that the drug had done that he didn't like was make him weak. Every time his stress level accelerated, he wanted the pipe. Whenever he thought, it was about the pipe.

In just a short time, the pipe had taken over his life. And at the moment, there was nothing he could do about it. Nor did he want to.

"*Ramon*," he heard a deep voice say.

He dropped the pipe and jumped up. "Who is it?" he asked.

"*Ramon*," the voice repeated, this time with an echo.

Ramon picked up his gun and the phone, then ran into the closet. He copped a squat on the floor with his gun pointed at the door. He cocked it, ready to unload on whoever came through it. Several terrifying minutes passed. Nobody came and the voices stopped.

He fished the phone off the floor, then dialed

Yawni's number.

Yawni sounded sleepy when she answered. "Hello."

"Yawni." His voice was a desperate whisper.

"Ramon?"

"I need you to come get me." He cracked the closet door, peeping through it. "They're trying to kill me."

Yawni cut on the lamp and sat up in bed. "Who? Who's trying to kill you?"

"Goddamnit, they're trying to kill me. They want me dead." It sounded like he was crying. "If you don't come get me, I'ma gonna ... I'm gonna kill myself." He sniffled. "And my blood will be on your hands."

"Where are you?"

"Oh my God!" Ramon yelled.

Boc! Boc! Boc!

# # # #

After Yawni heard the gunshots, the line went dead in her ear.

"Hello? Ramon? Ramon? Damn!" Yawni slammed down the phone just as Murphy walked into the room.

"You okay?" he asked.

Yawni tossed the covers to the side. She shot past Murphy on her way to the kitchen.

"Where're you going?"

"To make some coffee."

Murphy moved to the dresser where he opened up his laptop, logged on, and began checking his e-mail. His cheeks began to sag, and a knot began to form inside of his stomach when he read one message in particular. It read:

> *Frankie and Petey were found in an alley, shot to death this morning. Tulu's still alive. Be careful.*

The glass of Brandy that he was holding fell from his hand. He had tried to kill Tulu and failed. It was gonna be on now. With his crazy ass on the loose, there was no telling what was about to happen.

"Oh my God!" he cried.

His original plan was to kill Tulu and take the money so that the mayor would never receive it, assuming that the mayor would become angry and act on it by making Ramon step down. Then, Murphy would step in and take over. Corporate takeovers. That's what he lived for.

But now that he had fucked up, he didn't know what to expect. He'd have to consult with Molina.

# # # #

The next morning, Yawni woke early. She showered, ate and dressed in a hurry. Murphy was already at his office. She grabbed her purse and hit the door.

Neither on the news nor in the paper did she find anything about a man killing himself. She drove by a few motels, but didn't see Raomon's car. Jayde's car was parked in the driveway when she drove by Ramon's house.

It wasn't likely, but Yawni drove to the hotel to see if Ramon had shown up for work. Surprisingly, his car was parked in his private parking spot.

The elevator ride up to his office seemed to take forever. When the door opened, she sprang out into the hallway. Ramon's secretary was on the phone.

Yawni approached her desk. "Is the boss in?"

"Yes, but he is currently in a meeting."

Yawni sighed and took a seat.

# # # #

Inside Ramon's office, he sat on the edge of his desk while the mayor chewed his ass. He wanted to excuse himself so bad to go take a hit. All he had to do was go to the bathroom, but he didn't want to chance hearing that faceless voice inside his head while the mayor was present.

The mayor paced the floor with his hands on his hips. "Goddamnit, Delay! We were supposed to keep this quiet."

"I thought we did."

"Then why did I receive that e-mail this morning?"

"What e-mail?"

"Someone, I suppose whoever it was who's

responsible for trying to take out your guy, e-mailed me this morning threatening to go public if you retaliate."

Who could that be? he thought. *Fredrick or Murphy? Snug wouldn't know how to email anyone, let alone the mayor.* Fredrick was on his hit list anyway, so that left Murphy.

Ramon said, "I don't know how someone received word that Tulu was leaving here with the money. No one else knew, other than you. Yet and still, he got intercep—" Ramon cut his words off.

The mayor was curious. "What's wrong?"

While staring down at the waxed floor, Ramon spotted the reflection of a red light. He held up his hand, signaling the mayor to be quiet. On his hands and knees, he peered under the desk and spotted a small cassette recorder that was expertly fastened with Velcro.

He pulled it out. The mayor saw the recorder in his hand and freaked out. "Oh my goodness, someone's on to us."

Ramon tried to figure out why it was there. As far as he knew, the Feds didn't use cheap equipment so he figured it had to be Murphy's doing. But why? The answer came quickly—to monitor his business movements. That's how he knew what Tulu was holding and where he was on his way to.

Murphy didn't want Ramon to keep the casino because he wanted to be in charge. Let Ramon, the black fool, build the clientele back up, then Murphy would take it back over. That was Murphy's plan all along—to steal it back.

"It was Murphy," Ramon stated after a lengthy deliberation.

"Murphy? How in the hell do you know that? If word gets out that I'm taking bribes, I'm finished ... and so are you."

"There's no need for threats, Mr. Mayor."

"You need to fix this, Ramon. Now!" He left the office.

Ramon dropped the recorder on the desk, then plopped down in his chair. He needed a hit. He couldn't go up against Murphy; the man had the mob backing him. One phone call to Chicago from Murphy and a hundred unrecognizable men, all over fifty, would come looking for him.

He examined the recorder. It was the kind that you had to possess in order to listen to it. That would rule Murphy out because he hadn't stepped foot in the office since their argument. That means the only other person it could have been was ... Jayde.

# # # #

Yawni walked through the door, destroying his train of thought. He gazed up at her, shocked to see her face. His secretary followed.

"Mr. Delay, we're having problems with the delivery in the food court. The boxing promoter wants you to call him." She placed a stack of papers on his desk. "And I need your signature on these."

"Okay. Have the food court handle the delivery problem." She nodded, then excused herself.

Yawni took a seat. "Hey."

"Hey yourself," Ramon said solemnly.

Yawni was nervous and felt weird, because she had known him forever, but today, everything felt different. "What happened the other night?"

"The other night?"

"Yes. You called me the other night saying that someone was trying to kill you."

"Wasn't me," he lied.

"It wasn't you?" Her look was accusing.

"No."

Ramon stood and stepped around his desk. Yawni stood also. As he passed her, she reached out and hugged him tightly. She could feel his body accepting her embrace. It was a short moment before he pulled away.

Holding onto his hands, she asked, "Where're you going? Talk to me, Ramon," she begged.

He avoided all eye contact. "I gotta piss."

"Ramon, are you in trouble?"

After a short hiss, he said, "What kind of trouble could I be in?"

"Ramon, I'm serious."

"And so am I. Now, leave me alone, okay?" He snatched away from her and stepped into the bathroom.

The cold water that he splashed on his face felt refreshing. Several deep breaths were taken before he removed his pipe from the cabinet. Popping sounds came from the pipe while he sucked on it. When he finally came out some 20 minutes later, Yawni was gone.

chapter
24

"There you go, sucka," Tulu said. He was sitting in a stolen car, parked in the garage of Fredrick's office. Fredrick's limo had just pulled in.

Tulu pulled his gloves over his hands and checked the chamber of his gun. Fredrick stepped out of the limo talking on his cell phone. The car pulled away. There was a doorman waiting at the elevator.

"Evening, Mr. Bewig," he said with a smile.

Frederick nodded.

The doorman keyed the elevator.

Tulu started the car, put it in drive and gunned it toward the elevator.

When the doorman heard the roaring engine, he quickly turned around. "Mr. Bewig!" he shouted.

Fredrick turned around, saw the car coming and froze. Tulu hit the brakes, sliding dead into them.

Boom!

The sounds that escaped their mouths were sickening. Blood and saliva came up through their mouths, splattering the windshield.

Tulu exited the car with his gun drawn. Fredrick was still conscious. From the waist down, they were both crushed.

"You tried to kill me," Tulu said. Fredrick wasn't able to respond. "Now I'm about to send yo' ass straight to God."

Tulu raised his weapon. Fredrick looked like a retarded man, shaking like he was.

Boc! Boc! Boc!

Tulu moved the barrel to the doorman.

Boc! Boc!

Then he wiped the car down and fled on foot.

# # # #

"Tonight I'm having a get-together with some friends," Jayde informed Ramon. She was stocking their home bar with various bottles of liquor.

"Great." He yawned. "I'm going to bed. Wake me when the party is over."

After a long, hot shower, he crawled into bed naked. The silky satin sheets felt good to his skin. He fluffed his pillow and buried his face in it. Not long after, he was snoring.

Loud music blasting through the walls of the house woke Ramon. His eyes fluttered open as he rose with a frown on his face. He wondered why the hell Jayde was playing the music so damned loud, until he heard people chattering.

He climbed out of bed and peeped out the door.

All sorts of faces that he didn't recognize were in his living room partying. Ramon hurried into some clothes and went to see what was going on.

Women were in the middle of the floor dancing with other women. Couples were freaking on the sofas. The room smelled like weed and cocaine covered the coffee table. There were more white faces than there were was black.

Ramon fixed himself a drink, positioned himself by the bar and watched the crowd. Suddenly, he felt a pair of lips on his neck. A pair of arms clamped around his waist.

"Hey, baby." The voice belonged to Roberta. "Still mad?"

"Why wouldn't I be? I let you four bitches come along and fuck up my life."

Giggling, Roberta said, "Blame your wife, not me. And you can blame yourself for being so vulnerable and gullible when it comes to her."

A long-legged, blue-eyed blonde white woman sashayed over to them.

"Hi Roberta," she said with a wide grin. "Who's your friend? Does he party?"

"His name is Ramon. He's the husband of the host and owner of this big-ass house. And yes, he does party, Julia."

Julia took Ramon by the hand. "Well come on, let's the three of us go find a bedroom."

"Roberta, where's Jayde?" he asked.

A short white boy with a long ponytail stood up

on the sofa and yelled, "The bar is ours! Owww! Let's have a fuckfest!" He kicked off his shoes.

"Upstairs in the guest room," Julia answered for Roberta. Roberta shot her a look. "Well, he asked."

Ramon took off upstairs. Julia and Roberta followed.

"Ramon, wait!" Roberta yelled. "Listen to me first."

He stopped on the staircase and turned around. "What?"

"Umm, Jayde's high so prepare for the worst."

When he busted open the guest room door, he didn't like what he saw. Jayde was naked in the bed, sandwiched between two white boys.

"Ramon," Jayde said slowly. Her face was made up like a hooker's and she was stoned.

"You fuckin' tramp!" he hollered. He felt a hand touch his shoulder and looked back. "What?"

It was the short drunk guy that was standing on the sofa getting naked. He had on Ramon's robe, and held onto a beer.

"Excuse me dude," he said, "but I need you to leave my party." He pointed the beer can toward the door.

Ramon scowled. "What?"

"Buddy, you're up here tripping over one ho when there's a whole bunch of hoes downstairs. C'mon man, let's go get loaded and fuck some of these hoes together, just like they're doing Jayde."

"Yeah," Julia encouraged. "Forget about her, and

focus on these." She removed her shirt, revealing large breasts and pink, round nipples.

Roberta and Judd, the crazy white boy, led him back downstairs. They stopped in front of a group of women.

Judd said, "Now, you can have any of them, except for her ... her ... that one ... not Jamie either. You know what, why don't we move to another group 'cause all those hoes are mine." He snickered.

A redheaded girl with green eyes, body piercings and a lot of tattoos volunteered. Ramon, Julia, Roberta and the new girl went to his bedroom. Judd stayed behind. "Who wants to play spin the bottle?" he shouted.

The redhead, Shania, set out a bunch of coke. After they all got high, they climbed onto the huge bed. Woman on woman, man on woman, and vice versa, they went round after round. When they neared exhaustion, they took a crack break. Roberta loaded the straight shooter so everyone could take a blast. When the high kicked in, it was on, again.

Boom!

The door flew open. Everyone on the bed snapped to attention. Jayde came through the door with a loaded gun in her hand.

"Get the fuck outta my room!" she yelled sluggishly. Her eyes were barely visible.

The women did as they were told. Ramon was

high and spooked. Jayde knew it.

"Jayde," he said as he nervously inched toward her.

"Don't Jayde me, muthafucka. You're up in here fuckin' in our bed."

"Girl, put the gun down."

Judd walked in. "What the fuck is going on now?!" He peered down and saw the gun in her hand. "Oh shit!" he yelled. "She got a gun!" He ran out of the room.

While Jayde looked at Judd, Ramon tackled her to the floor. They tussled a while before Ramon snatched the gun from her hand. He raised it as if he were about to strike her with it.

"Bitch, I oughta knock yo' fuckin' head off," he threatened.

Jayde shielded her face with her arms. She got brave after she realized he wasn't gonna do it.

"Do it you crack head, coward-ass pussy. Up in here screwin' in my bed. You ain't shit," Jayde shouted. "You hear me?"

He grabbed her arm and snatched her up on her feet. She tried to break free, but it was no use.

"I'm tired of your shit, bitch," he said while dragging her through the house. The startled crowd made a hole for the fighting couple to get through. The guests in the house were regular swingers, and had never witnessed such a thing go on between a couple.

"Let me go, you fucking bastard!" Jayde clawed

at his arms. He still wouldn't release his grip.

The cold night air smacked her in the face as soon as the door opened. All she wore was a night-gown. Chill bumps spread over her flesh.

Her attitude quickly changed to a soft plea. "Baby, please don't throw me out. It's cold out here."

"Too late, bitch, you gettin' the fuck outta here," he growled. He tucked the gun inside his drawers, then slung her off the porch. When she still refused to leave, he fired two shots over her head.

Boc! Boc!

"Bitch, I said leave," Ramon said coldly. Then he closed the door. Soon after, she heard the music come back on.

"Okay, muthafucka. I got something for yo' ass."

# # # #

An hour later, Ramon sat on the sofa, between Shania and Julia, bent over the table and shoveling coke up his nose. He had gotten so high that he tried to snort a line, but the powder fell right back out. He had fallen in love with the girl, but it wasn't quite as good as the rock.

Everybody in the house was dancing, laughing and having a good time, when ...

Boom! Boom! Boom!

Someone banged on the front door.

"It's the police! Open up!"

Judd jumped up. "Oh my fuckin' God! Raid!"

Everybody including Ramon started picking up dope, pipes, bags and whatever else they could find, and dashed to the four bathrooms. The cops heard all the movement going on inside the house and asked Jayde for permission to enter. She granted it.

Upon entering the residence, they didn't know who to grab first. The entire scene was chaotic. Naked people were running around everywhere. To uncomplicate the situation, they set out to find the owner of the house. When they found him, he was in his bedroom bathroom, breaking up a crack pipe. He had already flushed the dope. He was arrested for domestic violence and possession of drug paraphernalia.

Jayde stood in the doorway with her hands on her hips, smiling deviously while they carried him away.

chapter

25

"I'm here to bail out Ramon Delay," Tulu said at the front desk. "I'll be paying cash."

"That'll be $2,500," the bailiff informed him. He placed a clipboard on the counter in front of him. "Sign here."

Tulu waited for Ramon outside. He sat in the car grooving to an Otis Redding CD when he saw Ramon come out.

"Thanks man," Ramon said.

Tulu mugged the side of his head while smoke flowed out of his nostrils.

Ramon said, "What?"

"What the hell you doing in the house with a bunch of crack pipes and naked white people?"

Ramon was too embarrassed to admit the truth.

Tulu sighed. "Don't tell me that bitch caught you smoking crack and turned you in."

"Take me home." Ramon took his Blackberry out of the sack.

Tulu put the car in drive. "I took care of our

Fredrick problem."

"I know. Seen it on the news."

"Fucked 'em up, didn't I?" Ramon nodded. "Un hunh. I told you, I don't play that shit."

"That's good. The detectives came to speak to me about ole Freddy. Said they were supposed to meet with him this morning."

"They probably thought you had something to do with his murder."

"Yeah. Now he don't have nothing to tell 'em."

Tulu hit his cigarette. "Murphy's next on my shit list. Fuck what ya heard. His ass is out, 'cause somebody tried to kill me."

# # # #

"Don't get any of that oatmeal on your shirt, Cindy," Molina said to his daughter.

He sat at the breakfast table reading the newspaper. His wife, Sarah, fixed his plate and sat it in front of him.

"Bacon and a boiled egg," he said as he put the paper down. "Yummy."

Sarah smiled. "You don't need to go to work full. Besides, I'm supporting the removal of that pouch you're growing."

Cindy found that humorous.

"Oh, you think that's funny, huh? You all just hurt daddy's feelings, I want y'all to know that."

Sarah and Cindy looked at one another. Then they both stood, walked around the table and sandwich-hugged their king.

"We're sorry, honey," Sarah said and kissed him.

"Yeah dad, we're sorry. We're gonna make it up to you by taking you to dinner and a movie tonight."

"Dinner and a movie? I'd love that. Your mother and I haven't done that since the '70s. Back then we used to—"

"Please spare her the details, Howard," Sarah said. "Time for you to go."

"Darnit, already?" He stood and walked to the front room. He holstered his Glock, hugged and kissed his family, then walked out the door.

Molina waved and smiled before he drove off. On his way to work, he started thinking. *How did we come to this point in the investigation?* Lawton had told him that he obtained the information from one of his informants. *What informant? And where, all of a sudden, did that informant obtain information about Snug's crew? What professionals would tell somebody about a joint they were casing before they took it down? Doesn't add up.*

Could Lawton be dirty? I was once upon a time, Molina thought. It was worth looking into.

# # # #

Yawni, Snug and Chico were at Snug's, preparing to hit the Resthaven. Ramon wouldn't know what hit him until it was over, but it wouldn't take him long to figure it out because he knew who he had snaked out. His friends. And they were the best thieves he had ever known.

The Thomas vs. Warren cruiserweight bout was going on at the casino that night. So much would be going on, they wouldn't even be noticed. If for some reason they were, the guns would come out and they would either kill or be killed.

Snug looked at his watch. "Where the hell is Bobby?"

Yawni placed her gun in her waist. "He should be pulling up at the jewelry store any minute."

Snug took a minute to admire the way Yawni looked in her black trousers and security shirt. Her ponytail brought out her face. She saw him eyeing her, but ignored him.

Chico walked into the kitchen carrying three Point Blank vests. He tossed one to each of them.

"It's time."

Yawni took two steps before Snug clutched her arm. She looked down at his hand, then up into his face.

"What?"

"You okay?"

She studied his face. "I'm fine. Why?"

He shrugged. "You look kinda funny, that's all." He released his grip. Yawni walked away.

# # # #

Inside the garage of the 63rd police station, Molina, Lawton and six members of their task force geared up for combat. Their destination was the jewelry store on the plaza.

Molina and Lawton drove a blue Ford Crown Victoria, followed by the black task force van. They arrived at the scene before Bobby did. They posted around the back of the building across the street.

From the roof of the building, Molina scanned the entire area through binoculars. Like any other day, people were walking by, heading to the nearby restaurants and shopping stores.

"Where the hell are those sons of bitches? Lawton, I thought your informant said they're supposed to be here."

"Relax. He said they'd be there. They'll be here."

Molina lit a cigarette. "I'd like to know how he knows so much."

Lawton ignored the question, just like Molina figured he would.

# # # #

Ramon shaved his face and head, showered and put on a tuxedo. He draped himself with some of his best jewelry. While he waited for his limo to arrive, the monkey started pounding on his back. The crack was calling him but he had neither crack nor pipe.

He was already out front when his car showed up. The driver got out to get the door for him. Ramon gazed into his eyes for any signs of a fellow user. The driver shot Ramon a look like he was either crazy or gay.

"Yes?" the driver asked in a feminine voice.

Ramon's eyes widened. "Nothing. Sorry. I thought I recognized you." He got inside.

"A closet Gump," the driver said, then closed the door with his ass.

# # # #

The casino was crowded. Kansas City wasn't accustomed to hosting fights, so it was a big turnout. At the present time, meaningless light-weight fights were going on, paving the way for the upcoming main event.

A lot of money was pouring into the hotel that night, so the count room was full. All suites were occupied. So much was going on that even the president could walk in and go unnoticed.

Tulu was in charge of keeping the promoters happy until Ramon arrived. It wasn't hard with the assistance of Francine, Roberta, Lashay and Jayde. With them around, dressed as they were, it was hard for anyone to concentrate on the fights.

Wearing a blue pinstriped Sean John suit, scarf, brim hat and Gucci framed glasses, Tulu sat ringside in between the promoters. He chewed on an unlit cigar, enjoying his moment as acting manager.

The lightweight division champion, Don Deal, pummeled his contender, Jay Rivers, in the 5th round. The crowd leapt to their feet cheering. Tulu threw down his cigar, because from the looks of things, he was about to lose $5,000.

"Get yo' gay ass up!" he screamed.

While the crowd was on its feet, Jayde checked her watch. Lashay saw her, then checked hers as well. They nodded to one another. Jayde excused herself.

"Where you going?" Tulu asked her.

Jayde stopped in her tracks and answered without turning around. "To the restroom."

# # # #

A white Astro van pulled up in front of the jewelry store, blocking Molina's view. The driver disappeared to the back. They couldn't see the other side of the van, but they knew someone was exiting out the side door. From their position, they couldn't see how many there were.

"It's them," Molina said.

"Let's go." Lawton jumped up, but Molina held him down.

"Don't move. Wait just a moment." Molina's eyes remained on the van. He glanced at his watch to time the robbery.

Lawton pretended to be impatient. "C'mon, man."

"Man, sit your ass down." The next time he looked at his watch, four minutes had passed. Too long for a professional robbery, yet the van was still there. "Something's wrong, don't you think, Lawton?"

"I ... I ..."

"Move in," Molina said into his radio.

Bobby was standing at the counter inside the jewelry store holding a platinum necklace when the police stormed in.

"Get down! Police!"

Bobby and the clerk heard the word "police" and immediately got down on the floor. Molina and Lawton entered the store after the area was secured. Molina didn't like what he saw. It didn't look like a robbery or anything else had gone down. He kneeled next to Bobby.

"Tell me what's going on, Bobby?" Molina asked. "That is your name, isn't it?"

"Yes, but I'm just picking up a necklace for my girl," Bobby explained. "Next thing I know, here y'all come."

Molina fired up a cigarette, thought for a moment, then threatened to put it out in Bobby's face. Bobby flinched.

"I know what's going on here, Bobby," Molina said. "Somewhere at this very moment, there's a 211 taking place, and you, pal, were used as a decoy to throw us off. It would've worked except for one thing." Molina pointed two fingers at Bobby's eyes. "Your eyes, Bobby. They're unique."

"What're you talking about?" Bobby demanded.

"I know a bank owner named Murphy. He showed us a video of one of his banks getting robbed," Molina lied. "In that video footage, we spotted a masked man. His eyes were green and brown, just like yours. We would've dismissed it until we found your face in our computer files. No one knows about this but me and my partner. We can keep a lid on it considering you help us locate your friends. If not, you go down for murdering a cop." Molina smiled. "What do ya say?"

Lawton stood by, sweating bullets.

chapter

26

The armored car pulled into the parking lot of the grocery store. Two of the guards got out of the back and walked into the store.

Snug and Chico were browsing through cereal in aisle D. They saw the guards pass their aisle as they headed toward the back room. Five minutes later, the door opened back up. One of the guards came out with a pistol drawn and down by his side. His eyes scanned the area for possible ambushers. Then, after the signal, the guard carrying the money bags came out.

Snug and Chico moved quickly. From their blind side they stepped forward producing two stun guns. Before the guards knew what hit them, they were on their knees, shaking uncontrollably. One dropped his gun and the other dropped the bags. The two thieves picked up the bags and gun and raced for the exit.

At almost the exact same time, Yawni stopped the stolen Chevy next to the armored car. The driver had his eyes locked on the store entrance. He didn't see her chuck the can of tear gas through the window on the passenger side. Seconds later, he leapt from the truck, gagging and coughing as he fell to the ground.

Yawni was sitting behind the wheel of the truck when Snug and Chico came out of the store. They jumped inside and she pulled off. Highway 435 was just down the road and it was a straight shot to the Resthaven.

# # # #

Ramon finally arrived at the hotel. He met and greeted the boxing promoters. Ronald Isley was on stage performing a song before the main event.

Ramon thanked the girls for helping to keep the promoters happy while he was away. Jayde had not returned.

The lights came on and Ramon took a seat next to Tulu. They whispered a few things in each other's ears. The waitress showed up with a message for Ramon. It read:

> *Meet me in suite 405. Now.*
> *I need to apologize.*
>
> > *Love, Jayde*

Ramon leaned toward the promoter and whispered, "Excuse me for a minute, please."

"Sure. Make sure you're around for the after-party." He laughed and pointed a jeweled finger at him.

Roberta touched Ramon as he walked past. He looked at her. "Watch yourself tonight, Ramon. Okay?"

He nodded thoughtfully and continued to walk away.

# # # #

"We got a 211 in progress at the Resthaven Hotel!" Molina yelled.

"Let's move," Lawton replied.

They jumped in their car and sped in the direction of the hotel.

"Did you know about this?" Molina asked.

Lawton frowned. "About what?"

"We'll talk about it later."

# # # #

Ramon used his master key to open the door to suite 405. Music was playing softly. Cautiously, he crossed the doorway. The table was set. Candles were lit. A bottle of champagne chilled inside an ice bucket. Jayde appeared out of nowhere.

She looked stunning in a red evening gown, diamond earrings, high-heeled stilettos and a rose in her hand. Slowly she stepped over to him.

Ramon took a step back. "This shit ain't gon' work this time."

Continuing toward him, Jayde said, "Unt unh, Ramon. This time I'ma take a different approach. You'll see."

"Bitch, you put me in jail," he reminded her.

Jayde stopped about a foot away from him. "Is that all? What else have I done to you, Ramon?" She looked at the champagne. "Wait a minute, hold that thought. Let me fix you a drink first."

# # # #

Yawni pulled the armored truck up to the hotel. Chico and Snug exited the back and walked inside looking like guards. They walked in flashing their badges on their way to the count room. Snug put the card into the slot, then the door opened.

The gamblers inside The Den were busy doing their own thing and the employees were busy running the tables and serving drinks. To them, it looked like a routine money pick-up.

The counters inside the count room already had four bags packed with money that was counted and ready to go. Snug was in awe of the room. The counters sat on straight-back chairs and counted the money on clear glass tables. There were steel shelves and floors to bear the tons of cash and coins. 10s, 20s and 100 dollar bills were sorted into inch-thick $10,000 bricks stacked on the shelves against the wall.

A sign posted on the wall read:
A million dollars in 100s weighs 20-1/2

pounds. 20s, 102 pounds and 5s weigh 408 pounds.

Snug guessed it to be guidelines for them to follow.

The two counters in the room saw the two guards pull guns. They immediately stopped counting money and stood, stepping away from the tables.

"No questions," Snug said. "Take out some more of those black bags and start filling them until we tell you to stop."

The counters did as they were told. Chico started lugging bags out to the truck, two at a time, starting with the four that were ready.

Yawni nervously glanced around while she waited. Seeing Chico rushing out with the two bags gave her some relief. He loaded them into the back, then left again, returning with two more. Before she knew it, he had loaded eight bags into the back of the truck.

She pointed at her watch. Chico acknowledged her signal then strolled back inside. Yawni sat up to get a look at the bags in the back through the little window. When she stood, the cell phone that Lawton gave her just in case he needed to alert her fell down between the seats.

"Yes!" she said excitedly. She didn't hear her phone vibrating over the sound of the loud truck. Lawton had sent her a text that read: *Abort!*

# # # #

Jayde sat at the table across from Ramon sipping champagne. "You were saying, Ramon?"

"Ever since I met you, I've been fucked up. I did everything I could for you. I bought you everything you wanted. So, I had to kick your ass a few times, but what choice did I have? I was hoping to knock some sense into your stubborn ass. For a while, you'd act like everything was all good, then all of a sudden, here comes the bullshit again. I'm sick of this shit."

Jayde sat there with a triumphant smirk on her face and Ramon couldn't understand why. That look almost put fear in him.

"What does all that sound like to you, Ramon?" she asked. "Doesn't it all sound like child's play? Hm? The beautiful young girl gets everything she wants, yet she's still unsatisfied. Why? Because she feels like it's all owed to her anyway. You catch the little tramp screwing in the house. What do you do? You spank her. After the spanking wears off, little girlie goes back to being mischievous again."

Ramon stared at her curiously. The conversation was headed someplace. He just didn't know where.

# # # #

"We have a 211 in progress at the Resthaven Hotel."

Yawni heard the announcement over the scanner inside the truck. "Oh, shit!" She got on her radio. "Snug, get out of there, now!" She put the truck in second gear, waiting to take off. "C'mon, c'mon, c'mon."

Inside the count room, Snug was helping fill four more bags when he heard Yawni on his radio.

"Let's go!" Snug commanded.

Yawni looked at the doors and still didn't see her partners. Loud sirens wailed. She pulled off just as Molina and Lawton hit the corner. Lawton saw the ass end of the truck going up the road. He smiled lightly and prayed silently thanking the Lord that his son would get a chance at life.

Snug and Chico walked out of the building. Molina slowed as he pulled into the entrance, glancing around.

Snug spotted Molina's car. "Go! Go!"

They took off running to a green Ford Bronco that they had parked in the east parking area. After they got inside, Chico removed an AR-15 from under the seat.

Snug bolted out of the parking spot. Molina heard the tires squealing and turned his head in their direction. The Bronco was coming at them, full speed. Hurriedly, Molina sped forward getting out of the way. Snug turned right out onto the street, damn near tipping the Bronco over.

Molina threw his car in reverse, backing all the way out onto the street, then took off after them.

The whole episode left Lawton trying to figure out what the hell was going on.

# # # #

Two left hooks and an overhand right to the jaw sent the champ down for the count. The crowd was on its feet. Everybody in the house seemed to be upset except for Tulu, who was jumping up and down.

"Take his muthafuckin head off!" Tulu shouted. "Ha! Ha!"

The promoters were all in stunned silence while the referee counted, and the champ slowly climbed to his feet. The fight resumed after a slow four count.

Lashay stood and excused herself. Seconds later, Roberta did the same. Francine waited until the crowd got hype again before she snuck out.

"Hey, man, where did the women go?" one of the promoters asked.

Tulu said, "What? Man, fuck them hoes. I'm about to win $50,000."

# # # #

Lashay led the girls to the linen closet. She unlocked and opened the door. "We've got to move fast before the fight is over."

Each girl changed into a pair of trousers, black T-shirt, bulletproof vest and a ski mask. Roberta passed out the guns to each of them.

Lashay looked at her watch. "Show time." She pulled the mask down over her face.

The gamblers inside The Den were having a good time. The fight was being shown on the big screens. According to Lashay's watch, the armored truck guards had just left. Four guards were posted up in The Den, and the rest of security was busy covering the fight. There was nothing that could stop them.

Inside the camera room upstairs, the security guards were so busy watching the fight that they didn't see the three women carrying guns through the casino.

Suzie, the bartender, brought the guards on duty some non-alcoholic beverages about five minutes earlier. Now they all found themselves nodding and sick. Lashay stormed in holding an AK-47 in the air. Suzie cut the music.

"Everybody line up against the wall, now!" Lashay ordered. "Don't fuck with me!"

Suzie politely relieved the paralyzed guards of their guns and walkie-talkies. They were gagged with their own ties and bound by their own cuffs. The gamblers and dealers all did as they were told. Wallets, jewelry, purses and everything else of value was ordered to be thrown on the floor.

Francine and Roberta used plastic hand ties to bind everybody's hands behind their backs. Lashay checked her watch again then waited for the word from upstairs.

# # # #

"What's up with you, Jayde?" Ramon inquired.

Jayde nodded toward a package sitting in front of Ramon. "Open it," she said. "Tell me what you think."

Ramon cautiously picked up the package and opened it. It was a photograph inside of a platinum frame. The picture stopped his heart as a jolt shot through his body. He could not believe what he was seeing, but now that he thought about it, it should've been obvious.

"You didn't see it because you're blind, baby," Jayde said. "All you see is Ramon Delay."

The photograph was of Hershey holding up two graduation certificates. There standing next to her with her arm around her, smiling proudly, was none other than Jayde. The names "Hershey" and "Trishay" were written across the photograph right above the word "Forever."

"Aren't you proud of me, daddy? I graduated from high school with honors. Unfortunately, Mama graduated from drug rehab. It's a good place. I strongly recommend it for you if you ever plan on kicking your habit."

No wonder I was so drawn to her, Ramon thought. *She's my seed.* His face wrinkled. "But we ... we ..."

"Never. We never had sex. You only thought we did. You couldn't tell the difference when I would sneak out of bed and let Roberta take my place.

That's because you're blind, daddy." She shrugged. "Although I would have done it to do what I'm about to do."

"You hid the tape recorder in my office? Why?"

"I wanted Murphy to kill Tulu, so I wouldn't have to deal with him trying to protect you. I listened to the tape while you were in the bathroom that day."

Jayde lifted her dress and pulled the gun that was strapped to her leg. She flipped open her cell phone. "I'm on my way down."

"So, why go through all this, Trishay?" Ramon asked.

She closed the phone. "I took you through everything you took my mother through and at the same time, I got to know my daddy. Got treated like the child I missed out on being. You whooped me, spoiled me, but now it's time for me to collect my back child support."

Ramon cracked a smile. "You're gonna try to rob my casino?"

"Not try, daddy. It's already happening right now, so get the fuck up!" She pointed the gun toward him.

"I have to admit, I'm impressed," he said as he stood. "Which way?"

"To your office, now!"

Jayde followed Ramon to his office. He fumbled with his keys at the door, trying to figure out what he could do. He peered back over this shoulder at her. The barrel of the gun was pointed at his back. The look in her eyes was cold.

The door unlocked, then they stepped inside. Ramon looked at her.

"Now, I want the security pass to the count room," Jayde demanded.

"I don't—"

"I bugged your office, remember daddy, so cut the lies." Ramon reluctantly walked to the safe and opened it up. "You're already dead to me, daddy," she said, "so don't think for one moment that I won't lay your ass down."

He handed over the card. Jayde led him back to the suite where she cuffed him to the tub and gagged his mouth. Then she took the elevator to The Den.

One of the security guards inside the camera room finally took the time to examine the screens. He gasped when he saw what was going on inside The Den. He snatched up the phone.

"Don't do that." His partner drew his gun on him. "Put down the phone and watch the fight."

After he put the phone down, his partner relieved him of his firearm.

# # # #

Snug sped through the park, going way too fast for the curvy road. Chico peered out the back window and saw the Crown Victoria on their ass.

"What're we gonna do?" Chico asked.

"Whatever you do, don't—"
Pow—Pow—Pow—Pow!
Chico fired shots at the police. It was at that moment that Snug felt like he was going to die. He had planned to avoid violence unless absolutely necessary.

Bullets covered Molina's front windshield. He veered to the right, then back left, damn near bumping the curb.
Pow—Pow—Pow—Pow!
Lawton returned fire.
Pop—Pop—Pop—Pop!
Pow—Pow—Pow!
Pop—Pop!
Molina fought for control of the wheel all the while dodging bullets. The windshield had so many holes through it that it was useless.

Snug shot past Gregory Boulevard and round-ed the corner by the lake. The truck was on two wheels for a brief moment. About a block before he would have jumped on the highway, he saw that the road was fenced off. Orange and yellow "Caution" and "Road Closed" signs cluttered the road. He wanted to run through the fencing, but there was a big hole in the road on the other side.

Left with no other choice, Snug hit the brakes.

# # # #

Jayde put on her mask before she entered the casino. The girls had everybody in line. She walked straight over to the count room door. Roberta stood beside her.

Jayde stuck the card in the slot. After the door opened, they stormed in with guns drawn. She saw all the empty shelves, coins and what was left of the money scattered all over the table and floors.

The grunting that they heard led them to the other side of the table, where they found the counters bound and gagged. Roberta pulled the tie out of one of their mouths.

"What happened here?"

A man looked up at the masked woman through pleading eyes. "The armored car guards robbed us."

Jayde didn't know what to think. It was a hell of a coincidence that someone decided to rob the casino on the exact same night. Unfucking believable. She spun on her heels and left the room.

"Hold it down." She took the elevator up to the security room. Her inside security guard saw her coming and let her in.

"What's happening?"

"I need you to roll back about 15 minutes of tape."

The man rewound the tape. They watched as the two armored guards entered the hotel. The two men seemed to keep their faces out of the camera's view. That right there told Jayde that they were familiar with the hotel's security system. But what really caught her eye was the unique swagger that the short one walked with. And he was the same height and weight as Snug.

"I should've known." Jayde left the room and headed back to Ramon.

# # # #

Ramon fell backward but the cuffs wouldn't allow him to go anywhere.

Jayde removed the stuffing from his mouth, squeezed his jaws until his lips parted like a fish and jammed her gun inside his mouth. "Your friends stole my money and I want it back." She kneed him in the balls.

"Owww!"

"You knew about this, didn't you?" She kicked him in the face.

"No!"

"Liar!" she yelled. "Give me my money you fucker! You owe that to me!" She took out her phone. "Move out!"

Jayde removed the cuffs and forced him to walk. They rode the service elevator down to the kitchen where they walked outside to the back parking lot. The girls were waiting in a van.

"That was a neat trick, daddy," Jayde said as she closed the door.

"I swear I don't—"

"Shut up!"

Lashay was driving. "Where's the money?"

"Yeah," Francine said.

Jayde shoved the pistol in Ramon's face. "Somebody's a little slicker than we thought. Did Joe pull the video tapes?"

"Yes."

"Good. I don't want nobody to be able to ID us."

Ramon said, "I can."

Jayde smirked. "But you won't. Trust me."

chapter

27

Snug could not see himself just giving up. Thirty to life in Federal prison didn't sound too tempting. He turned the truck around. When Molina's car rounded the bend, Snug took off, driving toward them.

"What the—" Molina covered his face, preparing for the collision.

Blam!

The big Bronco slammed into the Crown Victoria. Snug kept his foot on the gas, forcing the smaller car backward. Smoke came from all eight of their tires.

Errrrrrrrrk!

When Lawton and Molina collected themselves, they kicked out the windshield and fired at the Bronco.

Pop—Pop—Pop!

Chico caught two in the neck, killing him instantly. A bullet pierced Snug's left shoulder and grazed his ear. He put the Bronco in 4-wheel drive and continued to force the car backward.

"C'mon you muthafuckas!" he shouted. "C'mon you p—"

Molina fired a shot that hit Snug right in the nose. Then another to his head. Snug's dead hands released the wheel and his foot slid off the gas pedal.

When the cops finally stopped the car, they rushed the Bronco with their guns drawn. The two men inside the truck were dead. Lawton found the bags of money in the backseat. Molina called it in on his radio. Lawton picked up Chico's gun.

"Hey, Mo. Check this out. I found something," Lawton lied.

"What is—"

Pop—Pop—Pop!

Molina held his leaking torso as he fell down on the concrete. He could hear his lungs straining for air, and then he heard sirens. Help was on the way.

Lawton quickly lugged one of the money bags into the woods. By the time he came back, the police had hit the scene. Two of them were kneeling over Molina.

"The ambulance is on the way," one of them informed him.

Lawton walked up. "I'm Detective Lawton. This is my partner. One of those dead assholes got a shot off when we rushed the truck."

"Where're you coming from?"

Lawton, breathing rapidly, looked at the woods. "Uh, I couldn't get a signal on my phone here, so I started walking until I picked up one."

"Why didn't you just use the radio?"

He shrugged. "Shaken up. Wasn't thinking, I guess. I found the bag of money in the back seat."

The men peered through the back window at the single bag.

"Great."

Lawton peered down at Molina who was staring back up at him while taking quick, shallow breaths. He was trying to hold on, but it was his time to go. When Howard Molina finally closed his eyes, he slipped away into the unknown.

# # # #

The fight was over. The champ went down in the ninth round. It was the second upset of the night. The promoters did not appear to be happy about it either. They had lost a fortune betting on the champ.

Tulu suggested that they all go to The Den and have some drinks on him. To their surprise, policemen, detectives and paramedics were crawling all over the place. A crowd of people stood amongst a group of officers making statements.

One of the employees informed Tulu of the situation. He immediately got on the phone in an attempt to contact Ramon.

# # # #

Their hideout was a small house that sat at the

end of a dead end street. Roberta backed the van into an opened garage.

Hershey stood inside the garage.

Ramon looked away from her.

Hershey sneered, shocked to see him instead of a van filled with moneybags. "Where's the money, Trishay?"

Jayde stepped out of the van. "Somebody beat us to it. Step out, Ramon."

Ramon did. Blood stained the front of his suit and face. His lips and nose were swollen. Though she should not have, Hershey felt sorry for him.

"What happened, Trishay?" Lashay inquired.

On their way into the house, Jayde explained everything. Her theory was that somehow Ramon had caught onto her plan and robbed his own hotel before they could.

Ramon denied it all.

They led him to an empty room where Jayde kicked him in the back of the knees. He fell to the floor. She whacked him across the head with the gun, knocking him over.

Jayde stared down on him coldly, her chest heaving. "Tie his ass up." Then she left the room.

Hershey sat on the bed in the other room when Jayde stormed in, wiping blood from her face. She stripped the dress off then put on some leather pants, a jacket and a pair of boots. She felt her mother eyeballing her.

Jayde sighed. "What, mother?"

"Can I talk to him?"

Jayde pinned her hair back in the mirror, then gazed at her mother. "Sure."

Ramon sat on the floor against the wall. His hands were cuffed behind his back. Hershey walked in and looked down at him.

Hershey said, "Your daughter's out of control, but it's your own fault. You, her own father, threatened to kill her when she was a baby. Then you killed her uncle, my little brother, in cold blood. In cold blood, Ramon ... right in front of us."

Ramon spit blood on the floor. "Bitch, you had me locked away for 15 fuckin' years. I paid my debt."

"Even under the gun, you're still the same ole Ramon Delay." Tears glazed Hershey's eyes. "Pay for what, Ramon? For what you owe us? You killed my brother!" she yelled. She kneeled down. She could feel his breath on her face. "You fucked my friends and family. You beat me up in front of my own daughter. Even through all of your evil shit, the name-calling, the beatings, the put-downs, I still loved you. Sometimes, I think I still do."

Jayde listened through the cracked door, growing angrier by the second.

Ramon used the wall to push himself up. Hershey stepped back as he stepped toward her. She was nervous while she stared into his cold eyes.

"You still love me, huh?" He attempted to kiss her but she turned her head.

"You drove me to drugs, Ramon," she admitted.

Ramon stepped back, laughing loudly. "I drove you to drugs? You oughta see what that treacherous daughter of ours did to me. I get so fuckin' spooked when I'm at the pipe that I scare the hell out of my own goddamn self. I didn't deserve that."

"Neither did I. But you—"

Jayde and her girls stormed into the room.

"Enough of the lovey dovey shit." Jayde stared Ramon down. "I got you, pops."

Jayde peered over his shoulder at Roberta and nodded. She walked in carrying a chair and a phone. She placed the chair behind Ramon. He held still while his daughter sniffed his neck. At one time it would have turned him on, but now it was down right disgusting. He wanted to puke when she attempted to kiss him.

"Ah!" Ramon fell back in the chair after a knee to the nuts.

She threw the phone at his chest. "We're about to play a game that's very familiar to you, daddy. Call your bitch, Yawni, and tell her to bring me my money." She snatched the gun out of her waist. "Or you're a dead daddy."

"You'd stoop to my level and kill your own flesh over some paper?"

"Yes. See, you stole to enrich your life, but I steal to define mine. It's who I am." She laughed. "Look at what I came from. Two thieving-ass crack head parents." Her girls laughed. "Call her. Now!"

"She won't do it," he explained.

"Then you will die."

"Trishay Delay," Hershey called. "Please!"

Trishay peered at her mother through narrow slits. "Get out of here, mother."

Lashay led Hershey into the other room. She gazed over her shoulder at Ramon one last time before she was rushed out.

Ramon said, "Alright, I'll call her."

Ramon's hands shook as he dialed the number.

# # # #

Yawni had transferred the moneybags to a rented Dodge Magnum. At that moment she was flying down Highway 71, going south. She heard her phone ring.

"Snug?" she answered.

"No, Yawni. This is Ramon." His voice was full of stress.

Yawni didn't miss it. "What's going on?"

Jayde snatched the phone from him. "Look bitch, I'm not gonna beat around the bush. You got my money and I want it. If I don't get it, I will shoot this muthafucka in the head, then send the picture to your phone. I know you love him, Yawni, let's just see how much." She kicked Ramon in the shin. "This isn't a joke, so don't assume that it is. You have two minutes to call this number back with an answer." Jayde hung up.

# # # #

Ramon's memory reflected back to the night when Jayde asked him if he would have really killed his own daughter. Now he wished he would have lied. She had him in the same situation and he was terrified. He now imagined how she felt at six years old.

# # # #

In twenty seconds, the two minutes would be up. Jayde placed the gun to Ramon's temple and watched the clock tick. Hershey sat on the living room couch nervously rocking back and forth. Now that it had come down to it, she was no longer eager to kill him.

# # # #

Yawni glanced at the clock while she continued south on the highway. Her plan was to go to Texas and start over. She kept telling herself that the whole thing was a setup, and to keep moving. But the thought of someone actually killing Ramon kept haunting her. Five seconds left. Yawni made up her mind. She hit the brakes and pulled over on the shoulder.

# # # #

"Time's up, daddy," Jayde informed him. The phone rang. "Hello."

"Where do we meet?" It was Yawni.

Jayde smirked. "You're just like my mother. A damned fool. I married him and still don't get it."

She peered down at Ramon. "Meet us at the lookout point in 30 minutes. And come alone."

Jayde slammed the phone down. "Your bitch is gonna come through."

Ramon felt a sense of relief come over him. After all he had put her through, he wouldn't expect her to throw piss on him if he were on fire.

Francine and Lashay escorted Ramon back out to the van. Jayde grabbed her shades off the table. Hershey was drinking Scotch.

"Trishay," Hershey called out.

Jayde didn't look at her. "What, mother?"

"Don't hurt your daddy. We've hurt him enough."

"Have we? He paid us for all the pain we've suffered because of him? The depression? The loneliness that I felt while you were strung out, chasing your next hit? The proms, dances and field trips that I missed? I had to steal maxi pads and deodorant just so the girls at school would stop teasing me 'cause I stunk." She took a breath. "But it made me tough and independent."

She finally looked down at her mother. "I used that bastard to get back everything that I had missed out on. Material things, love ... even whoopins, but I still spent quality time with my daddy." Jayde held up her gun. "Now it's time to collect my dues, Mama. After tonight, there will be no looking back."

Hershey stood and hugged her daughter. "I love you, Jayde, and I understand, but I think we've done enough," she whispered in her ear. "Let it go. Ramon will hunt us down if we don't kill him and I can't live my life like that. I made a promise to the Lord that I would change if he got me off that evil narcotic, and he did."

Hershey's words only angered Jayde. "Mother, you're a weak coward and you have always been one." Jayde squeezed the trigger. *Pow!* And shot her in the stomach.

"Uhhh!" Hershey fell onto the couch, holding her bleeding stomach. Both shock and fear covered her face as she peered up at her demon of a daughter.

Jayde's eyes were cold orbs as she stood there waiting for her mother to die. At first, she wondered how her daddy could think about killing his own blood. Now she learned that it felt no different than killing a stranger.

"Before I see you turn on me, mother, I would rather see you dead in your grave." She kissed her on the lips. "Goodbye, Mama. I love you."

Jayde left her mother there to die alone.

# # # #

Thirty minutes wasn't much time, especially riding with as much stolen money as she was. Several times along the way back down 71, Yawni told herself to stop and finish what she had started. Go to Texas. Start a new life. But she was a loyal follower of Ramon.

The whole thing could have been a hoax for him

to get his money back. If it was, then one good thing would come out of all of this. It would prove to Ramon just how much she really loved him.

# # # #

Ramon stared out of the van window. Jayde sat next to him. She could just about imagine what was going through his mind. The great thief had been gotten by his own spawn. The very creature that slept with him every night and sealed their vows with a kiss on an exotic island. His own seed turned him out on crack and ghost pussy, and now she was about to escape with his bankroll.

Jayde spoke, "I remember when I was a kid, you, mother and I were having a barbeque at the house. Everybody was having a good time. That was until mother caught you with her cousin, Talisha, in y'all's bedroom doin' it. She tried to kill herself that night. That's why you caught me in the bed with those two dudes. How did it feel?"

Ramon licked his lips. "It hurt," he admitted. "I learned a helluva lesson fuckin' with you, Ja ... Trishay."

"Mother was a good woman."

Ramon thought curiously. "Jayde, you didn't—"

"No." She fired up a cigarette. "She killed herself. Doesn't matter. She was sick anyway," she lied. "I guess she only wanted to live long enough to see you get yours." She blew smoke in his face. "Cigarette?"

Ramon sneered. "You fuckin'—"

Jayde slapped him across the face. "Watch your mouth. That's no way to speak to a lady." Jayde thought about something. "Hey, how do you think Yawni would feel if she caught you high?"

# # # #

Yawni arrived at the meeting place. She drove into the circular parking area. The white van was parked, facing her direction. She didn't see any people inside. She parked beside it and exited.

Jayde appeared from out of nowhere. A chrome handgun protruded from her waist. She wore that slick-ass smirk on her face.

"Hi," Jayde said. "I'm Trishay Delay, Ramon's daughter."

Yawni's mouth fell open. "Trishay? How could you—"

"I'll do whatever it takes as long as I'm greatly compensated for it. I got that from my daddy. Where's the money?"

Yawni nodded toward the Magnum. "In the back."

Jayde opened the hatch. Four bags were sitting in the trunk. She searched each one of them.

"This all of it?" Jayde inquired.

"Yes. Snug and Chico went their own way with their split."

Smiling, Jayde said, "Trishay Delay, you pulled it off." She jammed two fingers inside her mouth and whistled.

Lashay and Francine came up the hill with Ramon. Yawni could look at him and tell that he was high on something. His eyes were wide open, his lips trembled and he was constantly looking around. Her first thought was that they had drugged him.

Jayde had given him a loaded pipe, knowing that he wouldn't be able to resist. She wanted Yawni to see him at his worst. To see that he really wasn't worth saving at all.

"Load the bags into the van," Jayde commanded her crew. She regarded Yawni and Ramon for a moment, then gave him a big hug. "Thank you," she said. She climbed inside the van and drove away.

When the van was gone, Ramon stood there avoiding eye contact with Yawni. "I'm sorry," he said pathetically.

"Sorry my ass. You owe me." Yawni's hard face softened. "I only did it because I love your stank ass." Ramon was acting jumpy. "Did they drug you?"

It took him a moment to answer. "No, I drugged myself. I let Trishay get me strung out on crack."

Yawni didn't know what to say. All that was left to do was for her to hug him. He hugged her back, and for the first time, he cried in her arms.

"It's okay. We're gonna get you some help, alright?" Yawni gently rubbed his back. "Let's go."

# # # #

Roberta sat low in the front seat of Jayde's Camaro. She was parked nearby waiting on Yawni's Magnum to come up the hill. She loaded a full clip into a Tec-9 and cocked it.

The Magnum's headlights came into view. Roberta started the car and let down the window. Slowly, the wagon crept in her direction. Twenty feet. Fifteen feet. Ten feet.

She could see both their heads sitting up in the front seat. Roberta bolted out of the parking spot, crashing into the wagon, pushing it back up against another parked car.

Quickly, she hopped out and jogged around to the passenger side of the Magnum. Ramon's head bobbled as blood seeped from the top of his head. He stared up at her dumbfounded.

Roberta drew the Tec. After all she and Ramon had been though, she couldn't find it in her heart to pull the trigger. Just as she began lowering her weapon, there was a loud bang, and the young woman's chest exploded right before Ramon's eyes. She fell to the ground.

It took a minute for Ramon to regain his composure. When he looked to his left, he saw that Yawni held the smoking gun.

Roberta lay on the ground, shaking, when Ramon kneeled beside her. Her eyes were as wide as they could get.

"I ... I ... I was ... wasn't ... gonna ... shoo .. ot ... you," she mumbled as she struggled to breathe. A single tear escaped her eye, followed by a deep breath. Then her eyes closed for the final time.

Yawni heard a cell phone ringing, then reached into Roberta's car and pulled it out. "Hello."

"Is it done?"

"Yeah, she's done," Yawni retorted. "So you'd better run far, you little bitch, 'cause you're next." She hung up.

chapter

28

Ramon was forced to resign as manager of the hotel. The building was temporarily closed, pending investigation of the robbery. Afterward, Murphy was to take over as the new manager—which was his plan from the very beginning.

Yawni confessed to Ramon that she had kept four of the bags from the robbery. Since Jayde didn't know how many there were, she couldn't complain. Besides, it was enough money in those four bags to last Jayde and her crew a lifetime.

Ramon was reluctant about checking into rehab, but he knew that it was the best thing for him. Yawni packed him a bag, then she and Tulu drove him to the same center that he helped the mayor build.

"I can't believe you's a crack head, man," Tulu said from the driver's seat.

Yawni nudged him, then turned to face Ramon. He was sitting low in the back seat with dark shades on.

"You okay, baby?" She rubbed his knee.

"I'm fine. Still trying to get over the initial shock of all of this."

"Yeah. She pulled a good one, didn't she?" Yawni said with admiration.

"Yes she did," Ramon admitted. "I'll catch up with her sooner or later. The world is not that big for her to hide from me."

"Remember, she's your daughter."

"Yeah. I created that monster."

Tulu pulled over in front of the rehab center. Ramon and Yawni stood outside the car eyeing each other.

"I'll be waiting when you return in six months," Yawni said. "Then we're gonna get married on some exotic island." She removed the old wedding band from his finger and tossed it.

"Thanks, Yawni," he said.

"It's only one way to thank me, and that's by meeting me at the alter in your white tuxedo."

"White? Not black?" She shot him a look. "You got it," Ramon said. When they hugged, he allowed real love to embrace him, and it felt good.

Tulu sat his bags in front of him. They wanted to hug each other, but didn't know how to go about it.

"You know I fucked Jayde on your wedding night," Tulu admitted.

"Dirty muthafucka."

"Couldn't help it. They gave me some of that same shit they gave you."

Ramon laughed and pulled Tulu toward him. "C'mere man. Thank you."

"I'll be here when you get out."

"In a minute." Ramon picked up his bags. "Don't fuck Yawni."

Tulu laughed.

After Ramon was shown around and settled into his new living quarters, they organized a special group session so everyone could introduce themselves. While the introductions were taking place, Ramon zoned out. He thought about the caper that Yawni had pulled off. It was too bad that Snug and Chico didn't make it. His friends left this earth before he could make amends.

Trishay, he thought. She got up under him, then vanished with what she came for. It was a lesson learned; Ramon had committed evil, and evil had returned to him.

# # # #

Tulu parked in the garage of Murphy's downtown office. He and Yawni took the emergency stairs to his floor.

Murphy was on the phone, arguing with someone, when the door flew open. The henchman on the sofa reading the paper jumped up. Tulu fired two shots through the "Sports" section. He crumpled to the floor.

The phone fell from Murphy's hand. He rose from his seat, peering at Yawni, who was walking toward him.

"Yawni?" he said as he backed up.

"Time for you to find out how long that jump is."

"No!" He grabbed the flagpole to use as a weapon. "Get back!" He swung it at Tulu, who dodged it, then rushed Murphy, clutching his throat.

"Yo' fat ass tried to kill me," Tulu said. "Didn't you know I did 30 years in the joint? Huh?"

"I'll pay you double whatever Delay is paying you. Please," Murphy pleaded. "Please!"

Yawni threw his office chair through the window. The cold winter air blew in on them.

"Please! Please!" Murphy begged. "Pleeeea—"

The people walking down below, and driving on the street, didn't know what to think when they saw Murphy come flying out of the window. He hit the ground with a loud thud.

Yawni and Tulu looked down on him.

"I'd say it's at least 40 feet," Tulu joked.

"At least," Yawni agreed. "Let's go."

# # # #

The drug counselor called on Ramon three times before he snapped out of his daze. He stood and adjusted his clothing. As he looked around the room at his fellow addicts of all ages and colors, he realized that drugs could affect anyone—no matter how young or powerful.

"*Ramon. Ramon,*" the voice called again. It was his conscience calling, and it was trying to tell him to wake up.

He took a deep breath and said, "Hi, my name is Ramon Delay ... and I'm a drug addict."

> *"Train up a child in the way he should go: and when he is old, he will not depart from it."*
>   Proverbs 22:6

ORDER FORM

Triple Crown Publications
PO Box 6888
Columbus, Oh 43205

ame: _____

ddress: _____

ity/State: _____

ip: _____

TITLES	PRICES
Dime Piece	$15.00
Gangsta	$15.00
Let That Be The Reason	$15.00
A Hustler's Wife	$15.00
The Game	$15.00
Black	$15.00
Dollar Bill	$15.00
A Project Chick	$15.00
Road Dawgz	$15.00
Blinded	$15.00
Diva	$15.00
Sheisty	$15.00
Grimey	$15.00
Me & My Boyfriend	$15.00
Larceny	$15.00
Rage Times Fury	$15.00
A Hood Legend	$15.00
Flipside of The Game	$15.00
Menage's Way	$15.00

HIPPING/HANDLING (Via U.S. Media Mail) $3.95 1-2 Books, $5.95 3-4 Books add $1.95 for ea. additional book

TOTAL $_____

FORMS OF ACCEPTED PAYMENTS:
stage Stamps, Institutional Checks & Money Orders, all mail in orders take 5-7 Business days to be delivered.

ORDER FORM

Triple Crown Publications
PO Box 6888
Columbus, Oh 43205

Name: _____

Address: _____

City/State: _____

Zip: _____

	TITLES	PRICES
	Still Sheisty	$15.00
	Chyna Black	$15.00
	Game Over	$15.00
	Cash Money	$15.00
	Crack Head	$15.00
	For The Strength of You	$15.00
	Down Chick	$15.00
	Dirty South	$15.00
	Cream	$15.00
	Hoodwinked	$15.00
	Bitch	$15.00
	Stacy	$15.00
	Life	$15.00
	Keisha	$15.00
	Mina's Joint	$15.00
	How To Succeed in The Publishing Game	$20.00
	Love & Loyalty	$15.00
	Whore	$15.00
	A Hustler's Son	$15.00

SHIPPING/HANDLING (Via U.S. Media Mail) $3.95 1-2 Books, $5.95 3-4 Books
add $1.95 for ea. additional book

TOTAL $_____

FORMS OF ACCEPTED PAYMENTS:
Postage Stamps, Institutional Checks & Money Orders, all mail in orders take 5-7 Business days to be delivered.

ORDER FORM

Triple Crown Publications
PO Box 6888
Columbus, Oh 43205

Name: _____

Address: _____

City/State: _____

Zip: _____

TITLES	PRICES
Chances	$15.00
Contagious	$15.00
Hold U Down	$15.00
Black and Ugly	$15.00
In Cahootz	$15.00
Dirty Red *Hardcover Only*	$20.00
Dangerous	$15.00
Street Love	$15.00
Sunshine & Rain	$15.00
Bitch Reloaded	$15.00
Dirty Red *Paperback*	$15.00
Mistress of the Game	$15.00
Queen	$15.00
The Set Up	$15.00
Torn	$15.00
Stained Cotton	$15.00
Grindin *Hardcover Only*	$10.00

SHIPPING/HANDLING (Via U.S. Media Mail) $3.95 1-2 Books, $5.95 3-4 Books add $1.95 for ea. additional book

TOTAL $_____

FORMS OF ACCEPTED PAYMENTS:
Postage Stamps, Institutional Checks & Money Orders, all mail in orders take 5-7 Business days to be delivered.